He even looked dangerous sleeping, dangerous, yet oh so sexy. Stephanie had been fighting her attraction to him since the day he walked into her office. She could no longer deny it. She wanted Jack.

She no longer kidded herself about their relationship remaining professional only. She and Jack had chemistry so strong it scared her. Stephanie knew it was only a matter of time before things escalated.

Jack Kaufman was like no man she had known. He wasn't exactly the three *w*s she was looking for, witty, warm, and wonderful. He was more, wild, wicked, and wanton. She had even gotten used to his cynicism and warped sense of humor. He believed in living life to the fullest and damned the consequences. He liked living dangerously and he played by his own rules. It infuriated her that he was always so cool and so in control of his emotions. The kiss they shared months ago had completely shaken her, while he appeared to be unmoved by it. Nothing she had done thus far had rattled him. He had even smiled when she threw water in his face.

Jack felt Stephanie watching him and wondered what she was thinking. He knew he had her where he wanted her. He was determined to make the most of their trip. Stephanie held the key to all his dreams coming true. In the process, he would do whatever was necessary to make her happy and ensure a future with her and his daughter. Everything he was doing was for Christina's sake.

Also by Sylvia Lett

Like Never Before

Perfect For You

Take Me Down

Sylvia Lett

Dafina
Books

Kensington Publishing Corp.
http://www.kensingtonbooks.com

DAFINA BOOKS are published by

Kensington Publishing Corp.
850 Third Avenue
New York, NY 10022

All Kensington Titles, Imprints, and Distributed Lines are
available at special quantity discounts for bulk purchases for
sales promotions, premiums, fund-raising, and educational
or institutional use. Special book excerpts or customized
printings can also be created to fit specific needs. For details,
write or phone the office of the Kensington special sales
manager: Kensington Publishing Corp., 850 Third Avenue,
New York, NY 10022, attn: Special Sales Department.
Phone: 1-800-221-2647.

Dafina and the Dafina logo Reg. U.S. Pat. & TM Off.

First Dafina mass market printing: April 2009

ISBN-13: 978-0-7582-3478-0
ISBN-10: 0-7582-3478-3

10 9 8 7 6 5 4 3 2 1

Printed in the United States of America

This book is dedicated to Michael Lett.

*Michael, basically you pushed me to follow my
dream of getting my first book published.
Without your encouragement and support,
I might still be writing in a notebook.*

Thank you for everything.

Acknowledgments

I'd like to take a moment to thank some very special
people in my life. I thank God for my family.

My wonderful children: Michael II and Courtney.
You guys are the best. Thanks for keeping the
noise and fights to a minimum so I can
concentrate on writing.

My mother, Mattie Willis, whose faith in me
has not faltered.

My sisters and brothers: C Earl, Johnnie, Liz,
Val, Sam, and Bessie, what can I say?
Your continued love, support, and
encouragement keeps me
focused and strong.

Nieces, nephews, cousins, friends, and coworkers,
thanks for your continued support.

I love you all.
Sylvia

Chapter 1

Stephanie looked over the impressive résumé of her next interviewee. She had posted a position for a security consultant three weeks ago. So far only amateurs had bombarded her.

What Stephanie needed was a professional. Someone who knew all the ins and outs of hotel security, and could hire and train a staff of security guards for the hotel chain. She wanted limited involvement in the process.

Jackson Kaufman appeared to be the man she was looking for. At least on paper. He had an engineering degree and experience, which gave him a leg up on the competition. His last two jobs were with Fortune 500 technology companies. Jackson worked as a security consultant for both of them. He was also an ex-Navy SEAL. His expertise was weapons and hand-to-hand combat. He possessed a black belt in tae kwon do and judo too.

The only thing that bothered Stephanie was the two-year gap between the navy and Jackson's first consulting job. If he could give her an acceptable answer—one that he could prove—she'd hire him on the spot.

She looked down at the thin gold watch encircling her wrist. Jackson was due to arrive in about ten minutes. "I guess we'll see if the man measures up to the résumé," she said aloud. "God, I hope so. I am so tired of interviewing."

There was a brief knock on her door before it opened suddenly and her mother came breezing into the room. Stephanie rolled her eyes heavenward. She was not in the mood for her mother today or any other day.

"Hello, dear. Sit up straight. You'll ruin your posture," chided Mildred Mason as she closed the door behind her. "That color looks dreadful on you. You really should take me or your sister shopping with you."

"Thanks, Mom," Stephanie said, pasting on a smile. "Seeing you always manages to brighten my day. I'm busy and I don't have time for fashion tips. What are you doing here? Shouldn't you be out shopping or looking for a husband for me? That does seem to be your favorite pastime lately."

"You know me too well, darling." Mildred sat down in the vacant black leather chair across from her daughter's desk. She held out her hand, inspecting her perfectly manicured red fingernails. "You received an invitation to the Waterfords' party on Saturday night. I accepted on your behalf."

Stephanie shot her mother a murderous glare.

"Now, don't be like that."

Stephanie laid her head down on the desk. *Why me? What did I do to deserve a social-climbing mother?* "Mom, why did you do that? You know I hate those things. I specifically told you I didn't want to attend this one. I had plans to curl up with a good book and a glass of chardonnay."

"Why snuggle up to a cold book when you can have a hot-blooded man? Honey, you could have your pick of men. You have a smorgasbord to choose from. Try a few different tasty morsels before you settle for the main coarse."

Stephanie's eyes narrowed on her mother. "Why do I

even bother? I talk. You don't listen. Some things never seem to change. I give up."

"Don't give me that look. I listen sometimes. You can't snub the Waterfords. It's simply not done. They are one of the most powerful families in the state of Texas. I'll go with you. It'll be fun, just us girls. There should be tons of eligible bachelors. Maybe you can make a connection with one of them. Who knows? Maybe I will."

"I wish you would. My bank account would thank him." She smiled. "I am not looking for a connection. It will be another boring dinner party with old lechers pawing at me. I always feel like I'm an appetizer or something. I hate it. I wish you would stop accepting invitations for me. I don't need a man in my life to be happy."

"You've proven that, dear, by dating Stanley," Mildred replied smugly. "You can be miserable with one or without one, but everyone needs companionship. Men have their purpose."

"Yeah, they are strong enough to hold all your shopping bags. I have companionship. I have Stanley." The words sounded lame even to her ears. Stephanie regretted them instantly.

"Stanley is not a companion. Stanley is your lapdog. You say jump and he asks how high. Honey, there is no fire, no spark, no nothing. He's too boring. You need excitement. You need romance. You need someone other than that limp biscuit. You are not going to find the right type of husband if you don't get out there and mingle with the right people."

Picking up her gold pen, Stephanie jotted down the date and time of the Waterfords' party in her monthly planner without giving it any thought. Despite her mother's plans, she had no intention of attending. Laying her pen down, she looked up at her mother. "You mean Stanley's not rich, don't you? Why is everything about money with you?

Stanley is not exactly destitute. He owns an accounting firm. He does very well for himself."

"Yes, dear, but you can do much better than Stanley. If you can't bring yourself to sleep with the man, then what would be the point of marrying him? He's boring and has the personality of pocket lint. Expand your horizons, dear. Reach for the stars. The sky is the limit when you're sitting on a gold mine. You are worth a fortune. The rich marry rich. That's how they stay rich."

"No, Mother, I'm not rich, but you seem to have selective memory when it suits you. I'm a pauper. Christina is worth a fortune."

"You could be too if you knew how to manage her inheritance. You could pay yourself a high six-figure salary and wouldn't have to drive a five-year-old SUV. You could buy yourself a nice Mercedes or BMW. I saw a black two-seater the other day I simply fell in love with. It would be perfect for me. I mean you."

"Mother, I am not having this conversation with you again. Listen closely. Christina's money is Christina's. Yes, I'm her mother, but the money is hers. I'm not touching her inheritance and neither are you. I used it to by our house, but there is no need to use it again. I make enough money to buy a new car, if I wanted one. At this particular time in my life, I don't want a new one. Besides, there is nothing I can do with a two-seater. I like my SUV. It's roomy and it's comfortable." Stephanie had never divulged the will to her mother. She let her believe everything went to Christina. If she knew that half of everything went directly to Stephanie, there would be no end to her greed.

"Well, I could certainly use a new car." Mildred looked down at her fingernails again. "My transmission seems to be acting up again."

"Mother, the car you have is only two years old. You wouldn't know the transmission from the battery. If something is wrong with it, take it to the dealership. It's still under warranty. If you just have to have a new car, then get a job and buy one yourself." Stephanie was quickly losing patience with her mother. "I am not buying you another car."

"You expect me to get a job?" Mildred gasped in outrage. "I gave your father and you girls the best years of my life. Is this is how you repay me? Your father walks out on me and you suggest I become a common laborer. Children are so ungrateful these days." She stormed out of the office, leaving the door wide open.

Coming to her feet, Stephanie rounded the desk to slam the door shut. She let out an exasperated growl. To her horror, it was that particular moment Jackson Kaufman chose to knock on her opened door. He smiled and she turned red in embarrassment.

Stephanie stared openly at the man in front of her. She wasn't sure what she was expecting, but this wasn't it. He was tall, a little over six feet with broad shoulders. His eyes were light brown with gold flecks shimmering in them. His skin was the color of smooth rich copper. His mouth was sensual, with full, inviting lips. The mustache and goatee gave him an almost sinister look. He was a handsome, but dangerous-looking man. He was dressed impeccably in a black suit, blue shirt, and tie. His feet were enclosed in designer shoes. Everything about him screamed *trouble* and *raw sexuality*.

In the same few seconds, Jackson appraised her from head to toe and back again. Until now he had only seen her from a distance; up close she was even more beautiful.

Stephanie stood about five-seven. Her skin was a soft honey color. Her eyes were a dark brown. Her small heart shaped face was perfectly made up. Her lips were formed in the same heart shape. Her long sandy brown hair was pulled back from her face with a clip. Her body was incredible. She was clad in a dark blue pantsuit. Her jacket was open and she wore a silky red camisole. What a pair of breasts. He guessed around a 36-D at least. Being a breast and leg man, Jackson knew he was pretty close in his estimation.

Stephanie had to tear her eyes from him as she moved back behind the oak desk and sat down. She felt safer putting some distance and an obstacle between them. She flushed under his direct gaze and quickly regained her composure.

"I growl sometimes too, but I don't bite, much," he teased, breaking the uncomfortable silence.

Her face turned a darker shade of red. *For some reason I don't believe that. You are anything but harmless.*

He smiled as if reading her thoughts. *I like a woman with fire.*

"Please come in. I'm Stephanie Mason," she said, holding out her hand to him. She tried to shake off the feeling of intimidation as she met his bold eyes.

He closed the distance between them in long powerful strides. "Jackson Kaufman. Call me Jack," he said in a deep, professional voice that did little to hide its sexiness. When his hand caught hers, they both felt the spark. Their eyes locked in silent communication.

Stephanie slid her hand back quickly and momentarily broke eye contact. She mentally counted to five and tried to compose herself. No man had ever rattled her the way this one had in less than five minutes. "Mr. Kaufman, please have a seat." She sat down and he followed her lead. "You have quite an impressive résumé. Can you tell me a little about what you did at each of your past jobs?"

"I was a Navy SEAL. I reenlisted when my time was up. After the navy, I took some time off and did some traveling. When I was ready, I put my training to good use. I became a security consultant. I had multiple duties with various companies. I hired and trained the entire security staff. I traveled from state-to-state recruiting and training. The chosen ones, I trained them in everything from recognizing a possible problem to hand-to-hand combat. They also had lessons at a firing range. I made sure every person carrying a gun was comfortable and capable of using one. My program included putting them all through a two-month rigorous training regimen. I shocked upper management by hiring a few ex-cons. The old saying is definitely true. Crooks do make the best security people, present company excluded. They are suspicious by nature and know the signs to look for. It was a win-win situation."

"Interesting philosophy. It makes perfect sense in a strange way, but I'm not sure I agree with it. How did you solicit these companies' business? Some of them are Fortune 500 companies. How did you get past the front door?"

"I had them put their money where their mouth was. They bragged about their wonderful security guards and their new security system. I told them I could not only break into their building, but I could make it all the way up to the CEO's office without being caught. The CEO laughed and told me I was crazy. He said if I could make it past the third floor, he'd hire me for double what I was asking." Jack smiled and Stephanie had already guessed how the story ended.

"And you of course made it all the way up to the CEO's office." She leaned back in the overstuffed leather chair fingering the gold pen in her hand.

"After observing and monitoring his security guards and hacking into his security system, I was sitting at his desk enjoying a glass of his hundred-year-old brandy when he came to work a week later. He gave me the bottle and hired me on the spot. Miss Mason, I'm the best at what I do."

"I'm sure you are. Tell me about the two-year gap between the navy and your first consulting job. You stated you took some time off and did some traveling. You don't seem the type to take a two-year sabbatical. What did you do in those years?" She laid her pen on the desk and folded her hands together. Leaning in, she waited for his answer.

"Are you sure you want to know?" *Don't do it, Jack. Don't tell her. You will send her running for cover. She's ready to bolt right now. She can't handle it. Make something up. You have this job in the bag. Don't blow it now. You have this job in the bag.*

"I think I need to know if you want to be considered for this position. I'll be honest with you. Your résumé is very impressive, but I get the feeling you are not being straight with me. I can't hire a man I don't trust. Were you in prison or something?" His reluctance to tell bothered her. She had a feeling that whatever he was hiding would be a bombshell. Maybe some things were better left unsaid.

"No, I wasn't incarcerated. After I left the navy, some friends and I went down to South America to work as soldiers of fortune. It was dangerous and exciting at the same time. The pay wasn't bad either." He saw her freeze up right before his eyes. He knew it would shock her. The truth would shock anyone. This was why he chose not to reveal his former line of business to many people. Men were envious of his daring escapades, but women were sometimes turned off by his past. He didn't need to be told which one Stephanie would be. He could see it in her eyes and her body gestures that she had become uncomfortable.

Stephanie was speechless at first. Her brain could not form one coherent thought. "You were a mercenary?" she asked tightly, folding her hands in front of her. Stephanie was aghast as she stared at him. This man was a gun-for-hire. She had read somewhere that mercenaries were loyal only to the highest bidder. She couldn't believe there was one sitting in front of her applying for a job at her hotel. Yet there he sat.

"Yes," he answered, meeting her startled eyes. He

watched her eyes twitch. "You wanted the truth. I gave you the truth. Ms. Mason, I'm the best man for this job. My past is my past. I'm no longer in that line of work. My résumé speaks for itself. You won't find anyone as qualified as I am."

That might be true, but Stephanie couldn't hire him. She would not subject the rest of the employees to him. She would continue her search. The interview was over. "Mr. Kaufman, thank you for coming in. I'll be in touch when I make my final decision." She came quickly to her feet and bumped the desk in her nervousness. The glass of water teetered and he caught it before a drop spilled. His hand moved so quickly, Stephanie thought she had imagined it. She watched as he set the glass upright.

Jack followed her lead by coming to his feet. He took two steps toward her, and Stephanie backed away cautiously, then eyed the door. Jack stopped when he noticed the alarm in her eyes. He smiled warmly. "I was only going to shake your hand and say thank you for your time. Thank you for the interview and your open-mindedness," he said as his eyes raked over her. "I hope you find what you're looking for. Have a good day, Ms. Mason. Good luck."

Stephanie felt foolish as she watched Jack back out of the office with his hands raised in front of him. He was sending a message. But Stephanie knew she wouldn't change her mind. She couldn't hire someone who'd preyed on the weak—even if it was a lifetime ago. And her attraction to him didn't help matters. No, she definitely couldn't hire Jack Kaufman.

Confident that she'd made the right decision, Stephanie took a deep cleansing breath and stared at the résumé one more time, and dropped it in the wastebasket.

* * *

Jack sat in his car staring at Stephanie's monthly planner. He had swiped it from her desk without her noticing. She was so flustered by his confession that she wouldn't have noticed much of anything. Jack didn't realize how intimidating he must have been until he saw Stephanie's reaction, but he was still surprised at how fearful she seemed.

Jack drove over to a quick copy place and photocopied Stephanie's entire planner. Now he had to get it back to her office before she realized it was missing.

He waited until he saw her walk out of the building for lunch and get into her SUV. That sign was an invitation to every would-be criminal in the city.

When she drove away, he went over to her parking space and removed the sign with her name on it. He took off his tie tack and put it in his pocket as a precautionary measure. If anyone stopped him, he could say he dropped it in Stephanie Mason's office and came back to retrieve it.

Jack frowned when he was able to walk all the way back to Stephanie's office without anyone stopping him. All the back office doors were unlocked. Her assistant was away from her desk and no one was around.

He walked into Stephanie's office and laid the sign on her desk. When he saw her computer was on and unprotected, he smiled wickedly. Sitting down in her chair, he pulled out the keyboard and began to type. He changed her password, and then logged off her computer. Picking up the notepad, he jotted down a quick note.

This place is an easy target. You should be more careful. A few tips:

- *Remove this sign. It makes you a target for every lunatic or kidnapper around.*
- *Get better security guards. I was able to walk*

*back to your office and leave this for you. No
one was around to stop me.*

- *Always lock your computer and your door when
  you leave for an extended amount of time. You
  never know when someone like me will walk in
  and change your password just to teach you a
  lesson.*
- *Buy a new car. Because of that stupid sign,
  everyone who has ever been here knows what
  kind of vehicle you drive.*

I look forward to our next meeting,
JK

Giving the room one last glance, Jack closed the door
behind him. Satisfied, he whistled a tune as he walked out
into the sunlight, slipping the dark sunglasses on his face.
He got into his black Porsche and waited.

Stephanie was puzzled when she returned from lunch and
her parking sign was gone. There was a car in her parking
space, so she picked a spot on the side of the building.

"Clarence," said Stephanie, setting her purse on the
counter in front of him, "my sign is missing. Do you know
anything about it?"

"Nope." He shook his head, but didn't bother to look up at
her. "Probably some kids. Just order a new one." He didn't even
have the courtesy to lay his magazine down and look at her.

"Can you go outside and look around?" she asked,
losing patience with him. Stephanie was infuriated by his
attitude. *He's worthless. I'm paying him to sit there and
read a magazine. Come to think of it, he was sitting there
reading when I left for lunch. He sits there all day. This has
to end. I have to find a security consultant soon.*

"It wouldn't do any good," he replied, looking up
briefly. "They are probably long gone by now." He got up
and stretched. "Guess I do need to stretch my legs a bit."

A lap or three around the hotel wouldn't hurt you either. Disgusted, Stephanie grabbed her bag from the counter and stomped back to her office.

Georgette was still on one of her extended lunches. A reprimand was long overdue, but Stephanie didn't know how to get her cousin to take the job seriously. And she didn't have the heart to fire her.

Stephanie turned the handle on the door and found her office locked. She frowned and fished in her purse for the key. *This is odd. I know I didn't lock the door.* Opening the door, she stopped when she saw her parking sign lying on top of her desk. She cautiously moved farther into the room. She saw a piece of paper taped to the sign. She ripped the note off and read it.

"You arrogant ass!" she hissed to the empty room. She balled the note up and threw it across the room. "You have some nerve." Stephanie turned on her computer and tried to log in. She was furious when, true to Jack's words in the note, she was locked out of her own computer.

Stephanie fished his résumé out of the wastebasket and pressed out the wrinkles. She hit the speaker button on her telephone and dialed his mobile phone.

"Jack Kaufman." He thumbed through the copy of her planner. He'd made notes on each page. *There's a couple of parties coming up. It should be interesting.*

Stephanie leaned both hands on her desk and tried to calm her emotions. "Mr. Kaufman, this is a childish prank. How dare you come into my office and mess with my computer? I could have you arrested for breaking and entering."

"Go for it if you think you can prove anything. No one saw me. Your security camera is disabled and your door was open. It wasn't a prank, Ms. Mason. It was a matter of security and you have none at your hotel. I'm surprised you haven't been robbed blind. If that hotel is any indication of what the rest of them are like, I wonder how you stay in business. I was able to walk freely through all the back offices. No one stopped me or asked me any questions. I don't know where your worthless security guard was hiding. The only thing he could catch is a supersized meal."

Stephanie had to stifle a laugh.

Jack continued. "I saw two people on my way up here, and they were so busy making out, they didn't even see me. You need me. Your hotels need me."

"No," Stephanie replied. "I may need someone like you, but I don't need you."

Click. Jack hung up the phone.

Stephanie stared at the telephone. "He hung up on me! The nerve of that man." She immediately dialed his number again. "I want the password!"

"I want a second interview. Meet me in the lobby in ten minutes and I will show you everything wrong with this hotel from top to bottom. After we're done, make up your mind about my qualifications, not about me as a person."

"Are you always so pushy?" she asked, playing for time. She knew giving him a second chance would weaken her position.

"I am when there's something I want. I want this job. I can do this job. I prefer to think of it as being aggressive."

"This goes against my better judgment, but make it fifteen minutes in my office so you can unlock my computer." Stephanie could hear Jack smiling as he said okay.

She removed the sign from her desk and placed it in her closet. Taking her compact out of her purse, she checked her makeup and then reapplied a layer of lipstick. Stephanie popped a breath mint in her mouth, and then dabbed a few drops of perfume on her wrist and behind her ear. She had a million thoughts.

What am I doing? I must be crazy. That's the only explanation for this. Why am I primping for this man? Mom would faint if she met him. That's an idea. I'll invite him to dinner one night. She did say I needed some excitement, but somehow I don't think Jack Kaufman is exactly what she had in mind.

Exactly fifteen minutes later, Jack knocked on her door. Stephanie opened it and stepped back for him to enter.

He's more handsome than I remember. That cologne is intoxicating. This was a very bad idea. "First things first. What's the password to my computer?"

Jack grinned and walked around to her desk and sat down.

"What are you doing?" Stephanie asked.

"I'm letting you back into your computer." He hit a few keys and looked up at her.

"Couldn't you just give me the password?"

"I could do that, but then I would have to kill you."

She paled and took an involuntary step backward. Jack laughed at the startled expression on her face.

"I'm kidding. I've never harmed women or children." He hopped up from her chair. "Okay, now you can change the password."

Stephanie moved suspiciously around him, making sure not to make any body contact. There was something way too intimate about him sitting in the chair she sat in. The chair was still warm from his body. She tried not to let on that she felt a tingle as she thought about her body being where his body had been.

But Jack noticed anyway. *She's incredible. I guess I didn't imagine the way she was looking at me. She's careful, but very interested. Well, at least she's not cringing in fear. That's a plus. She has backbone. I like that.*

Picking up her notepad, Stephanie rose from her chair. "Okay, so let's go take a tour." She looked down at her watch. "You've already used up three of those fifteen minutes."

Jack's eyes narrowed on her. "Aren't you forgetting something?"

She followed his eyes to her computer. Stephanie dropped her notepad and leaned over to lock the computer with her password. She faced him.

"You should do that every time you leave your office. So should your secretary, and if she ever comes back from her extended lunch, you can tell her."

Stephanie rolled her eyes at him and followed him out the door. She knew he was right, but she was not about to admit it.

Thirteen minutes turned into an hour. Stephanie was enthralled as they walked through the hotel and Jack inspected everything. She was more than impressed with his knowledge, and she was surprised at the hotel's shoddy security system. Halfway through the tour, Stephanie was convinced Jack was the person the hotel needed. Despite her concerns, she hired him.

Jack immediately blew off the first salary proposal and benefit package. He made several modifications and put the ball back in Stephanie's court. They finally came to a mutual agreement they could both live with.

As part of the deal, she agreed to put him up in the hotel until he could find a place of his own. She knew the six-figure salary she was paying him was well worth the money. With the robberies and burglaries at the chain in the past year, she was desperate and he knew it.

On Jack's first day of work, Stephanie called a special meeting to introduce him to her security staff. She let everyone know that in no uncertain terms, Jack had the power to terminate anyone for violating and/or not adhering to the security procedures he was putting in place. He went over some basic security dos and don'ts and passed out a security tips sheet. He let everyone know written procedures would be forthcoming.

After meeting and watching the current security guard, Jack immediately ran an advertisement for two new security positions. He knew the man there was not going to work out. He was fat, lazy, and didn't want to have to leave the front desk, except for breaks and lunch.

Stephanie more or less let Jack write his own job description. He also made his own hours. He had to work some days and nights to get the feel for the place.

Jack also wrote job descriptions for security guards. They were no longer allowed to sit idle at the front desk. They now had to tour the building and the parking lot hourly, taking different routes each time. It was mandatory they each attend a month–long security training program given by Jack. They also had to pass the training final exam to keep their jobs.

Jack wasn't surprised when the current security guard called in sick two days in a row. On the third day, he quit. Jack took over his shift, until he could hire and train a suitable replacement. He had interviewed several people, but he hadn't found two who stood out. Jack hated to do it, but he would have to pull double duty until he found someone. His commitment to the job would impress Stephanie, but it would leave him little time or energy to pursue her outside of work. His plans for Stephanie Mason would have to be put on hold temporarily.

He was a patient man. He could wait.

Chapter 2

Jack looked down at his copy of Stephanie's planner. Circled for tonight was a formal dinner at the Waterford Mansion. For several days, he had been trying to run into Stephanie outside of their work setting. He knew he wanted to see her again without all the talk about security keeping things strictly professional. He had no doubt that he could actually get into the party. The rest he would play by ear. But first, he had to find something appropriate to wear.

He fingered the tie around his neck, then removed it. He hated ties. He unbuttoned the white shirt he was wearing and tossed it on the bed. Instead he decided on a white turtleneck. Slipping on the black suit coat, he grabbed his keys off the dresser and left the room.

Jack smiled to himself, thinking about how easy it was to gain entrance into the party. His opportunity came when an older woman tripped. He was there to catch her and escort her inside. Once inside the house, he excused himself by saying his date was expecting him.

His eyes scanned the room until they lit on Stephanie. She wore a sleeveless black dress that reached her knees.

Though she was dressed conservatively, Stephanie's figure shone through. Her tight, muscular calves peeked beneath the dress, and she wore black high heels to match. She was as understated as her mother was flamboyant.

Mildred Mason was clad in a low-cut, backless mini-dress. She was an attractive woman, but the dress was more suited to someone her daughter's age.

From afar, Jack watched Stephanie's every move. Unlike her mother, she didn't seem to be enjoying herself very much. She mingled with a few people, but mostly she stayed to herself. She checked her watch several times, before slipping out the patio door. Jack followed her but kept his distance.

Stephanie sat in the gazebo. She was beautiful and elegant in the soft moonlight, her hair loosely pinned with wisps of it brushing her cheeks.

She kicked off her heels and took out her cell phone to place a call. Jack eased closer to hear the conversation.

"Hi, sweetie," Stephanie said, smiling into the cell phone. She leaned back on the bench and closed her eyes.

"Hi, Mommy."

Stephanie could almost see the smile on her daughter's beautiful little face. "How's my favorite little girl?"

Jack felt a tightening in his chest. She was talking to Christina. He closed his eyes and counted to ten to steady his racing heart. He shook himself out of his trance.

"I love you, sweetie. Be a good girl for Aunt Ashley and I will see you in the morning." As she closed the phone, Jack stepped into the gazebo. Stephanie gave a startled gasp.

"I'm sorry," he stuttered. "I didn't mean to frighten you." Jack's voice sounded choked even to his own ears. He was suddenly nervous.

"What are you doing here?" Her tone was more accusatory than she'd intended for it to be. But he really had taken her by surprise.

"I mean, I didn't know you knew the Waterfords," she said, trying to correct herself.

Jack saw how shocked Stephanie was to see him. For the first time that night, he wasn't sure if crashing the party was the best way to endear himself to her.

"Oh yes. The Waterfords. A friend of a friend mentioned he'd be here tonight and said I should drop by if I didn't have other plans. I didn't have other plans," he said, shrugging. "So here I am."

He paused to see if she was buying any of this.

"It's really nice to run into you here," he added. "May I?" he asked, indicating the seat next to her.

Stephanie had not moved an inch since she turned to see Jack standing there. Her hand was still in midair holding her cell phone. But she nodded and made room for him.

"I'm sorry," she began, dropping her cell phone back into her evening bag. "You just caught me off guard, that's all. I was saying good night to my daughter."

"I didn't know you were a mom." Jack smiled. "How old is your daughter?"

"Christina's four. Take a look." She handed him a picture from her wallet.

Jack's hand trembled slightly as it brushed against Stephanie's when he took the photo. He stared at the beautiful smiling little girl. Her long dark hair hung down her back in a mass of curls. Her bangs were cut just above her eyes. Twinkling gray eyes lit up her face and her dimpled cheeks were rosy. Her skin was a rich honey just like Stephanie's.

"She's beautiful," said Jack, staring at the picture. He looked at Christina as if he were seeing Alexia again, and was overcome with emotion as he gazed lovingly at the photo. A million questions came to his mind, but he knew now was not the time to ask them. He had to play it cool. Play it safe. "Does she take after her father?" Jack asked, fishing for information. His eyes were glued to the photograph.

"Her mother actually," Stephanie said, coming to her feet. "I've never had the misfortune to meet her father. Good thing too, because I would be torn between killing him and thanking him for the gift he's given me."

"You've never met her father? How is that possible? I can't imagine you looking through an album at a sperm bank."

Stephanie laughed at the very idea. She couldn't picture herself going to a sperm bank either. "There's nothing intriguing about my situation, I assure you. It's a short story. Christina's father was killed on some secret mission before she was born. Christina's mother and I met and became friends shortly after she moved here. We were best friends and she asked me to be her child's godmother. When she died in childbirth, I got custody of Christina. I adopted her right after I brought her home from the hospital."

"You said her father is deceased. You know for sure he is dead?"

Stephanie's surprised eyes met his.

"People disappear all the time," Jack continued. "Some may not even know they are lost or that people are searching for them."

"Alexia wouldn't lie to me about something like that."

Jack didn't think he'd heard Stephanie right. As she went on, she didn't notice Jack's stony expression.

"Besides, he walked out on her when she was pregnant. Even if he were alive, I doubt he would want the responsibility of raising a child. I would never give her up. Christina is my daughter and I will fight anyone tooth and nail to keep her."

Watching and listening to Stephanie, Jack didn't doubt

her love for Christina. But he was still processing everything in his own head. Could what he think happened really have happened? Jack needed to change the subject fast.

"Well, it's wonderful that Christina has someone as special as you in your life."

"Thanks."

Jack let out a big sigh. "Are you enjoying the party? I wouldn't have pictured this as your scene. Actually, you look a little uncomfortable."

"Is it that obvious?" She turned to face him and they both laughed. Her eyes twinkled with merriment. "I guess it is."

"A bit. Why are you here if you don't want to be?"

"Do you have a mother? One who is hell-bent on marrying you off to the highest bidder, no less? She's driving me nuts. My mother accepted the invitation on my *behalf*."

"You shouldn't let her run your life. You don't strike me as a pushover. Does she do this kind of thing often?"

"Afraid so. With my mother, I choose my battles wisely. She's made it her goal in life to find me a wealthy husband whether I want one or not. She's convinced I need a husband and Christina needs a father."

"And you're not convinced?" *Okay, I guess I'm just going to have to step up my timetable thanks to meddling Mildred.*

"Let's just say I'm in no rush to walk down the aisle of holy matrimony." She shifted in the seat. "I've seen my share of bad marriages and I've only seen a few good ones. It would be my luck I would pick someone who couldn't live up to my expectations and we'd end up in divorce court in a couple of years. That's not what I want for Christina. She's happy and content and so am I. I want stability for her."

"That's something we all want, Stephanie." She saw the

sincerity in his eyes. "You obviously don't think your expectations are too high?"

"If you think honesty, love, mutual respect, and trust are too much to ask for in a mate, then yes, I guess they are a bit high. I've yet to find those qualities in any man."

"It could be that you aren't looking in the right places." Their eyes met and held. Stephanie looked away first.

"And maybe those things don't exist in any man," she replied, folding her hands in her lap.

"Or woman," he shot back just as quickly. "I've encountered as many dishonest women as I have men. We all make mistakes. Some are a lot worse than others, but, Stephanie, we are all human."

"How are you liking this party?" she asked, changing the subject. This topic of conversation obviously was a sore spot for both of them. "I wouldn't have thought this was your scene, either. Jack Kaufman at a formal black-tie party?"

I'm here because you're here. "Normally it's not, but I'm adaptable. I can blend in anywhere."

"I guess you would have to be in your line of work." The comment had slipped out of her mouth before she could stop it. "It's not every day I meet or hire an ex-mercenary."

He smiled and she blushed. "I knew we'd get around to that. Are you having second thoughts about hiring me?"

"No, no, no, no," Stephanie said, shaking her head emphatically. "You will be good for the hotel chain. You already have us all on our toes and you've only been here two weeks. You're doing a good job. But how are you feeling about it? Hotel security isn't as exciting as what you're used to. Do you miss that kind of life, the danger, and the excitement?"

"Sometimes I do miss it," Jack confessed. "There's a certain rush to being chased through the jungle and shot at."

Stephanie laughed.

"But seriously, I have responsibilities now. You have to grow up some time. My daughter needs me. As much as I hate to admit it, I need her too. She's the only good and decent thing in my life."

"You have a daughter?" The surprise was evident in her voice and on her face. "You don't strike me as the family-man type."

"Don't sound so shocked. Aren't mercenaries allowed to reproduce?" Jack asked with raised brows. Stephanie returned his smile. "I was even married once, briefly. It seems like a lifetime ago." He stopped talking when he saw her mother leading a man in their direction. "Here comes trouble in a short black dress. Don't look now, but your mother is headed this way."

Stephanie closed her eyes and took a deep breath. "Please tell me she's alone. My mother has horrible taste in men. She thinks if they are rich and breathing, they are marriage material."

"No can do. He looks old enough to be your father. Maybe she should keep this one for herself. You only have a few seconds to make a clean getaway."

"Pretend we're together," Stephanie said, panicking and peering over his shoulder. "Too late to run now."

"What exactly do you want me to do? I'm no knight in shining armor." He was enjoying himself at her expense.

She glared at him. "Truer words were never spoken. You're the master of deception," she said, looking over his shoulder again. "Improvise." Before the words left her mouth, Jack lifted her onto his lap. Her startled brown eyes stared up into his laughing eyes. "What do you think you are doing?"

"I'm improvising," he said in a husky voice. Her breath got caught in her throat as his hand cupped her face and he gently pulled her head toward his. She had no time to react as his lips touched hers. At the first touch of his mouth on hers, liquid fire spread through her body. Stephanie was torn between pushing him away and pulling him closer. When her lips parted beneath his, there was no turning back. He deepened the kiss and his mouth became hot and demanding. It took control of her mind as well as her body. As she moaned softly, her arms went around his neck and she surrendered to the feelings he was arousing in her. Her tongue met his in an erotic dance before he captured it.

All was forgotten except for the feel of his mouth on hers as she eagerly returned his kiss. They both forgot the reason for the kiss as they were carried away by mutual desire.

Her heartbeat accelerated and her toes curled as she swayed into him. She had never been kissed so thoroughly or enjoyed it as much. Jack was the forbidden fruit and Stephanie couldn't resist temptation.

They slowly pulled away from each other. Stephanie peered down at Jack and wrapped her arms tighter around his neck. This time, she initiated the kiss. Her lips grazed his again and again.

Jack buried his hands in her thick hair as he plundered her mouth. Stephanie clung to him and returned his kiss. Her passion surprised him, but his reaction to her surprised him even more.

"Stephanie Andrea Mason!" Mildred gasped, approaching the couple hurriedly. "What do you think you're doing?"

Jack turned to face Mildred and held more tightly on to Stephanie. Stephanie's eyes fluttered open and she could feel desire swelling within her.

Stephanie was flushed and trembling as she rose from Jack's lap and came to her feet. Jack stood up also, slipping his arm around Stephanie's waist. She shivered beneath his touch.

"Hi, Mother," she said breathlessly stated as she struggled to regain her composure.

Mildred surveyed Jack with disdain. She snubbed him and turned her attention back to her daughter. "Who is this person? Stephanie, it's in poor taste to get caught making out with the hired help."

Jack's hearty rich laughter filled the air. He looked Mildred over and summed her up pretty quickly. She was like a miniature pit bull chomping at the bit. It was easy to see how she could intimidate and browbeat her daughter, but he was a different story.

"So, let me see if I've got this straight, Mother. It's okay to make out with the hired help, as long as I don't get caught? Great advice, Mom. I'll try to remember that."

"You are twisting my words."

"Doesn't sound like it to me," Jack threw in for good measure, all the while grinning at a furious Mildred. "I am the hired help."

"I'm not talking to you. I was speaking to my daughter. Why don't you go get us a drink or something?"

Stephanie was embarrassed by her mother's treatment of Jack. "Mom, stop it. Jack doesn't work here. He's an invited guest."

"I doubt that. Someone of his caliber would never be on the Waterfords' guest list. He probably crashed the party to prey on single, wealthy women."

"Then he certainly picked the right party, didn't he?" Stephanie snapped.

"I'm still standing here, ladies. Would you two like to be alone to discuss 'me'? Mildred, could you point out one of those wealthy ladies to me and I'll excuse myself?"

Stephanie elbowed Jack. "Behave. There's nothing to discuss. My mother is a drama queen. Let's go back inside, Jack. You promised me a dance."

"Honey, I am only looking out for what's best for you."

"Mrs. Mason, I'm Jack Kaufman." She refused to shake his outstretched hand, which spurred him into action.

"Your daughter has requested my services for the evening. They are expensive, but well worth the money." Stephanie couldn't resist a smile as Jack's twinkling eyes met hers. He winked at her. "If I can ever do 'anything' for you, let me know. I give family discounts."

Mildred gasped and grabbed her heart in outrage. "Stephanie, are you insane? You pick up a complete stranger at a party, a gigolo no less! Have you no shame? Have you lost your mind? This is ludicrous!"

"Jack is not a stranger, Mother." Stephanie was trying to hide her amusement as she enjoyed her mother's discomfort. "I hired him on Monday. He really is the best at what he does."

"Thank you." Jack smiled, caressing her arm. He leaned over and kissed her. "I aim to please."

"So far I haven't been disappointed. I can't wait to see what you teach me next. I'm a quick learner."

"You haven't seen anything yet, sweetheart." His eyes held a promise she tried desperately to ignore. "It was nice chatting with you, Mom, but the clock is ticking so to speak." His arms closed around Stephanie and his head lowered to hers again. His mouth feasted on hers and she responded wholeheartedly. "Meet me back at the hotel for that bubble bath and full body massage we discussed earlier." He gave her another quick kiss and then he was gone.

Stephanie stared at his retreating back. Her hand touched her still throbbing mouth. In that moment she knew she was in big trouble. She had been thoroughly kissed by a mercenary and had enjoyed every delicious moment.

Oh God. What have I done? I can't believe I let this happen. I can't make the same mistake again. I have to keep him at arm's length. He is so not the one for me. This was just for show. It was for my mother's benefit, nothing more.

When Stephanie turned to look at her mother, she

almost felt sorry for her. Mildred was sitting on the bench with her head in her hands.

"Mom, are you okay?" She couldn't stand the tortured look on her mother's face. Stephanie lowered her eyes in defeat.

"Am I supposed to be okay about this? You are acting careless and irresponsible, like me. What about poor Stanley? You won't sleep with him, but you pick up this gigolo and install him in your hotel for your pleasure. That's something I would do. That's not something you would do. You are too levelheaded. Honey, I know you run a multi-million-dollar hotel chain and you're an independent woman, but this is more than I can take. What's going on with you?"

It was confession time. She sat down next to her on the bench. "Mom, Jack is not a gigolo. We were playing around to get you riled up. He saw you coming with bachelor number three of the evening and I told him to pretend we were together. That's why he kissed me. It wasn't real."

"Oh, that's a relief," said her mother, exhaling a deep breath. "But be careful. That kiss I witnessed didn't look pretend. I saw the way you responded. Stephanie, stay away from that man. He's not for you. There's something about him that seems almost suspicious. I don't trust him for a minute."

You don't know the half of it, Mom, and my guess is right now is not a good time to tell you. You'd probably pass out.
"Mom, you don't trust any man."

"And neither should you. They are all liars and cheaters. They always leave in the end. The sex may be great for a while, but—"

"Please stop," said Stephanie, cutting her off before she started ranting and raving about her absentee ex-husband. "Jack is not a gigolo." Her mother looked at her skeptically. "Jack Kaufman is the new security consultant I hired

a few weeks ago. That's why he's staying at the hotel. He's
not my love slave. You can relax."

"He looks more like a criminal than he does hotel security. Where on earth did you find him? He's so imposing
and intimidating."

You have no idea how close to the truth you are!
"I posted an ad and he applied for the job. It takes a thief
to catch a thief."

"Stephanie, I think you are making a huge mistake. That
man spells trouble for all of us. He seems dangerous.
There's something about him. I can't put my finger on it,
but I have a bad feeling about him. Did you do a criminal
background check on him? I bet he's a criminal. A man
like that has to be wanted for something."

*Oh, he's wanted all right, Mom. I wanted him a few
minutes ago. I still do, but my common sense has returned.
I know he's not for me.* "You're overreacting as usual,
Mother. I can handle Jack. He's an employee, nothing
more." Even as she voiced the words, Stephanie wasn't sure
she could live up to them. Jack Kaufman was like no one
she had ever met. *God, please let me be able to handle Jack.*

Stephanie was lying in bed when her phone vibrated on
the nightstand. Frowning, she reached over and picked it
up. She laughed as she read Jack's text message.

Your bubble bath is getting cold. I owe you a
massage. You can collect any time you like.

Stephanie typed in her response. I could use a massage,
but I can't imagine you in a bubble bath.

She smiled at his response. Stranger things have happened, boss lady. How's Mildred? Has she calmed down
any?

She typed her final message for the night. *Not really. I told her who you really were, but I'm not sure if it made matters better or worse. Good night, Jack.*

Sweet dreams, Stef. Stephanie read Jack's message and placed her phone back on the nightstand.

Stephanie's sleep was anything but peaceful and restful. Imagines of Jack were invading her thoughts. As much as she would like to, she could not forget their kiss.

In the weeks that followed, she couldn't keep him out of her thoughts or her office.

She could barely keep up with his energy and zest for life. He didn't do anything halfway as he whipped both his staff and Stephanie into shape.

Stephanie breathed a sigh of relief when he flew out of town on business. He was at the hotel in Phoenix heading up security for an annual gala. He tried to get Stephanie to go with him, but she declined. He assured her it was for business only, but she wasn't convinced.

She had an entire week to get her emotions and her life back in check. Stephanie was not about to let Jack creep into her personal life any more than he had done already. She would draw the line between their business and personal lives. She owed it to her daughter and to herself not to get involved with someone with Jack's checkered past. There was no room in her life for a man like him.

Stephanie felt ridiculous even thinking about Jack this way. They only shared a few kisses the night of the Waterfords' party. He hadn't so much as made a pass at her since then. Still, she couldn't get him off her mind. She was thinking of reasons why they shouldn't be together when she had no reason to think he wanted to be with her in the first place.

I'm losing my mind. That's the only explanation. She glanced down at the calendar on her desk. Jack was due back today and she was torn between wanting to be there and not wanting to see him. She missed him and didn't trust herself to be around him right now. So she took the rest of the day off to clear her mind.

Stanley had invited Stephanie to a Halloween party, but she didn't want to go. She hated parties and she hated Halloween even more. Needing a distraction, she relented.

She waited until the last possible moment to find an outfit. The only outfits she found in her size were witches' costumes and Indian dresses. She chose the latter.

Stephanie stared at her reflection in the mirror. Parting her hair down the middle, she braided it and tied a piece of black leather on each end.

Didn't every little girl want to be a princess?

"Mommy, you look pretty," said Christina, running into the room. She jumped up on Stephanie's bed while hugging her favorite stuffed teddy bear. "Can I come too?"

"No, you can't come, sweetie," said Stephanie, walking over to the bed. Smiling, she tickled her. "It's past your bedtime. What are you still doing up? I know I tucked you in and read you a story at least half an hour ago."

"But I wanted to see your costume." Christina picked up one of her mother's braids. "You look like a real Indian princess."

"It's bedtime." Stephanie picked her up and carried her back to her bedroom. "Nana is downstairs if you need anything." She laid her daughter on the bed and covered her. "Tomorrow we are going to the park for a long-overdue picnic. I love you, pumpkin."

"I love you too, Mommy. Have fun. Are you going with Mr. Stanley? I don't like him. He doesn't like me either. I can tell."

"Of course he likes you. What's not to like? You are a

wonderful little girl." Stephanie leaned over and kissed her forehead. "No more talking. Go to sleep."

"Good night, Mommy. Maybe you will meet a real prince tonight." The sleepy little girl yawned.

"Maybe I will." Stephanie smiled, turning off the light. She went downstairs to wait for Stanley.

"Nice costume," said Mildred from the sofa. She glanced up at Stephanie, and then back at the television.

"A compliment from my mother. Will miracles never cease?" Stephanie sat down next to her on the sofa.

"I can't wait to see Stanley's costume. It will probably be something dull like he is." She smiled, picking up the wineglass from the coffee table. "He could be a wet blanket. That would be quite fitting."

"Mom, can't you ever say anything nice about anyone I date?"

"You haven't had a real date in four years. You remember what a date is, right? Dinner, dancing, and stimulating company."

The doorbell chimed. "Good night, Mom."

"Don't have too much fun," Mildred laughed. "Since you're with pocket lint himself, I'm sure you won't."

Stephanie was more than a little surprised to see Stanley dressed as Captain Hook. He looked ridiculous in the costume. Her mother probably would have laughed him out the front door. He couldn't pull off the pirate look. It wasn't him.

Chapter 3

Stephanie's eyes locked with Jack's from across the room. She blinked several times to make sure she wasn't imagining him. She knew he was due back in town today, but here, at a private party, was the last place she expected to see him. She had left work early to avoid seeing him and here he was.

How appropriate that he should come to the party dressed as a pirate. It was definitely in character for him. Their eyes held as he made his way over to her. Stephanie turned and fled out the patio door.

Jack followed, as she knew he would. She waited until he closed the door behind him, before she pounced on him. "What are you doing here? When did you get back?"

"I got back today midday. I dropped by your office, but you were already gone. I'll be going back in a couple of weeks to follow up with the manager. I put some new procedures in place and I want to make sure they are followed. To answer your other question, I'm here because you're here."

"What did you do, make a copy of my day planner?" she joked. He smiled wolfishly. "You did, didn't you?"

She poked him in the chest with her finger. "You are spying on me. You have me under surveillance."

"Do you mind?" He caught her hand in his. Stephanie jerked her hand away. "You have an overactive imagination, my Indian princess." His words belied his expression.

"No, I don't." She faced him squarely. This was no coincidence. He knew she would be at the party. He admitted as much. "Don't try and tell me this is another coincidence. You're stalking me? Why? What do you want? What am I missing, Jack?"

"I'm not stalking you," he said, advancing on her. His arm looped around her waist and he pulled her flush against him. "Believe me, if I were stalking you, you'd never know it."

She was mesmerized as she followed the descent of his mouth. The heat from his breath fanned her cheeks. His mouth had barely touched hers and she was melting in his arms. She swayed against him and her body brushed invitingly against his. The patio doors opened. The spell was broken and she extricated herself from his arms quickly. He caught her arm to stop her from fleeing. "You can run, but you can't hide from your feelings. There is something between us, Stef. I feel it and you feel it and it's got you running scared. Believe it or not, it scares me too. So, did you miss me?"

"Now who has the overactive imagination? Your ego knows no bounds, Mr. Kaufman. I feel nothing for you. You are not my type. You are not even in the ballpark. And no, I didn't miss you. I'm not into big scary men who carry even bigger guns."

"As close as you were to me moments ago, I can guarantee you it wasn't a gun you felt against you." Heat suffused her face. "You are as into me as I am into you. Care to put it to the test, Miss Mason? I do so love a challenge. Type has nothing to do with physical attraction. Normally, you're not my type either. You are way too high maintenance for my taste. I can see the ice princess starting to thaw." He stroked her cheek. "The kiss we shared proved the fire is there beneath the ice." He took a step closer and she stood her ground. "You don't need me to tell you what happens when fire and ice come together."

Stephanie was determined not to back down. She would not let him intimidate her. They stared at each other in silent combat.

"There you are," said Stanley, staring from Stephanie to Jack. He frowned when he saw Jack's hand on her arm. Stephanie moved out of his reach and his hand fell away. She took the drink Stanley offered her and took a step away from both men.

"We haven't met. I'm Stanley Jordan, Stephanie's boyfriend." Stanley didn't hold out his hand, nor did Jack extend his.

Jack simply raised his eyebrows in a question and Stephanie blushed. "I'm Jack Kaufman. I'm the new security consultant for Luciano Hotels."

Stanley's frown deepened. "You work for Stephanie. Funny, she hasn't mentioned you before."

"I'm not surprised. Don't take offense, Stanley, but she hasn't mentioned you either. I guess we both must have slipped her mind. She's under a lot of pressure running a hotel chain. I think she needs a vacation. Why don't you take her somewhere special for a couple of days? Some place warm so she can thaw, I mean chill out. Would you two lovebirds excuse me? I promised a dance to Lady Godiva inside. It was nice meeting you, Stanley. I'm sure I'll see you around." He winked at Stephanie. "Save me a dance later, Princess."

Stanley watched Stephanie as she watched Jack walk away. Folding her arms over her chest, she turned back around to face Stanley. She didn't like the look on his face.

"Did I interrupt something? You two seemed pretty intense when I walked up. He was touching you. Why?"

"It's not a big deal." She took a sip of her drink, glad for the distraction. "Jack makes a habit of being irritating."

"Then fire him," Stanley demanded. "I don't like him. I don't like the way he looks at you and I don't like the way you were looking at him."

Stephanie bristled in indignation. "I'm not going to fire Jack because you feel threatened by him. I need him." Stanley's eyebrows rose in question. Stephanie flushed. "What I meant was the hotel needs him. Luciano's needs his expertise," she corrected. "Do you know how long I ran that ad before the right man walked into my office?"

Stanley folded his arms over his chest and shook his head. He stared at her over the rim of his wire-frame glasses. "So now he's Mr. Right?"

"That is definitely not what I said. Jack Kaufman is as far from Mr. Right as you can get. Stanley, drop it. He's an employee, nothing more." The lie didn't even sound convincing to her ears. Stephanie threw her hands in the air. "I don't want to talk about this anymore. This is a party. Let's go have fun. You do know how to have fun, don't you?" She went back inside, leaving him no choice but to follow her. Her heart missed a beat when she saw Jack dancing with Lady Godiva. She felt more than a twinge of envy at seeing the other woman in his arms.

Stanley was glued to her side for the next half hour. When some business associates finally dragged him away, Stephanie was relieved and thrilled. She felt like a weight was lifted from her shoulders.

Her eyes scanned the room looking for Jack. *I must be insane. Why am I looking for trouble? Why am I playing with fire?*

"Would you like to dance?"

She tensed at the sound of that husky voice so close to her ear.

"I dare you."

As she turned around to face him, her eyes met his. "Let's add fuel to the fire, Stef."

"There is no fire. There is barely a flicker of a flame." His look told her he clearly didn't believe her. "Enough with the fire and ice references. If I dance one dance with you, will you go away?"

"If that's the way you want it. Who knows, maybe one dance will put out the fire, but then again, maybe not. You may just melt in my arms." He held out his hand to her.

"One dance." Stephanie caught his hand and trembled at the contact. She was powerless to stop him as he threaded his fingers with hers and led her to the dance floor. As his arm went around her, she knew she had made a mistake.

So much for keeping him at arm's length! I'm drowning. I need a life preserver to stay afloat.

Being this close to Jack was disturbing. He made her feel things she had never felt before. He awakened her body and her senses. She felt truly alive and reckless whenever she was with him.

His cologne was as intoxicating as the man himself. Her hand rested easily against the small of his back. They moved beautifully together to the sound of the music.

Jack was as affected as she was. Stephanie felt too damn good in his arms. His arm tightened around her waist and he held her close. He was in heaven and hell as her firm breasts pressed slightly against his chest. He had mentally undressed her with his eyes a thousand times and right now was no different. He wanted to take her out of the party and back to his room.

"Jack," whispered Stephanie, "the music stopped." His fiery eyes held hers. Stephanie was as dazed as he was. His eyes were molten lava, searing her flesh.

Bringing her hand to his lips, he kissed it. He felt her tremble beneath his mouth and smiled. Jack regrettably released her and took a step back.

"Thank you for the dance. It was everything I knew it would be. Don't waste all that fire and passion on a man like Stanley. He can't appreciate it. I can." He bowed slightly and then walked away.

A short time later, Stanley took the microphone and walked to the middle of the room. Stephanie felt a cold sinking feeling in the pit of her stomach. She was praying he was not about to do what she knew he was about to do.

Please don't say it. God, please don't let him ask me to marry him in front of all these people. No, Stanley. Don't do it.

He held out his hand to her and on wooden legs, she moved forward to take his hand. Her heart almost stopped when he dropped down to one knee and took a small box out of his suit coat. He opened the box and took out the ring. She stared in appreciation at the size of the ring.

"Stephanie Mason, will you marry me?"

Stephanie was immobilized with fear. *No!* She didn't really want to say yes, but she didn't want to embarrass him either. She heard someone choking and if she didn't know any better, she would have sworn it was Jack. Stephanie wanted the room to open up and swallow her. This was not what she wanted.

Before Jack Kaufman walked into her life, she could have been content with Stanley. Now the thought of spending the rest of her life with a man she didn't want to sleep with was not even an option.

"Stephanie, will you marry me," he nervously repeated. Stanley and the crowd waited expectantly for her answer.

Stephanie couldn't bring herself to embarrass him by saying no in front of everyone. "Yes," she said so softly only he heard her. Smiling brightly, he took the ring and placed it on her finger. She forced a smile when he came to his feet and kissed her in front of their audience.

The kiss left her unsatisfied and unfulfilled. She couldn't help comparing it to the passionate kiss she had shared with Jack. There was no spark between her and Stanley. The kiss was wet and unfulfilling.

As everyone moved in to congratulate them, Stephanie felt as if she were suffocating. She needed air. The ring felt as if it weighed ten pounds. She had to get out of there, and fast.

Her eyes peered around the room until they found Jack. His eyes were smirking as he raised his drink in salute. He made his way through the crowd.

She exited the side door for air. Breathing in deeply helped to calm her nerves. She felt Jack's presence behind her. "Did you come to congratulate me?"

"No, I came to ask you, what the hell were you thinking?" he snapped. He caught her elbow and turned her around to face him. "Why did you accept his proposal? And please don't insult my intelligence by telling me you love him. Clearly you don't. Hell, you didn't even look like you were enjoying him kissing you. The kiss we shared was real. That was a performance and a lousy one at that."

"I don't have to explain anything to you," she bristled, shaking off his hand. "I couldn't embarrass him in front of all those people. They are his friends."

"It sure as hell beats the alternative. Can you see yourself married to that cardboard cutout of a man? He'd bore you to death inside a week, maybe less." He held up her hand. "This is some rock. It must have set him back a pretty penny." He examined the ring closer. "The stone is a good quality. He shouldn't have any trouble returning it when you give it back to him."

"And who says I'm going to give it back? It's a beautiful ring." She jerked her hand from his.

"Common sense says you're giving it back if you have any. He is clearly not the man for you."

"And you are?" she asked incredulously.

"I didn't say that," he hedged.

"I didn't think so. At least I know he'll be around tomorrow and not off somewhere pillaging the countryside and ravishing maidens."

"My pillaging days are over and as for ravishing maidens, you are the only woman I want to ravish." His dark eyes raked over her, stripping her naked in a glance and making her blush. "As for that wimp, he'll be around because when he looks at you he sees dollar signs. You could be standing in front of him naked and he would still be trying to balance your bank account."

"Show me a man in this room who doesn't see money when he looks at me and I'll marry him. Men generally marry for two reasons, obligation or money. Since I'm not pregnant, I guess that leaves money."

"You forgot sex."

She flushed under his heated gaze.

"That's the third reason men marry. If I married you, it would definitely be for sex."

"I should slap your face for that."

"Try it and I will kiss you until you swoon. That should give everyone here something to talk about. Straitlaced balls-to-the-wall Stephanie Mason accepted dull, fortune-hunting Stanley's marriage proposal less than ten minutes ago and already she's bored. She's out on the patio making out with the hired help. Let's see how good you are at faking happiness, Stef. Pretend for the rest of the night you are on top of the world. Pretend Stanley is everything you have always wanted in a man. Even you aren't that good an actress."

"Haven't you heard, Jack? Women can fake anything," she fired back, pivoting to leave.

His hand on her arm stopped her from leaving. His touch sent a jolt through her. "Is that what you do in his bed? Is that how you get through the night?"

Her face turned bright red. "Whether or not I'm in his bed is none of your business," she hissed.

"I guess that answers that question. If you were with the right man, you wouldn't have to fake it."

"I hope you are not considering yourself Mr. Right," she shot back. Glaring at him, she jerked her arm away and left him staring after her.

You never know, Stef. We are not finished by a long shot. Stanley Jordan is a nonissue. He's an obstacle easily removed. As for me being Mr. Right, I can guarantee you that's something I've never been called.

Jack was walking to his car when he heard someone calling his name. He turned around in surprise to see Stanley heading his way. He slowed his pace, but didn't stop.

He knew this confrontation was bound to take place sooner or later. Stanley would have to be blind not to miss the sparks flying between him and Stephanie.

"Hold up a minute, Kaufman. I think we need to talk." Stanley had to almost run to keep up with Jack's long, sure stride.

Jack stopped and waited for the other man to catch up with him. "I can't imagine what we would have to talk about," he said coyly. "Do you need some security consulting at your firm? I can recommend someone, but I'm under contract with Luciano's and I don't moonlight."

"No, I don't need a security consultant. What I need is for you to back off. I saw the way you were looking at Stephanie and I don't like it. Stephanie Mason is mine," he said, getting straight to the point.

"So it would seem, but I wouldn't bank on it if I were

you. It was pretty ingenious of you to propose to her in a roomful of people you both know. Stephanie is too much of a lady to embarrass you by saying no in front of your friends, but there's always tomorrow. I'm sure she'll come to her senses by then and realize what a mistake she would be making in settling for someone she doesn't really love or want."

"You know nothing about our relationship. I'll have you fired if you try to interfere." Stanley threatened, bristling at Jack's audacity.

"You're welcome to try, but I have a contract. I'll be around long after you're gone. My guess is you'll be gone by tomorrow. Good night," said Jack, turning to walk away.

"A good lawyer will rip that contract and you to shreds. Contracts are broken every day."

"So are engagements. Go enjoy your celebration while you can, Stanley. It'll be the shortest engagement in history. You will never get your hands on Stephanie or the Luciano fortune. She's much too smart to marry you."

"I'll take that bet, Mr. Kaufman, and raise you a million. Stephanie will marry me and you will be left out in the cold."

"I guess the first one of us down the aisle with Stephanie Mason wins the lottery. Stephanie is smart enough to know what you're after. With me, it'll be a surprise. No one will see it coming."

"You have no idea who you are messing with. I have friends in low places. They could make you vanish without a trace," he threatened.

Jack laughed at Stanley's attempt at intimidating him. Catching him by the collar, he shoved him against his car. "Don't ever threaten me again or you won't like the consequences," he warned. "I wouldn't need to call anyone to make you disappear, Stanley. I've been in low places. I would do it myself, with pleasure." Jack released the other man and took a step back. Stanley took a swing at him and he ducked. "I was hoping you'd do something stupid like that." Jack decked him before he saw it coming. Stanley fell back against the car and then slid to the ground with one punch. *What a wimp. I only hit him once. I sure as hell hope Stephanie can defend herself, because you sure can't defend her.*

Hefting Stanley over his shoulder, he carried him to the lawn and dumped him just as the water sprinklers turned on. Jack was walking to his car when Stanley started to wake up. He drove out of the driveway and waited on the street for Stanley.

Mr. Jordan, you have no idea who you are tangling with, but welcome to my world. Let me show you how things are done.

Everyone stared and pointed at wet Stanley as he struggled to get to his feet. He dripped his way to the front door. He asked someone to go inside to get Stephanie while he waited outside and tried to wring some of the water from his outfit.

She was bewildered as she made her way to the door. She slipped outside, eyeing his wet clothes with a frown. "What happened to you?" she asked, noting his black eye. She had a sneaking suspicion she already knew the answer. Stephanie had seen him leave the house immediately after Jack left, and prayed he didn't confront him. His next words confirmed her suspicions.

"I want you to fire that man immediately," blustered Stanley, wringing water from his shirt. "That mongrel attacked me for no reason. I should have him arrested for assault. Look at my suit. I'm definitely sending him the dry-cleaning bill. What is everyone staring at? It's not like they haven't seen a man wet before."

"I'm looking at your eye," said Stephanie, hiding a smile. "It's turning black already. Sending him the bill will really show him who is the bigger man. I can't fire Jack. He has a contract. What happened out here? What did you say to him? He doesn't rattle easily."

"You should be more concerned about what he said to me. He's after you, Stephanie. That fortune-hunting bastard is after your money. He admitted as much."

If that's not the pot calling the kettle black! I'm not stupid, Stanley. I know what you're after and you will never get your hands on Christina's inheritance.

"I have no interest in Jack Kaufman. You shouldn't have provoked him. He's not someone to mess with, Stanley. You started this. I saw you follow him outside."

"I just wanted to talk to him. I saw the way he was leering at you. I was defending your honor."

"Stanley, there's nothing to defend. Jack has been a perfect gentleman." The lie slipped easily from her lips. "Leave the man alone. The party is over. Let's go. I think you need to get out of those wet clothes before you catch a chill. Can you drop me home? I have to get up early tomorrow." She got in the car and waited for him.

"Stephanie, we just got engaged. Aren't you coming home with me? We could have a real celebration." His hand slid to her thigh.

"Stanley, you know the rule." She picked up his hand and placed it on the seat beside him. "I don't believe in premarital sex."

"But we're engaged," he whined. "Can't we just once?"

She shook her head and turned her face away from him. She had milked this excuse for all it was worth. Her feelings on premarital sex had nothing to do with her reasons for sleeping with him. Simply put, she didn't want him in that way.

"You win," snapped Stanley, putting the car in gear. "I don't know how much more of this I can take."

Jack watched the guests leave and waited patiently for Stanley and Stephanie. He followed Stanley from Stephanie's house. He was puzzled when instead of heading home to change, Stanley drove to a popular area frequented by prostitutes.

Hello. So, what do we have here? Stef, you are falling down on your job by not pleasing your man.

He parked a short distance and watched as two young hookers got into the car with Stanley. Smiling, Jack took several photos of them getting into the car. He followed as Stanley turned into a seedy motel a short distance from where he picked up the girls. He handed one of the girls some cash and she went inside to get a room key. Holding up the key, she got back into the car and he drove to the back of the motel. Jack zoomed in on them getting out of the car and going into the room.

Jack was still smiling an hour later, when he looked over the developed photos. Stanley Jordan was now out of the picture, he was sure of it.

Stephanie's mother hit the roof when she saw the engagement ring. She begged and pleaded with her daughter to reconsider. The more she was against the idea, the more Stephanie stuck by her decision to marry Stanley. After all, she could do a lot worse.

Christina took the news even worse than her mother. She didn't like Stanley and didn't want her mother to marry him. She cried in her room for hours.

The weekend at the Mason household was one of anger, confusion, and frustration. Ashley laughed when Stephanie told her about the engagement. She wanted to know what she was drinking the night she accepted. She told Stephanie, Stanley would bore her to death in less than a week.

By Monday, Stephanie decided to give the ring back to Stanley. She knew she couldn't marry a man she didn't love or want physically. They were having dinner tonight and she would give the ring back to him and break the news to him as gently as possible.

Stephanie was having lunch in the hotel restaurant when Jack yanked out a chair and sat down across from her. She ignored him, hoping he would eventually go away.

"Today is Monday and you are still wearing his ring. I guess that makes it official, either that or he avoided you yesterday and you couldn't give it back to him."

"It is official. I am marrying Stanley. Did you want something in particular or just to ruin my appetite?" she asked sweetly.

"You say the sweetest things. Talk like that could turn my head. I wanted three things actually. You left your computer on again when you left your unlocked office. I resisted the urge to lock you out again. Second, I'm teaching a self-defense class Thursday in meeting room 102, encourage everyone to attend. I'll send you an e-mail with all the specifics."

"You said three things." She laid down her fork and folded her hands on the table in front of her.

"Here's an early birthday present for you." He took the envelope of pictures out of his jacket pocket and dropped them on the table in front of her. "Pictures from the after party Saturday night. It looks like you missed all the fun." He picked up the fork in front of her. "This looks wonderful. Are you going to eat that?" he asked, pointing to the succulent shrimp basted in a warm butter sauce.

"Be my guest." Against her will, she followed the shrimp

to his mouth. He moaned in appreciation and waved the waiter over.

"I'll have whatever this is and a Coke. Thank you." He waited until the waiter was out of earshot. "That's where he went when he left your place on Saturday night. Stef, you're not pleasing your man."

Stephanie picked up the envelope and took out the pictures. She was shocked at the first one. There were two half-dressed women all over Stanley. One was wearing a tank top and short shorts; the other one was clad in a red minidress. His arms were around both women and his hands on each of their breasts.

There was little doubt in her mind what profession the women were in. It was apparent in their dress. They were prostitutes. Stanley was with two hookers. She should care, but she didn't. She dropped the photos back on the table.

"You followed us." She was amazed at his audacity. "You followed him. Why? What was the point?"

"Of course I followed him. I was curious to see if you would sleep with him in celebration of your engagement."

Stephanie choked on her water. After a fit of coughing, she was able to catch her breath. She picked up her napkin and dried her eyes.

"Have you ever slept with him?" She refused to answer or to meet his eyes. "I take that as a no. I can understand his need for looking elsewhere for pleasure, but he could have been a little more discriminating. These two aren't exactly high-dollar working girls."

"And you know this how?" she shot back. "Don't answer that. I don't want to know. It's none of my business."

He merely smiled. "Stanley and two women, go figure. I never would have guessed he could please one. Maybe he just watched them. What do you think? Is he any good in bed?"

"I think this is none of your business." She coughed. "So he paid for sex. Big deal. He's not the first man to pay for pleasure and he won't be the last. Have you ever paid for pleasure?"

"I've never had to pay. Although I do remember a few times they offered to pay me." He winked. Jack reached across the table and ran his fingers over her hand. Stephanie snatched her hand away. "Let me see if I've got this straight. You don't care for his kisses. You don't want to sleep with him yourself and you couldn't care less that he sleeps with prostitutes. Therefore, what is it you don't like, Stef, sex or men? Did I miss something? Are you a closet lesbian?"

Stephanie gave it no thought as she picked up her glass of water and threw it in his face. Furiously she got to her feet and stalked away.

I guess not. Jack picked up his napkin and dried his face. *Maybe I pushed her a little too hard this time.*

Stephanie was furious with Jack as she left the hotel. She didn't know why she bothered having a conversation with him unless it was in regards to business. The man had a one-track mind and he was driving her nuts.

It angered her that he was right on target about her relationship with Stanley. She knew it wasn't the real thing and she knew it was a matter of time before she broke things off with him. She just hated the fact Jack could read her so well.

She dialed Stanley's office on her way over. She wanted to catch him off guard. She needed to surprise him, so he would be available to see her. It was time to end their engagement as soon as possible. She also knew Stanley was more motivated by money than love. He didn't love her any more than she loved him.

"Tami, it's Stephanie Mason. Is Stanley in?"

"Just a moment, Miss Mason."

"Hi, honey," said Stanley brightly. "Are we still on for dinner tonight?"

"Actually," said Stephanie, getting on the elevator to go up to his office, "I'm in your building. Do you have a few minutes to spare?"

"For you, anything."

"Great. I'm right outside your door now." She hung up her phone and dropped it in her purse. She took a deep breath for courage before the door opened.

"What a pleasant surprise." He held the door open for her. Stanley moved forward to kiss her, but she stopped him. She stepped inside and he closed the door behind them. Stephanie held the ring in her fist. Catching his hand, she dropped the ring in his palm.

"I think this belongs to you."

He stared at the ring and then at her.

"I can't marry you, Stanley. I don't love you and I don't think you love me either."

"Honey, I do love you. I've loved you for years. I thought you felt the same way. We are perfectly suited for each other. What happened between Saturday night and today to change your mind?"

"Saturday night you took unfair advantage of me. You knew or were hoping I wouldn't turn you down in front of everyone. We both deserve more. We deserve someone who is going to love us with all their heart. Our soul mates are out there, Stanley. We just have to wait a little longer to find them."

His expression changed as he watched her. "It's because of him." They both knew what *him* he was referring to.

Stephanie flushed and broke eye contact momentarily with them.

"What did he say to turn you against me? I have a right to know."

"Jack didn't say anything. He didn't have to. I wouldn't have married you, Stanley. This is not about Jack or anyone else. This is about us." She handed him the packet of pictures. "I think these speak for themselves." She watched him blanch as he looked at the photos.

Quickly sticking them back in the envelope, he put them in his desk and then looked up at Stephanie. "Who took these? I can explain. It's not what it looks like."

"There's no need to explain anything. Stanley, I'm not judging you or what you did. I understand men need sex. This doesn't even bother me and it should. It would if I loved you."

"If you would sleep with me, I wouldn't need hookers. This is what you pushed me to. This is partially your fault."

"My fault," she laughed without humor. "How is this my fault? I didn't force you into bed with them. If you wanted sex so badly why didn't you just sleep with Gloria? She's been after you for months. You could have kept your money. Her father has plenty."

"That empty-headed little twit. I'd have to gag her first. She talks nonstop. She'd talk all the way through it." He waved the question away with a sweep of his hand. "He did this, didn't he, your new security man? He followed me from the party. He followed us. Don't you find it a bit unsettling that he's stalking you? He's monitoring your movements."

"Jack is not stalking me. Stanley, it really doesn't matter who took them. I wouldn't have married you anyway. I was giving the ring back to you at dinner tonight. I can't marry you. I'm sorry." Stephanie would neither admit nor deny his accusation about Jack. For his own safety, she didn't want him to tangle with Jack. She knew he would lose if he did.

"He's the one who's going to be sorry," he threatened.

"I'll make him pay for this. Someday and some way, he will pay for interfering in my life."

"A word of warning, you really don't want to mess with someone like Jack Kaufman. It could be very hazardous to your health. He's a dangerous man, Stanley. For your sake, steer clear of him."

Chapter 4

Stephanie went back to her office and sat down. She was swamped. Minutes after she got back, Jack popped his head in the door.

"Got a minute?"

She ignored him and continued working. When she looked up again, she only saw a white flag waving in the air.

"If I say no, will you go away?" She closed the folder on her desk and folded her hands together.

"Probably not." Jack smiled, filling the seat across from her desk. His eyes followed the movement of her hands. Her ring was missing.

"What do you want, Mr. Kaufman?" she asked tiredly, putting her elbows on her desk and resting her chin on them.

His eyes gleamed with mischief and his eyebrows rose suggestively. "Now, that could be interpreted as a leading question. If I answered truthfully, you would turn red in embarrassment and then throw me out of our office."

Her eyes narrowed on him.

"I came to apologize for the crack I made earlier."

Her eyebrows shot up in surprise. The last thing she had expected from this man was an apology. She wasn't even sure he knew how to form the words.

"No lesbian would have responded the way you did when we kissed at the party."

Hot color suffused her face and her eyes dropped momentarily.

"We seem to have this attraction."

"I accept your apology," said Stephanie, cutting him off. She came quickly to her feet and rounded the desk to see him out. He caught her arm to stop her. They both felt the jolt of electricity. He let go just as quickly.

"I'm not finished. You can run from the truth all you want, but we both know something happened when we kissed. We are attracted to each other. Ignoring it won't make it go away. Do I make you all hot and bothered?"

She flushed again and her eyes dropped.

"Are you ready to throw that life of celibacy out the window for a walk on the wild side with big, bad Jack? Are you afraid of me, Stef, or the way I make you feel?"

"I don't know what you're talking about," Stephanie lied, moving a safe distance away from him. "You give yourself way too much credit. You aren't nearly as appealing as you think you are. There is nothing between us and there never will be. We have a professional relationship such as it is and a very shaky one at that. I happen to like my life of celibacy. I am not foolish enough to become involved with you or anyone like you. Stay out of my personal life or find yourself another job. Do I make myself clear?"

"Not really." His eyes bored into hers. "Your mouth is saying one thing, but your body seems to be sending out a totally different message." Breaking eye contact, he headed for the door. Turning back around to face her, he winked. "I guess we'll have to wait and see which one wins the battle. My bet is on the body. Sometimes it has a mind of its own."

Blushing, she turned her back on him. She prayed turning away from him would break the connection between them. The air was charged with emotions as he closed the door behind him.

She let out the breath she was holding and collapsed in her chair. *This can't go on. I'm smart enough to follow my head. I just have to be strong enough to listen to it.*

Pushing Jack from her mind, she opened the file on her desk and began to read. A few minutes later, her secretary buzzed her to remind her of Jack's security staff meeting.

Stephanie looked around the room, pleased at the turnout for Jack's first meeting and demonstration. This meeting would serve as an introduction for Jack to the entire staff.

She watched him walk through the room and mingle with everyone before going up to the podium. He had everyone's attention even before he spoke.

"Good afternoon, I'm Jack Kaufman. I've met most of you already, and for those of you I haven't met, you're the lucky ones." This was followed by laughter. "I'm the new security specialist for Luciano Hotels. I bring with me several years of knowledge and practice in the security industry. The binders in front of each of you go over some of the new policies for the hotel. Read them. Learn them. I'm only going to hit the high points today, and then for the second half of today's meeting, I will be teaching you some basic self-defense moves."

Stephanie listened and watched every move Jack made. They made eye contact several times and each time she would break the connection. Jack went through the material with ease. He was a born public speaker. He had a presence that demanded attention and respect.

When it came to demonstration time, he took off his jacket and tie and laid them on the table. Rolling up his sleeves, he asked for volunteers. Every woman in the room raised her hand except for Stephanie.

In the next hour, they all learned various techniques. Jack started with giving them tips on not putting oneself into a situation to become a possible victim.

"Who can tell me what type of clothing has the easiest access?" Stephanie rolled her eyes when all the men raised their hands. "Jerry?"

"A miniskirt."

"That's one. Darryl?"

"Short pants."

"Yes and no. Stephanie?"

Startled, she met his eyes. "Overalls." She had read this somewhere.

"That's right. Two cuts of a knife and you become a victim. Georgette?"

"A short dress."

"There goes Georgette's wardrobe," laughed Jerry as Darryl gave him a high five. "That's what I'm talking about."

"Okay, guys, settle down. Clothing does send out a message. Whether it's the message you want to send out, who can say for sure? I'm not saying throw away your miniskirts and short dresses. What I am saying is think about where you are going and whom you are going with before you dress. A perfect example would be some place with a parking garage. If at any time you are going to be alone or if it's night and you're alone, don't wear anything that is easily taken off. Wear your jeans and a T-shirt. Wear as many layers, buttons, and ties as you like. Don't wear overalls or jumpsuits. Anything one-piece could make you a possible target. The most important factor in all of this is staying alert. Always be aware of your surroundings. Don't get on or off an elevator digging in your purse for your car keys. Put them in your hand before you leave your office. If you are at a shopping mall and it's dark when you leave, never, ever walk alone to your car. Make sure there are other people around. Women should walk in groups. If no one is around, ask the security guard to walk you to your car. Once you get to your car, lock the doors and leave. Don't sit in your car and balance your checkbook. Don't call your best friend on the cell phone and tell her what a great sale J.C. Penney is having. Leave the premises. If it's night, don't stop at the money machine if you are alone. Pay the dollar fifty and walk inside a well-lit store or gas station. It's worth it. You have to be alert at all times. I think that's enough for today, I don't want to overload you. We'll meet again in a few weeks. In the meantime, I will be coming by to check on everyone to make sure you are following the new procedures I put in place. Thank you for your time." This was followed by applause.

Stephanie remained seated while everyone else filed out of the room. Jack had impressed her again. He had managed to hold everyone's attention. He got everyone involved in the discussion, which made the time pass quicker. He used different people in the room to demonstrate different self-defense techniques.

"Pretty impressive," Stephanie said, clapping her hands as she came to her feet. "Great job."

"Thank you. You sound surprised." Jack closed the distance between them. "I told you I'm good at what I do. I've had years of practice."

"I have a feeling you are full of surprises. I can't wait until the next class."

"I also do private demonstrations." Before she had a chance to react, he put his hand over her mouth and hauled her against him. Their bodies touched from breast to thigh. She felt so good in his arms he almost forgot why she was there. Her perfume was hypnotic. "Now, what would you do if someone grabbed you like this?" He held her steadfast, but then dodged when her knee came up near his groin and she tried to bite his hand. "I knew you would try that. It's not always successful." He released her and took a step back. "If you were paying attention in class, then would you know there are other places equally as sensitive."

"It was a natural reaction," she defended. "I was paying attention. The shin and the nose are also sensitive. I'll also try to remember to wear jeans everywhere I go and not go by the money machine at night."

"I'm glad to see you were paying attention. You don't have to wear jeans everywhere, just be aware of your surroundings."

"Are you going to grab me again?" she asked, eyeing him uneasily.

"Would you like me to? I'd be more than happy to oblige." Not bothering to answer him, she turned and walked away. She had gone no more than three feet when he grabbed her from behind. Stephanie's reflexes kicked in and, remembering an old karate move, she flipped him.

Jack and Stephanie were equally shocked by the action. He lay motionless on the floor with his eyes closed.

"Jack," said Stephanie, looking down at him worriedly. "Jack, this isn't funny. Open your eyes." When she received no response, she kneeled down beside him. Stephanie let out a startled squeal when he grabbed her and she landed on top of him. Her startled eyes locked with his. He quickly reversed their positions and smiled down into her flushed face.

"Great reaction, but never stick around to find out if your attacker is going to get back up. I'm touched you cared enough to find out." His hot breath fanned her cheek.

"I don't care. Get off me," said Stephanie breathlessly, shoving at his massive chest. "I can't breathe."

"If I must." Pushing himself up, he caught her hands and pulled her to her feet.

Stephanie removed her hands from his and smoothed the wrinkles from her suit.

"Where did you learn that?"

"Four years of karate," she stated proudly. "I made it all the way to brown belt before I quit."

"Now I'm impressed. Any time you need a good workout, let me know. It's like riding a bike. Once you learn it, you don't forget. Are you going to pass up an opportunity to kick, punch, and flip me?" he teased.

"Not when you put it that way," she laughed. "You always manage to say something to make me want to hit you."

"Stephanie," Georgette interrupted, sticking her head in the door. "Stanley is waiting outside your office for you."

Stephanie sighed in exasperation. "Thanks. Tell him I'll be right there."

"So Stanley is still sniffing after you? Some people are gluttons for punishment. Why do you bother with him? Are you that desperate for a man?"

She bristled at his question. "Stanley and I are still friends. Why am I explaining myself to you? My personal life is none of your business. I think I'll take you up on that workout. You're back to being irritating again."

"I have an idea. Are you up for a ride?"

"Excuse me?" Stephanie wasn't sure she understood the question. She knew he could be uncouth, but surely he wasn't suggesting what she thought he was suggesting.

Jack laughed at the expression on her face. "On my Harley, Stephanie. Have you ever been on a Harley?" Embarrassed, Stephanie turned on her heel and walked away. "I have an extra helmet," teased Jack to her departing back. She left him staring after her.

On Sunday night, Stephanie and Christina were watching a movie when the doorbell rang. Stephanie left her daughter and went to answer the door. Her mother was out and Ashley was upstairs getting ready for a date. Maybe her date was early.

Stephanie frowned when she looked out the peephole to see Jack standing there. He was clad in jeans and a polo shirt. Looking down at her T-shirt and denim shorts, she felt a bit self-conscious. Her hand shook slightly as she opened the door.

"Hi. What are you doing here?" she asked, wiping her sweaty palms on her shorts.

He eyed her appearance in appreciation. Stephanie was a knockout dressed up or dressed down. "I'm flying out to Atlanta in a couple of hours and I wanted to see you before I left."

"Why?" she asked softly. "Was there something we forgot to go over? I thought we pretty much covered everything." As their eyes held, they both knew the answer to her question.

He took a step toward her, but stopped when a movement out of the corner of his eye caught his attention. His gaze softened as it rested on the little girl with long flowing dark hair in the pink pajamas. She was holding a brown teddy bear in front of her. It wasn't just any bear, but the musical bear he had given Alexia on their wedding night.

Stephanie followed his gaze to Christina. She was leaning against the door watching them. Smiling, she held out her hand and Christina ran to take it.

"Jack, this lovely precocious little girl is my daughter, Christina. Christina, this is Mr. Kaufman. He works with Mommy."

A lump formed in Jack's throat as he came face-to-face with his daughter for the first time. She was even more beautiful up close. He kneeled down to her and held out his hand to her. His heart pounded loudly as he waited for a response from her.

She hesitated only briefly before taking his outstretched

hand. A sense of warmth and love spread through him at the first touch.

"It's nice to finally meet you, Christina," he said in an emotion-filled voice. He reached out and brushed a strand of hair from her face. He wanted nothing more than to take his daughter in his arms, but he knew he couldn't do that. Not yet anyway. He had to wait and be patient.

"Want to watch the end of the movie?" she asked, smiling. "It's almost over."

"Honey, Jack has a plane to catch. He has to get going. Maybe he can watch some other time." She was embarrassed by her daughter's question. She knew Jack had better things to do than spend time with her daughter.

"I have time. I'd love to see the movie," he said, coming to his feet. Catching his hand, Christina led him to the den. "What are we watching?" His voice trailed off as he left the room with Christina.

Stephanie was speechless as she watched them go. *Did I miss something? My little girl has just asked Jack of all people to watch a Disney movie with her and he has said yes. Mr. Macho is watching a kid flick. What is wrong with this picture? I must be in la-la land. That's the only explanation. My daughter has hated every man I brought home and now she latches on to Jack Kaufman, the one man who is off-limits for me. It figures.*

She stopped abruptly when she entered the den to see Christina and the teddy bear curled up in Jack's lap. He seemed way too comfortable holding her daughter. His rich laughter filled the air at something Christina said.

She didn't hear Ashley approach and jumped at the sound of her voice next to her ear. Stephanie backed out of the room, pulling Ashley with her.

"Who is he, and can I have one just like him for Christmas? You finally brought home a man she likes. For a four-year-old, she has great taste. Forget Stanley. This one is a definite keeper. Can we keep him? Does this mean Stanley is history?"

"No, we can't keep him and no, Stanley is not history. Be careful what you wish for, little sister. That's the infamous Jack."

"The Jack Kaufman, gigolo, mercenary extraordinaire. You're kidding, right?" Stephanie shook her head. "Come on. You've got to introduce me."

The movie ended and Christina hopped off Jack's lap to go stop the videotape. Jack came to his feet when he saw Stephanie and her sister coming his way.

He knew who Ashley was from all the surveillance he did while formulating his plan. She was an intern at a local hospital.

"Jack Kaufman, this is my sister, Ashley Mason."

He caught Ashley's outstretched hand. "Hello, Ashley, it's nice to meet you. I'm sure you've heard all about me from your sister."

"You got that right. The tales I could tell. Do you have any brothers?" blurted out the beautiful petite miniature of Stephanie. "How do you feel about cloning?" They all laughed at her suggestion.

"Somehow I don't think your sister could handle another me." He liked Ashley instantly. Her openness and honesty were refreshing.

"Who's talking about Stef? The clone would be for my personal entertainment. I now know what I want in my Christmas stocking."

"And you're the meek, shy one, I suppose," he teased.

Christina yawned loudly and then covered her mouth with her hand in hopes no one heard her. They all laughed again as Ashley swung her up into her arms. "Say good night, Christy."

"Good night, Christy," she giggled, resting her forehead against her aunt's. The loving bond between them was very evident. Ashley spent as much time as she could with her niece.

"Come on, silly. It's bedtime for you. Let's give Mommy and Jack a few minutes to talk."

"Good night, Mr. Jack," said Christina lunging for him. He caught her and returned her warm hug. Again, Ashley and Stephanie were amazed by her attachment to Jack.

"Good night, sweetheart. Sweet dreams."

"Come back and see me," she whispered for his ears only, but everyone heard her. Stephanie was embarrassed, while Ashley merely smiled.

"I promise," he whispered, kissing her cheek.

A knot formed in Stephanie's stomach as she watched the two of them. She knew her daughter missed the attention of a father figure and Jack was obviously missing his daughter. She would have to make sure her daughter didn't get too attached to him. That shouldn't be a problem, because she had no intention of getting attached to him. He was definitely not the father she had envisioned for her daughter.

"I'll be up in a little while to tuck you in, sweetie."

"Okay, Mommy."

With a heavy heart, Jack watched his daughter leave. It took all his inner strength to let her go. He closed his eyes and took a deep relaxing breath. When he looked up, he saw Stephanie watching him intently.

"I'd better be going," Jack said, abruptly leaving the den. He knew he had to get out of there before his emotions got the best of him. Jack was always so in control of his emotions. He couldn't talk to Stephanie right now. He was too emotional. He wasn't ready for her to know the truth. He needed more time.

"Jack." Stephanie rushed after him. She caught his arm to stop him from leaving. "Christina reminds you of your daughter, doesn't she?" It was more a statement than a question.

"Yes," he answered, but didn't turn around to face her. *She is my daughter!*

"Then go see your daughter. It's obvious to me you love her and you miss her. Go see her."

"You don't understand the circumstances. It's complicated. My daughter has no idea who I am. I have never been part of her life."

Stephanie was floored by his answer. She never considered this possibility. "It's not too late for you to have a relationship with her. She's four years old. You need her. She needs you. If you don't go see her, you will regret it the rest of your life."

He turned around to face her at last. "If you were the woman who is raising my daughter, could you honestly say you would want me in her life?" he asked pointedly.

Stephanie felt a chill go down her spine as she wrestled with her answer. If the situation was hers, she knew for a fact that she would not want him anywhere near Christina given his background. She would fight him tooth and nail to keep him away.

"You know who and what I am. Would you let me in your daughter's life without a fight?"

"I honestly don't know what I would do," she said softly, lowering her eyes.

"Yes, you do," he said, turning away. "You wouldn't, Stef, and we both know it. I'm not exactly father-of-the-year material."

"Jack, this is not about me. This is about you and your daughter. You have to at least try. You don't strike me as a man who gives up easily. She's your daughter and you have rights. Make her see you mean no harm. Make her see you only want to spend some time with your daughter. You don't strike me as a quitter. Don't give up."

"I never give up on something I want." His hand caressed her flushed cheek. He leaned forward and his lips touched hers tenderly. Stephanie didn't move as his lips grazed over hers in a gentle caress. She felt her resolve begin to crumble just as he moved away from her. "I'll see you in two weeks." Jack closed the door behind him.

Stephanie went through two weeks of soul searching. She missed Jack's presence in the hotel. She had weighed the pros and cons a thousand times about getting involved with a man like him. There was no future in it and she realized it. He was good looking and charming, but he was also dangerous and unpredictable.

Jack had little time to think about Stephanie or his plan. He was busy from sunup to sundown. He encountered problem after problem at the hotel. The manager was on a power trip and less than cooperative.

He implemented new security measures and hired new security. He took them through an abbreviated training course. In a month or so, he could come back and evaluate how things were running.

Stephanie was working diligently when there was a brief knock on her door. She looked up as the door opened and Jack strode into the room. Her smile lit up the room. She didn't realize she was smiling, until Jack smiled back at her.

"Did you miss me?" he asked, watching her closely. His eyes moved over her in a soft caress.

Although she had missed his overbearing presence in the office, wild horses couldn't force it out of her. "Were you gone?" she teased, still smiling at him. "That would certainly explain all the work I've been able to accomplish over the last two weeks."

"Aah. So you did miss me." He sat down in the chair in front of her desk.

Her eyes drank in the essence of the man in front of her. His cologne tickled her nose and tantalized her hormones.

"Anything interesting happen while I was gone?"

"Things ran pretty smooth. How was your trip? Please give me the good news first. I can't handle any bad news right now."

"Do you want the brief synopsis or do you want to wait for the full report? It will probably be just as brief."

She dropped her head to the desk in answer to his question. "Okay. Give me the synopsis."

"I hope you're ready to open your wallet. The hotel needs a complete overhaul. The security system is outdated. The computers are outdated. The manager was not very cooperative. He was personally offended by the fact I was there. We had words on several occasions."

"Is he still in one piece or should I send out a search party to look for the body parts?"

"He's barely in one piece. The urge to beat the crap out of him was always in the back of my mind. Lady, you have no idea of the self-control I've held on to lately."

His eyes bored into hers and Stephanie wasn't sure if he was talking about James Maroney or her. She shifted uncomfortably under his twinkling eyes.

"I'm planning a trip to Jamaica to check out the hotel there. Want to come along?"

"You're kidding, right?" Stephanie looked up at Jack. "I can't just pack up and take off to Jamaica with you. I have a daughter. I have commitments. I have a hotel to run."

"This is purely business. I know you have commitments, Stef. Bring your daughter along."

"Now I know you're kidding. I would never get anything done with Christina around. She's way too adventurous and inquisitive. Kind of like you are."

Jack bit back the retort he wanted to make. *That's because my daughter is just like me.* "Admirable qualities. The more you inquire, the more you learn. There's nothing wrong with being adventurous and inquisitive."

"There is when you're four. You can't be serious about bringing her along. We wouldn't get anything accomplished. Parenting is not an nine-to-five job."

"I'm totally serious. Christina and I get along great. I'll even teach her to swim. When was the last time you took her on a vacation? Have you ever taken her on a vacation? Have you ever taken a vacation?"

"No, not really, but now is not the time either. I have to much to do." Stephanie was tempted. She did so need a vacation. She needed a break, but she wasn't sure whether a trip to Jamaica with Jack would help or hurt.

"And this has been your excuse for how long? Come with me. It's not exactly a vacation. There's a lot of work to be done there. I've gone over the blueprints and the place is a mess. You might be better off tearing it down and starting from scratch."

"Okay," said Stephanie. "We'll go. I'll go. I don't know. Let me think about it overnight." She was tempted to throw caution to the wind and go with him.

"Think fast. I book my flight in two days. I'd love for you to be with me. Just think about it."

Her eyes followed him as he left the office. Stephanie came to her feet and paced the room like a caged animal. Jack's suggestion was so tempting. She had never been to the hotel in Jamaica. She hadn't really gone anywhere since adopting Christina and inheriting the hotel chain. Her life and her daughter were her work.

There's nothing stopping me from going. I have a nanny. I have a mother and sister who help me take care of my daughter. Truth be told, I'm scared. I'm afraid to be alone on a Caribbean island with Jack. I'm attracted to him and I can't help myself.

She worried about her decision the entire weekend. It didn't help matters when Jack called her on Saturday night and grilled her about why she should go. He had a lot of valid points. All communication and staff meetings with senior management were through conference calls and e-mails.

On Sunday, she decided to throw caution to the wind and go. When she called Jack and told him, he said he'd see her at the airport with her ticket. He purchased one for her when he purchased his. She was a bit miffed that he was so sure of her.

Stephanie dreaded telling her mother about the trip. She knew she was in for a lecture, but she had already waited until the last minute. Their flight was scheduled to leave in the morning.

They were in the den after putting Christina to bed when she broached the subject with her mother. Her palms were sweaty and she felt like a teenager all over again. "Mom, I'm going to Jamaica for a few days to work."

Mildred looked at her in surprise. "This is a first. What kind of work do you have at the hotel in Jamaica?"

"I'm going with Jack to go over some new security options." Stephanie waited for the other shoe to drop at her declaration. She didn't have to wait long.

"You're what?" Mildred asked, staring at her daughter in disbelief. "For a minute I thought you said you were going to Jamaica for a week with that mercenary you hired."

"His name is Jack, Mom, and that's exactly what I

said." Her defenses were up and ready to block whatever objections her mother would throw at her. "This is not a wild fling. It's a business trip. I'm going up to pack." Stephanie left the room. She knew the conversation was not over, so she left her bedroom door ajar.

Mildred followed her up the stairs and into the bedroom. "Honey, the man is trouble with a capital T. You are not thinking clearly. You are letting your hormones think for you." She walked around Stephanie and picked up the purple nightgown from the suitcase. "And I suppose business is the reason you bought this."

Stephanie flushed hotly under her mother's close scrutiny. Grabbing the gown, she threw it back in the suitcase.

"This is a seduction gown if ever I saw one. You don't wear things like this, I do. You wear cotton and flannel. You bought this for him."

"I bought the gown because I liked it." This was the truth. She saw the gown, and fell in love with it. What was not to like? It made her look and feel sexy.

"You are kidding yourself. You have never bought sexy lingerie in your life until a few weeks ago. I see the connection, don't you? I have seen the way the two of you look at each other. I know sexual attraction when I see it. I'm surprised you've both resisted each other this long. Honey, you are a beautiful and wealthy woman. You could have any man you want, but not him. He is not the one. Jack Kaufman is a handsome, sexy, and dangerous man. He's not for you. Sleep with him if you must, but don't ever lose your heart to him."

"Thanks for the advice, Mom, but there is nothing going on between Jack and me. He is an employee, end of story."

"The story is far from ended. There is plenty going on with the two of you. It may not be sexual yet, but once you reach the Caribbean, will you be able to say the same? I know all the signs. You have been lusting after that man since the Waterford's party. Mark my words, you two will come back from this trip as lovers. It's inevitable. You have too much chemistry to ignore it. He won't let you ignore it. Honey, it takes a predator to know one."

Chapter 5

Mildred's words were ringing in Stephanie's ears as she studied the profile of the man sleeping in the seat next to her. *You two will come back as lovers.* Her face flushed at the idea.

He even looked dangerous sleeping, dangerous, yet oh so sexy. Stephanie had been fighting her attraction to him since the day he walked into her office. She could no longer deny it. She wanted Jack.

She no longer kidded herself about their relationship remaining professional only. She and Jack had chemistry so strong it scared her. Stephanie knew it was only a matter of time before things escalated.

Jack Kaufman was like no man she had known. He wasn't exactly the three *w*s she was looking for, witty, warm, and wonderful. He was more, wild, wicked, and wanton. She had even gotten used to his cynicism and warped sense of humor. He believed in living life to the fullest and damned the consequences. He liked living dangerously and he played by his own rules. It infuriated her that he was always so cool and so in control of his emotions. The kiss they shared months ago had completely shaken her, while he appeared to be unmoved by it. Nothing she had done thus far had rattled him. He had even smiled when she threw water in his face.

Jack felt Stephanie watching him and wondered what she was thinking. He knew he had her where he wanted her. He was determined to make the most of their trip. Stephanie held the key to all his dreams coming true. In the process, he would do whatever was necessary to make her happy and ensure a future with her and his daughter. Everything he was doing was for Christina's sake.

He had been pleasantly surprised when he phoned her and she agreed to come with him. He knew she was softening toward him and this was his chance to make his move. Before the trip was over, they would be lovers, he was sure of it. Wooing Stephanie Mason was only a small part of his plan. With that thought in mind, he drifted peacefully off to sleep.

The hotel had sent a driver for them. When they arrived at the hotel the manager greeted them at the front door.

"Miss Mason, it is a pleasure to finally meet you," said the handsome man with the thick Jamaican accent. "I'm Louis Devereaux, the manager."

He was tall, about Jack's height, thin, and dark. He wore a black business suit.

Stephanie caught his outstretched hand. "It's nice to finally meet you too, Louis. This trip was long overdue." Removing her hand from his, she turned to Jack. "This is Jack Kaufman, our security consultant. Jack is to have full access to everything while we're here."

"Welcome to Jamaica, Mr. Kaufman." The two men sized each other up as they shook hands. "Is there anything you two would like to see before I show you to your rooms?"

"Lead the way," said Jack. "Be careful you don't step in drool," he whispered for her ears only.

"Be nice," she whispered, elbowing him in the ribs.

"That was nice. He's foaming at the mouth like a rabid dog."

"Is there a problem?" asked Louis.

"No," Stephanie answered quickly. "Jack was just admiring the hotel. He was commenting on how beautiful the island is."

Stephanie was very apprehensive upon learning Jack was in the room next to hers. If she didn't know any better, she would have thought he planned it.

Stephanie was lounging on the bed after taking a relaxing shower when she heard Jack's door open and close. Seconds later, she heard a knock on her door. Getting up from the bed, she opened the door.

"You didn't ask who it was," he scolded. "Care to join me for dinner?"

She looked down her at robe. "I'm not exactly dressed for dinner. How about I meet you downstairs in ten minutes?"

"No need to get dressed on my account." Jack smiled wickedly. "We could always stay here and order room service, later."

She laughed, shaking her head. "Nice try, Jack, but I don't think so. Make that fifteen minutes in the lobby."

"I'm a patient man." He winked at her. "I can wait until you're ready. I'll wait for you downstairs in the bar." They both knew the double meaning behind his words. Stephanie closed the door on his smiling face.

Jack was sitting at the bar chatting with the bartender when Louis walked over and sat down next to him. He ordered a ginger ale.

"Is this your first time to the islands?"

"To this island, yes." He finished off his rum and Coke and ordered a plain Coke. "It's beautiful here."

"I call it home," laughed Louis. "How long are you planning on staying?"

"Possibly a week, maybe longer. It all depends on how much we get accomplished over the next couple of days."

"I can arrange for some female entertainment, that is, unless you brought your own with you." Louis laughed at his own sense of humor.

Jack caught his meaning and merely smiled. He looked down at his watch. He was weighing his answer carefully.

"I can assure you I'm no man's entertainment," Stephanie bristled from behind them. They both turned at the sound of her voice. Louis had the good sense to look embarrassed.

"I can attest to that," Jack mumbled into his drink. She shot him a murderous glare and he raised his glass in salute to her.

"I meant no disrespect, Miss Mason. I incorrectly assumed you two were together."

"We are not 'together,'" she assured him with not much conviction.

"I think she doth protest too much. Lighten up, Stephanie. It was an easy mistake to make. Louis, please show us to a table."

"This way. The chef is preparing a special meal for you. Shall I tell him to begin?"

She nodded and they followed him to a table. He held out the chair for her and then excused himself.

"Do you have to be so uptight? Relax. You're a beautiful woman and he wanted to make sure he wouldn't be stepping on my toes if he made a pass at you."

She folded her hands in front of her on the table and met his eyes. "And how would you have answered the question had I not answered for you?" she asked curiously.

"To save you from being pursued by a lusty Jamaican, I would have said yes, we are involved."

She smiled at his carefully worded answer. "As opposed to being pursued by a lusty American."

Jack laughed. "I like to think I have more finesse than Louis."

"Maybe. Shall we put it to the test?" His eyebrows rose in question. Before he could respond, she waved Louis over to the table. "Please join us for dinner, Louis." He visibly relaxed and sat down. "And call me Stephanie."

"You never told me which approach you prefer," Jack said, following her down the hallway to their rooms. Stephanie stopped in front of her door and turned to face him.

"I've always liked the direct approach," she said, smiling up at him. She nervously wet her dry lips.

Jack followed the movement of her tongue across her lips. "So do I." Placing his hands on either side of her head, he trapped her between his body and the door. Stephanie raised her hands to push him away, but the instant they made contact with his muscular chest, she was lost. The heat from his body seared her already hot flesh and she was powerless to resist when his head slowly lowered to hers. Her eyes closed as his mouth touched hers in a soft gentle kiss. She swayed toward him and his arms closed around her. Her lips parted under the gentle pressure of his and her hands moved up his chest to circle his neck. She clung to him as he deepened the kiss and transported them both to paradise. She moaned softly in protest when he lifted his mouth from hers and ended the kiss. His hand came up and stroked her flushed cheek. "I think at this point you should either invite me in or say good night." His words had their desired effect. Stephanie blushed furiously at his statement. He saw the indecision in her eyes as she weighed his words heavily.

"Good night," she whispered softly, unlocking her door and ducking inside.

Jack leaned against her door. *I knew you would say that. I was hoping you wouldn't, but I knew you would. It's the thrill of the hunt.*

During the day, they worked from morning to late afternoon. Stephanie went over the books, while Jack went over the hotel from top to bottom. He took her through the hotel and instructed her on all the changes he wanted to make. Stephanie agreed with him completely until he showed her the cost of what he wanted to do. After several revisions to his original plans, they finally agreed on a plan of action. Jack and Stephanie made a toast as they sat in the restaurant.

Jack watched Stephanie giggle like a schoolgirl as she drank a fourth fuzzy navel. Her face was flushed and she smiled brightly at him.

She ordered another round of drinks. It hadn't taken Louis long to see the sparks flying between the two of them and he excused himself.

"I think you've had enough." Jack took the glass from her hand. "You are going to be sick in the morning."

"I've never had this much to drink before."

"No kidding," he teased. "I wouldn't have guessed."

"Is it true drinking makes you lose your inhibitions?"

"I wouldn't know. I have none." Jack winked at her. "What you see is what you get."

She giggled again and her eyes turned sultry. "I like what I see. You have a great physique. I bet you've been with women all over the world."

"Pretty much."

Her hand caressed his on top of the table. His other hand covered hers and their eyes locked. "Stephanie Mason, are you making a pass at me?"

"No, I'm letting you catch me. You've been pursuing me

for months. I'm giving in to you. We both want the same thing. This may come as a surprise to you, but you'll have to teach me what you want me to know." He stared at her in confusion. "My experience with men is very limited. You were right about Stanley and me. We were never lovers. I've only been with one guy in my life. I was seventeen years old. It was right after my father walked out on us. I needed to be held by someone, to feel loved. I made love the very first time for all the wrong reasons. It was painful and it was awful. We were both two inexperienced kids who didn't know what we were doing. The only smart thing we did was use protection."

Jack was touched by her confession, but he knew if she hadn't been drunk, she never would have shared this much of herself with him.

"I've never had any desire to repeat the experience, until now. Come back to my room and show me what it's really like to make love. I want you to teach me, to show me what I've missed out on. Prove to me sex is not overrated. I want you, Jack. You were right. There is something between us. I can't deny it any longer. I've wanted you from the beginning. You scare me to death, but you also excite me. You make me feel things I've never felt before." She brought his hand to her lips.

Jack looked around the room to see if they were being watched. When he saw several employees eyeing them curiously, he knew he had to get her out of there. "Come on," he said, helping her to her feet. His arm went around her waist as he led them out of the bar. She snuggled suggestively against him in the elevator and it was all he could do to keep a rein on his own spiraling hormones.

Little did she know it, but Jack was taking her to her room to put her to bed. He had no intention of taking her up on her offer in her present condition. He wanted her stone-cold sober when he made love to her. She would remember the details explicitly the next day.

Back at her room, he took her key and unlocked the door. He helped her over to the bed. She kicked her shoes off and collapsed on the bed. Giggling, she pulled him down on top of her. Her mouth met his in a ravenous kiss. In the process of unbuttoning his shirt, she passed out.

Bringing his emotions under control, he rolled off her and sat up on the bed. His hands shook as he stripped the sleeping woman down to her red lace bra and matching panties. His eyes raked over her body, devouring every inch and curve of her. He picked her up, placed her between the sheets of her bed, and covered her.

Jack unlocked the connecting door that led to his room before leaving her room. When he got back in his, he unlocked his side of the connecting door and opened it slightly. He knew she was going to be sicker than a dog in the morning and he couldn't wait to say "I told you so."

Stephanie's eyes opened slowly. The pounding in her head made her quickly close them again. She sat up in bed holding her aching head. Looking at the clock on the nightstand, she saw a glass of water and two aspirins. She leaned over, took the aspirin, and drank the water. Setting the glass down, she swung her legs to the side of the bed. Stephanie frowned when she looked down at what she was wearing. She paled when bits and pieces of the previous night came back to haunt her. Her last coherent thought was asking Jack to make love to her.

Surely he didn't. If he had, I would surely know it, wouldn't I? I would be naked.

As the soft sounds of music caught her attention, her eyes flew to the partially opened connecting door between their rooms. Groaning softly, she fell back on the bed and covered her face with the pillow.

"So Sleeping Beauty is finally awake." Jack smiled, leaning against the connecting doors.

Stephanie gave a startled squeal and dove under the comforter to cover her nakedness.

"It's a little late for modesty. Who do you think undressed you and put you to bed last night?"

His words brought the blood rushing to her cheeks. "Please tell me you didn't take advantage of my inebriated condition last night."

"I never kiss and tell." He winked. Stephanie hurled the pillow at his smirking face. Jack caught it and tossed it back at her. "Go shower and get dressed. We have a lot of work to do today. Meet me in the lobby in, say, half an hour." He turned to leave the room, but stopped. "Stef, if we had made love last night, you would definitely know it. You wouldn't have to ask."

When he closed the door behind him, she jumped up from the bed. She quickly closed her side of the connecting door and locked it.

After an uncomfortable few minutes for Stephanie, she relaxed when Jack made no mention of the previous night. He was all business.

She could only remember bits and pieces of the previous evening, but she remembered enough to be embarrassed. She had thrown herself at him and he had walked away. She didn't know whether to be insulted or grateful.

They spent the day working diligently. Stephanie was impressed with Jack's professionalism and with his vast knowledge. He pointed out potential problems she never even thought about.

They shared a working lunch in the restaurant while

continuing to go over various details. He showed her several options the hotel could take to upgrade the hotel to today's standards. Stephanie asked for his recommendations and totally agreed with his suggestions.

They also met with Louis and various employees to discuss some of the issues Jack had brought to her attention. By the end of the day, they had accomplished at least half of what they came to Jamaica for. At this rate, they would be done in another day or so.

Stephanie was hesitant when Jack asked her to join him for dinner. She dressed in a casual red wraparound rayon dress that stopped just above her knees. Jack wore khaki pants and a white button-down Havana shirt.

To her surprise, they left the hotel. He rented a car and they took a drive. They ended up at a competitor hotel.

"What are we doing here?" she asked as the hostess seated them.

"It's always a good idea to check out the competition from time to time. Once we're finished with the meal, we'll take a stroll around the hotel. I'm interested in seeing what security measures they have in place."

"You asked me to dinner to look at security locks?" she asked unbelievably.

"Among other things." Jack smiled, winking at her and opening his menu. His sole purpose was to get her out of her safety zone. He wanted her away from Luciano's and away from the prying eyes of her employees. Jack wanted to see her let go and have fun.

They talked easily during dinner about their childhoods. Jack was easy to talk to and Stephanie shared more with him than she had with anyone in the past.

Her father was a doctor and he and her mother divorced when she was seventeen. She hadn't seen or spoken to her father in ten years. Stephanie blamed him for the breakup of their family.

Jack grew up in a small East Texas town. His parents were killed in an automobile accident when he was ten and an elderly aunt raised him. His aunt died right after he graduated from high school. After high school, he joined the navy. He liked it so much he stayed for two terms. Then he joined up with his ex-captain and a few friends and they formed their own elite squad of guns for hire. His wife died several years ago, and a family friend was raising his daughter.

To change the subject and lighten the mood, he turned the conversation to Christina. He knew this would bring a smile to Stephanie's beautiful face.

As they walked through the hotel, Jack pointed out different security features to her. He educated her on the different types of locks and doors. Stephanie was trying to stay focused on the topic at hand, but her mind began to wander after an hour. She finally told Jack she'd had enough for one night.

He surprised her when he suggested they check out the nightclub in the hotel. A few hours later, he was tired and ready to go, but Stephanie was having a wonderful time. He could hardly keep her off the dance floor.

Jack smiled as he watched her dance. She even sang a very sexy and suggestive karaoke song to him. Afterward, she had sworn him to secrecy about telling anyone.

Mission accomplished. She is having a great time. Her smile lights up the room. He imagined for the tenth time tonight, untying the knot at her waist and watching the dress cascade to her feet.

When a slow ballad started playing, Stephanie made her way back to the table. Jack caught her hand and led her back out to the dance floor. She stepped into his arms as if it was the most natural thing in the world for her to do. They moved beautifully together to the island rhythm.

Several more slow songs followed, before they finally

called it a night. They laughed and talked all the way back to the hotel. Still chatting, they took the elevator up to their rooms.

"Thank you for tonight," Stephanie said, smiling up at him. "You really didn't take me there to look at locks, did you?"

"I wanted you to let your hair down and have a good time and I think you did." They stopped outside her room. "It doesn't have to end here, Stephanie." As he raised her chin, his mouth lowered slowly to hers. The kiss was light and very unsatisfying, but he wanted her to be the one to initiate more.

Stephanie definitely wanted more. She craved more. As she moved closer to him, her arms went around his neck. Stephanie brought his head back down to hers. Her lips grazed his. She teased and taunted him into a response.

His arms closed around her and he returned her kiss. Jack still held himself back. He didn't want to scare her away.

"Oops," said a voice behind them. Jack's mouth left hers, but he didn't release her. They both looked at the young girl and her mother who were in the room across the hall from Stephanie. They watched them go inside their room and waited for the door to close.

"I think we should say good night," said Stephanie with a great deal of uncertainty.

"If we must. Good night," Jack repeated, watching her unlock her door. Their eyes met momentarily before she slipped inside her room.

Stephanie's breathing was shallow as she leaned against the door. Stripping off her clothes, she made her way to the shower. "One cold shower coming up."

The initial spray from the showerhead jolted her back

to reality. She squealed, jumped back, and then leaned forward to adjust the water temperature.

Minutes later, she patted her glistening body dry with the fluffy white towel. Slipping into the soft bathrobe, she padded over to the bed with a bottle of lotion in her hands. She parted the robe and applied a generous amount of the sweet-smelling moisturizer to her legs and arms.

On impulse when she was finished, she shimmied into the paisley thigh-high gown. She glimpsed her reflection in the mirror as she paced the room.

She heard Jack's shower turn off and she stopped in her tracks. This brought vivid images of Jack naked to her mind. She could see the water droplets running in rivulets down his muscular chest, then farther down to his flat stomach before disappearing into the thick white towel he wrapped loosely around his waist.

Towel! What towel! Even my fantasies are G-rated. It's not fair.

Throwing caution to the wind, she left her room. Stephanie stood outside his door nervously debating on knocking or going back to her room and taking something to help her sleep. Even when she closed her eyes, she could picture Jack in his swimming trunks coming out of the pool. That was an image she couldn't erase from her mind. She had wanted him then and she wanted him now.

I can't do this! I'm not ready. Okay, I'm ready, but I'm terrified. I'm not even experienced. What if he laughs at me? What if I make a fool of myself?

She went back to her room and collapsed on the bed. Picking up the remote, she turned on the radio. Soft jazz filled the air.

Great! Mood music, just what I didn't need to hear.

The soft knock on the connecting door startled her. Stephanie vaulted off the bed. Her hand trembled slightly as she tried the door. To her surprise, it opened when she turned the knob.

She took an involuntary step back when Jack came into view. Her greedy eyes spanned his bare chest and bulging biceps. He wore only a pair of black silk pajama bottoms. The desire to reach out and touch him was overpowering.

When their eyes clashed, she saw an unmistakable yearning in his gaze. Her eyes mirrored his craving. She wanted him as much as he needed her.

She stood before him in her seduction gown, as her mother had called it, covered by the thin matching wrapper. Her long hair was piled on top of her head with a barrette. The wrapper was also low cut and stopped at midthigh.

Glossy brown eyes undressed her. Without a single word, he reached out and untied the sash holding her green and purple paisley wrapper together. He slid the wrapper from her shoulders, and it pooled at her feet. She stood uncertainly before him in a matching short chemise.

As his head dipped, Samantha reached up on tiptoe and met his ravenous mouth. Her hands splayed across his chest and journeyed upward to encircle his neck. Jack swung her effortlessly up in his arms and carried her through the connecting doors to his room.

Without breaking the kiss, he pressed her back into the downy soft mattress. His mouth feasted on hers and she whimpered in protest when his lips left hers. He slid the silky material from her body with a sweep of his hands. His gaze darkened as her breasts sprang free from the confinement of the silk. All the air left her lungs and returned in a huge sigh of delight when he took her breast into his hot mouth and gently suckled. Stephanie held his head to her frenzied flesh. His other hand brushed the material past her thighs to her feet.

Raising his head, he stared down at the naked temptress

in his bed. His eyes committed to memory every inch of her body. Jack had dreamed about this moment for what seemed like forever. He was going to take his time and enjoy her beautiful body.

His tongue flicked her neglected breast as his hand skimmed down her body. He felt her tremble as his hand slid between her legs. Her thighs clenched involuntarily at the intrusion. He rubbed his palm against her in tiny leisurely circles.

Stephanie trembled in apprehension. She was fearful of what was to come almost as much as she was scared of disappointing Jack.

"Relax," he whispered against her ear, biting gently and then kissing the injured lobe. "Trust me, Stef." His mouth captured hers and her body was his to do with as he pleased. Her legs parted and she inhaled sharply as he slipped one finger inside her already moist body. As his hand worked its magic on her lower body, his mouth moved back down to pay homage to her breast.

Stephanie felt a storm building inside her. She quickly grabbed the pillow to smother her scream as her body shuddered against him. Her first orgasm left her weak, trembling, and euphoric.

She collapsed on the bed unable to move a muscle. She was puzzled and then horrified when he kissed and licked his way down her body.

I know he's not going to do what I think he's going to do. Yes, he is. She closed her eyes and put her trust in her skilled lover.

Jack eased her legs farther apart, planting kisses and nips on the inside of her thighs. Slipping his hands under her hips, he elevated her just enough to reach the treasure he was seeking.

Stephanie almost vaulted off the bed when his hot tongue plunged deeply into her hot quivering flesh. Her loud gasp filled the room as her body exploded again. She squirmed beneath his tender ministrations as he sucked and nibbled at her sensitive flesh. Before long, she was clawing at the sheets and alternating between begging Jack to stop and never stop. Stephanie grabbed the pillow and buried her face once again to keep from screaming out when she reached her peak of gratification yet again. He took her over the edge again and again, enjoying the pleasure he was giving her and knowing no other man had made her feel this way.

Jack eased on a condom, slid back up her body, and gently eased into her tight, wet body. He groaned in pure bliss as her body engulfed him inch by inch. The feel of her tight body wrapped around him almost made him come to an end before he began.

Stephanie struggled to breathe at the feel of him inside her. She wanted all of him. She raised her hips to meet his slow entry.

He wanted to go slowly, but she was so hot and tight that he gave up the fight. She moved seductively against him, speeding up the pace.

Stephanie fervently met him thrust for thrust. Her body was starving and eager for his. This time when she reached out and touched the stars, she was not alone. They both captured a small piece of heaven on their descent.

Jack let out a guttural groan and collapsed on top of her. It took him a couple of seconds to regain enough strength to ease from her still quivering body. He maneuvered Stephanie with him and she cuddled into the crook of his arm.

"Okay, so it's not so overrated." Stephanie smiled, kissing his chest and snuggling against him.

Jack laughed as she dropped a kiss on his parted lips.

"I never dreamed it would be like this."

"I did. It just took the right touch and the right man."

"Oh, it did?" she asked, straddling him playfully.

"Give me a few minutes to recuperate and I'll show you." Stephanie started to move off him.

"Don't move. You're right where I want you for lesson number two."

"Lesson number two? And how many of these lessons are there?"

He drew her face down to his. "As many as you can handle and for as long as you want them."

Jack told Stephanie they had several chapters in the book of love to cover before either one of them could leave the bed. In the wee hours of the morning, they fell into an exhausted sleep in each other's arms.

Over a late breakfast, they agreed it would be better to keep their personal relationship separate from their professional one.

"There's something else we need to discuss. Me. My past and how it could potentially affect us. There are things in my past we can't ignore or sweep under the rug. I need to know you can deal with it, if and when it rears its ugly head."

Stephanie pushed aside the plate in front of her. Her appetite was gone. She knew she couldn't ignore Jack's past. She also knew she would have to eventually face it, deal with it, and move on, if they had any chance of having a future together.

"I can deal with it as long as it's in the past. If you are still involved in that line of work, tell me now and I will walk away. It won't be easy, but I would do it in a heartbeat. I have a child to think about Jack and she comes first in my life."

"Stef, I'm not ashamed of my past. It's part of who I am and I make no apologies or excuses for it. I am who I am, sweetheart. It's a total package." His hand covered hers. "I'm no longer in the business. It is most definitely in the past. I have way too much at stake to get pulled back in."

His gentle hands brushed a strand of hair from her cheek. "I wouldn't risk losing you."

She caught his hand and pressed a kiss to his palm. Stephanie got up from her seat and held out her hand to him. His words warmed her heart and she was too choked up to speak. She couldn't tell him with words, but she could show him how much he meant to her. Jack caught her outstretched hand and stood. Stephanie led him to her room. Untying his robe, she pushed it from strong broad shoulders. She untied her robe and it joined his on the carpeted floor. He lay back on the bed, pulling her with him. It was midday before they left the room.

When making the decision to keep their relationship private, neither realized how hard it would be to keep their hands off each other. It was extremely difficult, but worth it as they made up for lost time each night in each other's arms.

The last night in Jamaica, after dinner, they went strolling on the beach hand in hand. Neither wanted the night to end.

When they got back to their rooms, Stephanie hopped in the shower to wash some of the sand off her. She squealed in surprise and then delight when Jack joined her. It turned out to be the longest and most exhilarating shower of her life. They made love most of the night and into the wee hours of the morning. They barely made it to the airport to catch their flight home.

Chapter 6

Jack drove Stephanie home from the airport. She invited him to have dinner with them. He jumped at the opportunity to spend more time with her and his daughter.

She smiled as she watched Jack and Christina have a tea party. Her mother was horrified that she would bring "that man," into their home. Stephanie shocked her even further when she told her she might as well get use to seeing Jack around because they were involved.

Jack simply smiled and made no comment to Stephanie's fuming mother. He did, however, wink at her, which made her even more livid.

When she informed her mother he was joining them for dinner, Mildred refused to eat at the same table with a mercenary and voiced her opinion very loudly. Stephanie stood her ground and told her Jack was staying and Mildred left the house in a huff.

Jack entertained Christina in the den while Stephanie threw something together for dinner. She smiled as she watched Jack with her daughter. Jack was a natural with kids. She guessed part of his interest in Christina was the fact that his own daughter was so far away. The harder she tried to get him to talk about his daughter, the more he clammed up. Stephanie gave up trying to talk to him about her.

She and Jack were by the front door kissing when it opened. Mildred Mason stood there watching them with her hands on her hips in disapproval.

"I feel like we've come full circle now. This is where I say good night." He brushed his lips across Stephanie's. "I'll see you tomorrow."

"Good night." Stephanie smiled, kissing him again. She closed the door behind him, still smiling.

Mildred set her purse and keys on the hall table. "I'll be right back. Don't interfere, Stephanie. I mean it. Do not come out that door." Moving Stephanie aside, her mother went out the front door.

Stephanie stood frozen as the door closed. It wasn't so much the tone of her mother's voice that stopped her from following. She knew Mildred and Jack were bound to have a confrontation. It was probably better to let them have it out right now than wait for the storm to build inside Hurricane Mildred.

Jack wasn't sure why he was still outside, but something made him stay. When the door opened and closed, he wasn't at all surprised to see Stephanie's mother coming toward him like an avenging angel. Okay, so maybe *angel* wasn't the right word to use.

"You may have my daughter fooled, but not me," said Mildred, advancing on him. "I don't trust you. I know you're up to something. You're hiding something and I'm going to find out what it is. When I do, Stephanie will drop you like the trash you are."

Jack said nothing as he listened to her tirade. He let her get it all out of her system without interrupting. "I'm glad you got it all out of your system, Mrs. Mason. It's always such a pleasure chatting with you. Well, see you around."

"Don't you dare turn your back on me! Stephanie is too good for you! Mark my words, it won't last!"

Jack turned and left the fuming woman standing there. He would not disrespect Stephanie's mother or Christina's grandmother. His mother would be proud of him for remembering his manners and respecting his elders.

He didn't even burn rubber leaving the house. He didn't even give Mildred a second thought. By the time she figured out who he was, it would be too late. There was nothing she could do to hurt him.

From that day forward, Jack included Christina in the majority of their plans. The three of them spent a lot of time together doing family stuff. Jack and Christina's growing bond pleased and frightened Stephanie. If things didn't work out for her and Jack, Christina would be devastated.

Stephanie didn't know what kind of future the world held for her and Jack, but she was willing to try and take it one day at a time. She had no choice. She was in too deep now to walk away from him.

Jack had known it was over for him the minute Stephanie got up onstage and sang to him. He knew he loved her. All his scheming and planning went right out the window when he held her.

When they made love, it was like nothing he had ever experienced before. Stephanie was shy, yet passionate. She wanted to give him as much pleasure as he gave her. She learned quickly what turned him on and how to drive him crazy. Sometimes with them, it only took a look or a touch and they each knew what the other was thinking.

What bothered him most was losing the closeness he and Stephanie had. Jack had no idea how he was going to tell Stephanie the truth. He knew that day would come, but he kept putting it off. He enjoyed being with her and Christina too much to risk telling her right now. He was falling in love with her and there was nothing he could do about it.

Still beaming from their exhilarating shower, Stephanie dried off and was getting dressed when the phone started to ring. "Jack, phone!" She rolled her eyes. He was singing so loudly in the shower, she doubted he heard her. "Oh well, the answering machine will pick it up."

She smiled when the shower stopped and so did the horrible singing. Jack was great at a lot of things, but singing was not one of them.

When the machine clicked on, she stared at it in surprise as she finished dressing. The volume was up.

"I'm not in. You know what to do. Leave a message after the beep and I'll get back with you." *Beep.*

"Hey, D.J. what's up, man?" Stephanie frowned. It must be a wrong number. "Well, are you a millionaire? Has that Mason babe let you see your kid yet? Tell me, does Stephanie Mason look as good out of her clothes as she does in them? Being 'the wolf,' you know by now, I'm sure." Stephanie froze and then paled as the implication of the speaker's words sank in. The hairbrush slipped from her fingers as she stared at the answering machine. "Hey, let me know what happens. Maybe you can finance our next expedition instead of Uncle Sam."

Stephanie could barely breathe. She was trembling uncontrollably as she looked up to see Jack standing in the doorway.

Oh God! Roper, your timing stinks as usual! His hand was rubbing against his forehead.

Stephanie felt a sinking feeling in the pit of her stomach.

Jack was D.J. She'd heard that name before. Something about his name rang a bell. *No. He couldn't be. Yes, he could.* She didn't want to believe it. This was a nightmare. Jack Kaufman was Christina's father. It all made sense now, his desperation to get the security job at the hotel. The questions he asked her at the Waterfords' party about what if Christina's father wasn't dead? He told her he had a daughter. He had even gone so far as to say a friend of his dead wife's was raising his child.

She had even urged him not to give up on his daughter. His bonding with Christina was premeditated. Even his interest in the hotels now made sense. She should have put it all together. She should have made the connection. He had used her.

Fumbling with her shoes, she threw them at Jack's head and rushed from the room. She didn't want to talk to him or face him. She wiped furiously at her tears.

This was a game to him, a maneuver, operation seduce-the-Mason-babe. Make her care about you. Make her fall in love with you. None of it was real.

I was a means to an end and that end was either Christina or Christina's inheritance. The wolf is what the man had called him. How appropriately he was named. I knew better than to trust him. I knew he was trouble and I got involved with him anyway. I only have myself to blame. This is my fault. He made a fool out of me.

"Stephanie, wait." Jack, panicking, followed her into the living room. Running his hand over his head, he didn't know what to say as he faced her. He had faced a million and one angry betrayed women in his line of work, but none had ever affected him as much as this one. He felt her pain slice through his heart.

"Why, D.J., or Jack, or whatever the hell your name is? What would be the point?" she asked furiously. "That phone call said it all. You were using me. You were after the Luciano fortune like every other man in this town. Is Jack Kaufman your real name?"

"My name is David Jack Kaufman. I wanted to tell you a hundred times and a hundred ways. I am Christina's father."

She whirled on him angrily. "Christina doesn't have a father! The man who happened to sleep with her mother and donate a few sperm cells does not make him a father! I am the one who has been there from the beginning of her life. No, I take that back. I was there during Alexia's entire pregnancy. Where were you? You ran out on Alexia when she told you she was pregnant. You went off on some mission and supposedly got yourself killed."

"I didn't run out on Alexia. I was captured, but not killed obviously. I was rescued by my squad a short time later."

"What a pity you were rescued at all," she stated cruelly. "All these months you've been lying to me. You've been playing this sick game with me. Why? What was the point, Jack? Why bother? I am so stupid! I was so naïve I didn't realize I was sleeping with the enemy. That's what you are, isn't it? You are the enemy. When were you going to tell me the truth?"

"Soon." Jack didn't know what else to say. He knew there was no reasoning with Stephanie right now.

"Soon," she repeated past the lump in her throat. "That's a hell of an answer, but then you're a man of few words. Now I know why you were so closemouthed about your daughter. You had every opportunity to tell me and you didn't. So what was the plan, Jack? Why were you waiting to drop this little bombshell on me?" She picked her purse up from the coffee table.

"Stef, I know you're upset, but we need to discuss this rationally."

"Rational. You expect me to be rational after what you've

done. You would have to have the heart of a mercenary to do what you do. You prey on people's needs. You win their trust, you make them care, and then you stab them in the back while looking them straight in the eye. A person who does that doesn't have a heart." She wiped furiously at her tears. "You were right, Jack. You are damn good at what you do. If I ever need someone completely humiliated and emotionally destroyed, I'll be sure to look you up." She walked to the door and opened it. "Don't bother coming back to the hotel. You're fired."

"You can't fire me. I have a contract."

"So sue me, or was that the plan all along? You're a soldier of fortune, so I guess this was all about money. It was never about me, or Christina. It was all about the money. How much do you want? How much will it cost me to get you out of my life permanently? Whatever the price is, it'll be worth it?"

He hauled her kicking and fighting back into the room and closed the door.

"Don't touch me!" She jerked away from his grasp. "Don't ever touch me."

"I am not going anywhere. Okay, I admit, when this started I was after the money. I also wanted to see that Christina was happy and loved. I wanted to meet her and be a part of her life. I would have split the money and everything with you fifty-fifty."

"How kind of you considering the past four years I have been running everything. You are such a liar. You wanted the money. You couldn't care less about Christina and what she needs and I was a means to an end."

"You're wrong, Stef. I never wanted to hurt you. You mean more than that to me and I love my daughter."

"Love her. You don't even know what love is. All you know is lies, trickery, schemes, and manipulations. You have never had to consider anyone's feelings before.

You never once considered my feelings when you started this scam. You had your plan and you went full speed ahead and damn the consequences."

"That's not true." He tried to touch her and she slapped his hand away from her face and moved away from him.

"Yes, it is and I am a fool. How many women like me have you seduced and made a complete fool out of to serve your purpose? Do you even know? Do you even care? I guess not. You would have to have a heart to care and we both know you don't have one. You are quite the skilled actor. It must have been a stretch for you to make love to me, to pretend you care about me."

"I do care about you. There was never any pretense regarding the way I feel about you."

"Please don't insult my intelligence any further. Let's be honest. You care about money, your daughter's money. You knew everything there was to know about me when you came here. You did your research. You must have a file on me for your friend to know what I look like. So, how long did it take you to plan this little operation?"

"A few months," he answered honestly. "I followed you, watched you, and took pictures of you and Christina. I know your schedule, your daily routine. I know everything about you and your family. In doing my research, I even went to see your father. He misses you."

"You saw my father. I haven't seen or talked to my father in ten years," she said sadly, "but you already know that. So why bring him up?"

"He wants to see you, Stef, and Ashley. He wants you in his life. He regrets walking away," said Jack, guessing, but not really knowing the truth. He was taught to divert someone's attention by using their weakness to distract them. He knew Stephanie's was her father.

"You are unbelievable, you know that?" she said, seeing right through his ploy. "This is not about my father. This is about your betrayal, not his. Forget it. I can't talk about this anymore. I have to get out of here."

"Stef, wait."

"Why? What would be the point? It's over, Jack. This is my fault as much as it is yours. I knew who and what you were when I became involved with you. None of this should come as a surprise to me. Everything you did and said to me was motivated by greed. It's what you are and who you are."

"Not anymore! I want you, Stephanie. I want you and my daughter."

"I will never believe another word that comes out of your lying mouth. You don't want me. You want your daughter's inheritance. You never wanted her or me! It was all about the money! The game is over, Jack! You don't have to pretend anymore! The blinders are off. I see you for who you are, who you've always been. You're a mercenary and you will always be one! You have no heart and you have no soul! You're an unfeeling monster! You're not even human!" Tears clouded her vision as she shoved him aside and ran from the room.

Jack stood there and took everything she had to dish out. He knew he deserved her anger and her scorn. He also knew she needed some time to cool off before he saw her again. He would give her some time and space before trying to explain his side to her. She was so wrong. He did have a heart and he did care about her, more than he wanted to admit. There had been no pretense when he took Stephanie in his arms.

Stephanie gave up wiping her tears about a mile from Jack's condo. Her face and blouse were wet.

How could I have been so stupid? I knew what he was. I knew and I still got involved with him. I should have my head examined for letting myself fall in love with someone like him.

At the stoplight, she leaned forward and laid her head on the steering wheel. She raised her head slightly and stared as the turn lane got a green turn arrow. She laid her head back on the wheel, and the tears continued to fall. The light had barely turned green when the pickup truck behind her plowed into her car, sending her headlong into the intersection. The impact caused her head to slam into the steering wheel right before the airbag deployed. Stephanie panicked as she saw two cars coming toward her. One was apparently turning, while the other had obviously run the red light. She braced herself and swerved the car to try and miss the cars. Her reaction was too late and they all crashed into each other.

Stephanie was barely conscious after that. Her hand touched her forehead and she saw the blood on her fingers. She tried to move and pain racked her body. She was trapped in her car. The driver's-side door was caved in to almost touching her side. She was startled when the passenger door opened. She turned her head and the shooting pain was back. Stephanie winced and closed her eyes.

"Ma'am, don't try to move. The ambulance is on the way," said a woman's voice. "Can I call someone for you?"

"My cell phone is in my purse," she whispered hoarsely. Pain unlike anything she had ever experienced racked her body. It hurt to breathe.

The woman opened the purse and took out the phone. "Got it. Who do you want me to call?"

"Jack," whispered Stephanie, wincing in pain. "Tell Jack I love him. Tell him I forgive him." The words were torn from her throat as she lost consciousness.

Jack was sitting on the couch playing over in his mind the events of tonight. The evening had been perfect until

Roper called. He knew he couldn't blame his friend. He was the one who forgot to turn down the volume on the answering machine and he was the one who had started this mess. Now the cat was out of the bag. Stephanie knew the truth. He had no idea what to do next. For once, he had no backup plan. He was in love with a woman who despised him.

I have to go talk to her. I can't let it end like this. I can't let it end period! Stephanie and I belong together.

Jack left the condo. When he opened the car door, his cell phone was ringing. He saw Stephanie's number and immediately picked it up.

"Stef."

"No," said the woman's voice. "Does Stephanie drive a new red BMW?"

"Yes," said Jack, immediately knowing something was wrong. His grip tightened on the phone. "Where's Stephanie?"

"She's been in an accident." Jack closed his eyes in anguish. He fumbled with his keys and then started his car.

"Stephanie asked me to call you."

"Where are you?"

She quickly gave him the location. Jack put the car in gear and sped away. She was only about a mile from his place. "How's Stephanie?"

"I don't know," said the soft, hesitant voice. "She lost consciousness a few seconds ago. She asked me to call you."

"I'll be there in five minutes or less," said Jack, ending the call and dropping the phone on the passenger seat. The drive to the scene of the accident was the longest drive of his life.

Jack blamed himself. He shouldn't have let her leave in her condition. She was too upset to drive.

Stephanie Mason was everything he had ever wanted yet everything he feared. He had fallen deeply and madly in love with her, which made him vulnerable. He couldn't lose her.

When he stopped at the site, it chilled him to the bone. Killing his engine, he ran to Stephanie's car. Jack froze as he stared at the car. The back was caved in and so was the door on the driver's side. The front was also smashed in. He was trembling as he approached the passenger door. The lady who called him was in the car with Stephanie. Just as he opened the door, the paramedics swarmed around the car.

"Stef!"

"Sir, ma'am, please step back."

Jack was numb as he watched them ease Stephanie out of the car. The sight of blood all over her terrified him. He paled when he saw the cut on her forehead.

"We have a head injury over here, we'd better move fast."

Oh God. I can't lose her. Fear like nothing he had ever known gripped him and held him paralyzed.

"Jack," said the woman, putting her hand on his arm. "Stephanie gave me a message for you. She said to tell you she loves you and she forgives you."

Jack froze. Those anguished words didn't make him feel better. They made him feel worse. He prayed those were not Stephanie's last words. She had to make it. There was so much he had to tell her.

Jack was on pins and needles as he followed the ambulance to the hospital. He called Stephanie's mother to let her know what had happened.

He asked the nurse to page Ashley to the emergency room stat. He was pacing the floor when he heard Ashley asking the nurse why she was paged.

"Ashley," Jack said, rushing toward her. Her smile faded as she stared at him. She could tell by his expression something was wrong. "Stephanie's been in a car accident. She's back there somewhere."

Without a word, Ashley rushed through the double doors.

Jack sat down and leaned back with his eyes closed. *This is my fault. I shouldn't have let her leave. She was in no condition to be driving. I knew better. I did this to her. If she dies—no, she can't die. I won't let her. Christina needs her. I need her.*

"Excuse me," said the woman who had called him about the accident. "How's Stephanie?"

"I don't know yet. Thank you for helping her." He held out his hand. "I'm Jack Kaufman."

"Sally Aames. I thought you'd like to know the police arrested the man in the pickup truck who hit Stephanie. He was way over the legal alcohol limit."

"What exactly happened?"

"I was in the car next to Stephanie's. I saw her with her head on the wheel like she had been crying or something."

Jack felt an ache in his heart. He was the reason she was upset and crying.

"The moment the light changed, the guy went. He rammed into Stephanie and sent her straight into traffic. Someone on the other side ran the light and someone else was turning. She was hit by both cars."

"Was anyone else hurt?"

"Not as seriously as Stephanie. She got the worst of it."

"Thanks for telling me." Jack spotted Stephanie's mother. He excused himself, and headed in her direction.

"How's Stephanie?" she asked worriedly.

"I don't know anything yet. Ashley went back to find out." Ashley chose that moment to appear. "How is she?" asked Jack.

"She's conscious."

Thank God! Jack closed his eyes and said a silent prayer.

He hadn't been a praying man before tonight, but Stephanie needed all the help she could get to pull through.

"Thank God," cried Mildred Mason, folding her hands in silent prayer. "Can we see her?" she asked, wiping her tears.

"She's conscious, but in a lot of pain. She has a cut on her forehead that took about ten stitches to close. Her right wrist and ankle are sprained and she has tons of bumps and bruises. They are going to keep her for observation for a few days because of the head injury. You can see her for a few minutes. They're taking her up to do a full CAT scan. She has a concussion and doesn't remember anything about the accident. Come on."

Jack hung back. He didn't want to intrude. Besides, he knew Stephanie would not want to see him. She wouldn't want to be anywhere near him.

She doesn't want to see me. I should leave now that I know she's going to be okay, but I have to see for myself that she's okay. She knows the truth now and there is no turning back. I want Stephanie and I want my daughter.

"Jack, are you coming?" asked Mildred unexpectedly. She didn't wait for an answer, but turned to follow Ashley.

Jack winced when he saw Stephanie's bruised and battered body for the first time. From looking at her car, it was a wonder she survived at all. The car was totaled.

He hung back as he watched her mother rush to her side. He was preparing himself for her to send him away. As their eyes locked, she looked away quickly, but not before he saw the flicker of pain in her eyes.

"Honey, how do you feel?" asked her mother.

"Like I was hit by a truck." She winced. "They gave me a local, but they didn't want to give me anything else until after the CAT scan."

"You were hit by a truck," replied Jack, "and two cars."

"I don't even remember the accident, but I remember everything before it," she said softly, closing her eyes against the pain. This time it was Jack's turn to wince. She wouldn't meet his eyes. She wouldn't even look at him.

"Okay," said a nurse, coming into the room. "We are taking her down for a few more X-rays and then we'll take her to her room. She'll be in 519. It's a private room if you folks want to go there and wait for her."

"Mom, why don't you and Jack go wait and I'll go with Stef?" suggested Ashley. "We shouldn't be too long." She led them back to the waiting room.

Stephanie looked up when Ashley came back into the room. "I did what you asked. I didn't tell Mom or Jack how extensive your injures are."

Tears splashed down Stephanie's cheeks as she touched her stomach. She didn't want to think about the fact she might never be able to have children. Ashley caught her hand and squeezed it.

After a few minutes of being ignored, Jack gave up trying to make polite conversation with Stephanie's mother. The woman hated him and there was nothing he could do to change that. She didn't think he was good enough for her little girl and in truth he probably wasn't. If Stephanie knew half the things he had done, she would run in the other direction. He did whatever it took to get a particular job done, which included lying, cheating, and stealing. Jack lives a life of survival of the fittest.

Chapter 7

He sat quietly by Stephanie's bed until her mother had closed the door behind her. Stephanie removed her hand from his and closed her eyes.

"Why didn't you tell them the truth about me, about us?" Jack asked.

"Which truth would that be? I'm not sure what the truth is myself. Why would I subject myself to an I-told-you-so sermon from my mother when I can't exactly get out of bed and walk away from hearing it? I'm a captive audience for a lecture from my mother right now. I'm not giving her any ammunition until I can leave under my own steam."

"I'm sorry, Stephanie. I never meant for this to happen."

Her eyes met his and she saw the sincerity in his expression. She also saw something she had dreamed of seeing, or maybe she was imagining it with all the pain medication they were giving her. "This wasn't your fault. This was the idiot in the truck's fault. I hope they lock him up and throw away the key."

"He's in jail for DWI. He may have rammed your car, but I put you behind the wheel. To say you were upset is an understatement. I feel responsible for what happened."

"Maybe you're finally developing a conscience." Her

eyes dropped. "That could be dangerous in your line of work, a mercenary with a conscious. It makes for a strange combination."

"Stef, don't," came his anguished voice.

"Don't what? Don't be honest? You see, that's the one thing that was missing from our relationship. I was honest with you. I let you in my life, my bed, and my home. You never let me in. I didn't see the real you until tonight. Once the blinders were off, I saw the real Jack Kaufman in all his glory. I was a means to an end for you. You lied to me from the day you walked into my office and applied for a job." She closed her eyes and took a deep steadying breath, which hurt like hell to do. "The doctor tells me I'll be out of work for six to seven weeks minimum." Her eyes met his again. "You know the day-to-day operations of the hotel like the back of your hand. The employees fear and respect you. I want you to fill in for me in my absence," she said, surprising him. She saw the shock and puzzlement in his eyes as he did a double take.

"Me?" he questioned in disbelief. "You're kidding, right?" He saw the seriousness in her gaze. "Stef, I'm a security specialist. I know nothing about being a hotel manager. I don't want to know anything about being a hotel manager."

"I'll teach you what you need to know. I don't really have a choice, Jack. It's either you or Georgette."

"Then God help us all." He stood up and looked at her IVs.

"What are you looking at?" she asked, frowning.

"I'm trying to see what kind of mind-altering drugs they're feeding you through that tube. They're apparently affecting your thinking."

"There's nothing wrong with my thinking. You are the only one on staff capable of being in charge."

"Now I know it's the joy juice talking. You trust me to run the hotel chain?" he asked in disbelief.

"No, I don't trust *you*," she said honestly, "but I do trust you to look out for your own interest. It's in your best interest for the hotels to continue to do well. Will you do it?"

"I would do anything for you," said Jack as his hand covered hers. Stephanie drew back as if burned by his touch.

"Please don't go there," she said, closing her eyes. He watched with a heavy heart as a tear escaped the corner of her eye. She quickly wiped it away. "This is strictly a business arrangement until I am back on my feet. I'll have Georgette e-mail the chains letting them know you are temporarily in charge effective immediately. As for our personal relationship, it's over. It takes two people to have a relationship. What we had wasn't a relationship. It was a premeditated and engineered seduction. Please go, I have a splitting headache."

In truth, the pain medicine dulled her body, but nothing could take the pain away of Jack's betrayal. Her heart ached.

Jack leaned against the wall outside Stephanie's room. She didn't remember the accident or anything after it, which meant she didn't remember saying she loved him, or she forgave him.

Jack had no idea what his next move should be. Everything had changed for him. He wanted Stephanie and Christina. He wanted to be part of a family. The money didn't seem as important to him now. Stephanie loved him and he loved her.

He was a patient man and he knew now more than ever his patience would be tested. Stephanie would not easily forgive him or let him back into her life. He had won the battle of her heart; now the war was about to begin.

* * *

"Stephanie," came the soft voice.

She opened her eyes to see her lawyer, Michelle Atkins, smiling down at her.

"I heard about your accident on the news. How are you feeling?"

"Battered and bruised," said Stephanie, elevating the bed to a sitting position. "Please have a seat. I called you because I need some legal advice." Michelle sat down in the chair next to the bed. "It's about Christina's adoption. Her father isn't dead. He's here in Dallas. What does this do to the adoption?"

"I don't understand. You told me he was dead. We filed the papers based on Christina's father and mother being both deceased."

"I thought he was dead. Alexia told me he was dead. According to Jack, he was captured and presumed dead, but he was rescued shortly after that. Maybe she was notified of his death, but by the time he was rescued she had moved. I don't know what happened. All I know is he's here. Can he have the adoption overturned? Michelle, I can't lose my daughter."

"Where has he been all this time? It's been four years and he's just now showing up to claim his child. Why now? What's he like? Can he be reasoned with?"

"I'm not sure he can. I'm not sure I can. Jack Kaufman can be dangerous. After his enlistment in the navy, he worked as a mercenary. Now he's working at my hotel as a security consultant. I discovered his identity purely by accident."

"He's working at the hotel? This is incredible. So what does he want other than the obvious?"

"I don't know and that's what's scaring me. He was playing this cruel game with me to get close to me." Stephanie stopped talking and bit back her tears. "I became involved with him and I just happened to be there when one of his old buddies called and left him a message. That's how I found out who he really was."

"Wow. I don't know what to say. When was this?"

"The night of my accident. If he wanted to take Christina from me, does he have a case? If I refuse to let him see her, can he take her from me? Is my adoption legal without his signature and consent?"

"Stephanie, I'm not going to lie to you. As her father, he can try and have the adoption overturned. He never signed the adoption papers. The court would probably be in his favor. He can always lie and say he never knew about Christina until now. There are a million and one reasons he could use to explain why he is here now as opposed to four years ago. Was he married to Alexia?"

"He says he's been married, but I'm not sure what was real and what was a lie. Alexia never mentioned being married to him. She hardly talked about him at all. I didn't even know what he looked like."

"A blood test is the only way we can be sure he's Christina's father. Are you prepared to have him take one? If he is her father, the test results will work against us, but we have to know for sure he's not a phony. If she was married to him, your guardianship can be thrown out the window if he challenges it."

Stephanie felt a chill go down her spine. This was what she had been dreading. "What do you mean?"

"Under state law if you are married to someone and die, they become guardian of your children automatically. You could still be named as trustee of the estate, but he also becomes the executor. This could get real sticky. A judge could rule either way in a case like this. You need to find out for sure if he's her father. If they were married at the time of Christina's birth and/or Alexia's death, the best advice I can give you would be to find out what he wants and give it to him. If he's only after money, a quick payoff and a binding legal agreement signed by him relinquishing his rights will save you from months of pain and aggravation in the courtroom. A custody trial is a no-win situation for everyone involved. This could be such a mess. Alexia left everything to you and Christina jointly. You are her heirs, but the fact she didn't mention Mr. Kaufman, he can contest it. You could have him tied up in court for years, but in the end, he could win. Has Christina met her father?"

"Yes, and she adores him, but she has no idea he's her father. I don't know what's going to happen if I am forced to tell her."

"Before we do anything, we need to determine paternity. Next we find out what he's after. My office will contact Mr. Kaufman and we'll make the arrangements for the paternity test."

"I'll have Ashley contact you. She will help with whatever you need. I don't want my mother to know anything about any of this. The fewer people who know right now, the better."

"I understand. I know this is impossible in your situation, but try not to worry. If he's waited this long, chances are he's not after custody."

Stephanie was drifting off to sleep when the door opened. Stanley came in carrying a bouquet of flowers. He set the flowers by the sink.

"I came as soon as I heard. How are you feeling?" he asked, kissing her cheek and then taking the vacant chair beside the bed.

"Sore from head to toe. I guess that can be expected when one is sandwiched between a couple of cars and a truck. Thank you for the flowers. They're beautiful."

"I know this is not a good time to tell you this, but brace yourself. Stephanie, there's something I have to tell you about your new boyfriend. He's not what he seems. I had him checked out. You are not going to believe what I found out."

"Jack's not my boyfriend. I could have saved you the money and time had you asked me about him. I know more than I care to know about the man."

"I'm afraid you don't, sweetheart. He's been conning you Stephanie. He's after your money."

"Isn't everyone? No one sees me. They all see dollar signs. Isn't that what you see, Stanley?"

He was taken aback by her harsh response. "He's Christina's father." Stanley paused to let his words sink in. When they didn't have the effect he was hoping for, he frowned. "Did you hear what I said? He's your worst nightmare come true. He's your daughter's father."

"That's not news to me. I already know, Stanley."

"You know?"

She nodded.

"How? Did he tell you? Of course he didn't tell you. How did you find out? Did you know he's a mercenary too?"

"Afraid so. Sorry to burst your bubble, but I know everything. Was there something else you wanted? I'm tired."

"Have you contacted your lawyer? Stephanie, this man could take everything from you, the money, the hotel chain, and your daughter."

"Glad to see you have your priorities in the order of importance to you. It's always money first with an accountant."

"You could be left penniless," he said, ignoring her sarcasm.

She didn't bother to correct him with the fact that she in fact was half owner of the hotel chain. It was her best-kept secret. The only two people who knew were her attorney and her sister. Her mother didn't know for obvious reasons. "And me being a pauper would bother you?" she asked perceptively. "Is that the appeal? Would you want me if I were flat broke?" She saw the truth in his eyes. It's what she had always known. Holding up her hand, she stopped him from saying anything. "Don't bother answering that. I don't even care anymore. Jack can have the money. I am more concerned about my daughter than I am money right now."

Stanley was appalled by her response. "I hope you haven't told him that. He could take everything. What does he want?"

"That's the million-dollar question. I don't know what he wants, but I'm sure he'll tell me when he's ready. He's the closemouthed type."

"Surely you fired him when you found all this out. He could rob you blind."

"No, actually he's running the chain until I'm back on my feet. He's in charge. Maybe I should call the kitchen and tell them to hide the silver."

"Are you insane putting someone like that in charge? He could steal everything right from under you."

"Yes, he could, except for the fact that Jack is anything but stupid. I'm not worried about the hotel chain or the money."

"You should be. Stephanie, I know some people who could make Jack Kaufman disappear from your life permanently. Just say the word and he's gone like that," Stanley said, snapping his fingers. "There wouldn't be so much as a smudge of him on the sidewalk."

As his words sank in, her shock turned to fury. "Stanley, don't even think about doing something so utterly stupid," she snapped angrily. She could not bear to think of Jack being hurt, not unless she was the one inflicting the pain. "He's Christina's father. I would never be able to face my daughter if I were responsible for something happening to her father. Do not, I repeat, do not harm one hair on his miserable, conniving head. I mean it, Stanley. If anything hap-

pens to him, I will make sure you are held responsible. Jack
Kaufman is off-limits. Do I make myself perfectly clear?"

"You're in love with him. You would protect the man
who played you for a fool. He must be real good."

"Touch him and be prepared to face the consequences."
Her voice was filled with emotion. She was furious at Jack
and she might never forgive him, but she wouldn't stand
by and let anyone harm the man she loved. The man she
would probably always love.

"Stef, that almost sounds like you care," came a very familiar voice. Her face turned red as she looked up to see
Jack standing in the doorway. "Why hire someone, Stanley?" Jack asked, coming farther into the room. "Aren't
you man enough to do the job yourself?"

Stanley blanched and took a step back. "I wouldn't dirty
my hands on you, Kaufman."

"That's too bad," said Jack, advancing. He grabbed
Stanley by the lapels of his suit jacket and slammed him
against the wall. "I'd sure as hell dirty my hands on you.
Just give me a reason to rip your head off, please. This
makes twice you've threatened me, you sniveling coward.
The third time may possibly mean your life."

"Stop it!" Stephanie cried, coming painfully to her feet.
She winced in pain and fell back against the bed, hitting
her hip. Jack released Stanley and rushed to her side. He
lifted her in his arms and placed her on the bed.

"Are you out of your mind?" scolded Jack. "Stay in bed
where you belong. Aren't you in enough pain already
without adding more bruises?" He pressed the drip on her
IV to administer pain medicine.

Stephanie glared at Jack. "Stanley, I think you should
leave. Please don't do anything crazy."

"I'll check in on you tomorrow," said Stanley, trying to
press the wrinkles from his suit. "One day, Kaufman, you
will get yours."

Jack lunged and Stanley ran out the door. "Stef, your taste in men has a lot to be desired, present company included." He winked. "Glad to hear you didn't take Stanley up on his offer to have me knocked off. Although I'm sure it was quite tempting."

"Very tempting, but if anyone is going to inflict pain and suffering on you, I'd rather it be me."

"Touché. I didn't know you were such a bloodthirsty little wench. I guess I'd better watch my back."

"An eye for an eye."

"I thought it was a heart for a heart."

Her eyes lowered. "Stanley is harmless," said Stephanie, changing the subject. "He was trying to protect me."

"I don't take threats against my life lightly. You may think that spineless wimp is harmless, but I don't. A coward can be more dangerous than a mercenary. Fear makes them careless. He sees me as a threat. If he comes after me, you know he'll lose."

Stephanie felt a chill go down her spine. She hoped and prayed Stanley would heed her warning and leave Jack alone. Jack's threat was not an idle one.

"I don't want to talk about Stanley. How was your first day as acting manager? How did the conference call go?"

"As well as could be expected. Louis sends his regards. Stephanie, I'm a fish out of water. Are you sure you want me to do this?"

"The truth is, I could run things from home," she admitted, "but I need the break, Jack. I'm mentally and physically exhausted. I need some time for me and for Christina. You owe me this much."

Jack hated emotional blackmail, but she was right. He did owe her. "Take as much time as you need. I'll come by once a week and keep you abreast of things."

"I'd rather you call instead. Try not to run Christina's inheritance in the ground while I'm gone, or we all lose."

"I just love your pep talks. Keep them coming, babe. Mildred did one hell of a job on you. She must be very proud."

A few days later, Stephanie was released from the hospital. She settled back into home life without too many obstacles. Having to sleep in the guest room downstairs was a pain, but until she could make it up the stairs on her own, she was stuck there.

Not one to sit idly by, she was baking a second batch of cookies when the doorbell rang. "Just a minute!" yelled Stephanie as she used her crutches to make it to the front door. *What idiot was playing with the doorbell?* She unlocked the door and yanked it open. Stephanie frowned when she saw Jack standing there leaning casually against the doorbell. She stepped outside and closed the door behind her. "Do you mind?" She pointed to the doorbell and he got off it. "What are you doing here?" she asked quietly.

"We need to talk. Can we do this inside and sit down where you will be more comfortable?"

"Not a chance. You are not coming inside my home. You can forget it. You are not stepping one foot inside my home."

"Fine. Let's stand here in the doorway and discuss the blood test results. I have mine and I know for a fact you have yours. I want to see my daughter, Stef. It's time she knew the truth. We tell her right now. I've given you two weeks to get used to the idea and to tell her, but apparently you haven't."

The door opened and they both turned to see Christina holding the phone. "Mom, it's Stanley." Her eyes lit up when she saw her father. "Jack!" Christina ran to him and hugged him. She stared curiously from Stephanie to Jack. Stephanie took the cordless phone from her.

"Hi, honey." Jack smiled, swinging her up in his arms. "You have no idea how much I've missed you."

"I missed you too. Are you two still mad at each other?" she asked, looking from Stephanie to Jack.

Stephanie turned away from the sight of father and daughter. "Hi, Stanley. Where are you? I thought you were coming by tonight?"

"I'm still home. My brand-new car is dead. I'm having it towed to the dealership."

Her eyes flew to Jack's smiling face.

"I'll have to take a rain check on tonight."

"No problem, I'll talk to you later. There's someone at the door." She gave the phone back to Christina. "Honey, can you hang this up for me? Jack and I need to talk."

"Jack, don't leave without saying good-bye," said Christina, squeezing his hand.

"I promise." He kissed her cheek and then set her on her feet.

Stephanie waited until Christina was out of earshot before she whirled on Jack. "What did you do to his car?"

She watched him take a cap out of his pocket and toss it in the air. "Nothing much. Any experienced mechanic will find it in a couple of hours. They'll replace it and Stanley's car will be as good as new. Are you going to let me in or do I need to put a full-page ad in the local paper about Christina being my daughter? Our ill-fated romance would make one hell of a story. What do you think?" He paused to gauge her reaction. "I'm through trying to reason with you, Stephanie. Did you forget the little speech you gave me? 'It's not too late for you to have a relationship with her. You need her. She needs you. If you don't go see her, you will regret it the rest of your life.' They were just words, Stef, meaningless words. Now that you know you are the woman who has my child, it doesn't apply anymore. I know how much I hurt you and I'm sorry. I know you despise me, but it doesn't change the fact that I'm Christina's father."

"You have no idea how I feel about you," she hissed.

"I think I have a pretty good idea. You love me and you hate my guts at the same time. Is that a fair assessment?"

Stephanie remained silent. She would never tell Jack she loved him. She wouldn't give him that kind of power over her.

"You can't keep her from me. I'm through waiting. We tell her I'm her father, right now."

"And what happens if the next mission you accept, you don't return. What do I tell her then? I am not setting her up to be hurt when you decide to run off again just for the thrill of it. You had better be damn sure this is what you want, because if you hurt her, I might be tempted to take Stanley up on his offer."

"I am finished with that business. I am here and I am not going anywhere. She needs me, Stephanie, just as much as she needs you. Don't force me to take legal action to see her. I will if I have to and you can be sure it will only be the beginning."

Stephanie shivered at the icy tone of his voice. She knew he was capable of almost anything. He had proved that much to her. She wasn't strong enough to fight him yet. She wanted to be standing on both feet when she did.

Stephanie knew they should tell Christina the truth, but it didn't make the decision any easier. She couldn't put it off any longer. Jack wouldn't let her.

Chapter 8

She opened the door and waved him inside. He held the door open for her and they came face-to-face with her angry mother.

"I'm not in the mood to slay the dragon," mumbled Jack under his breath.

Stephanie hid a smile. This was the first meeting between the two of them since she had confessed the truth to her mother about Jack's real identity.

"What are you doing here?" she asked, glaring at Jack. "Haven't you done enough damage? Haven't you hurt my daughter enough? You almost got her killed. Wasn't that enough for you? I suppose now you are back to finish the job."

"Mom, please stop," Stephanie said softly. As much as she wanted her mother to read Jack the riot act, now was not the time. She didn't want Christina to witness any of it. "Where's Christina?"

Jack stood his ground, but said nothing in his defense. He was not about to get into a shouting match with Stephanie's mother. He could well understand her anger at him for hurting her daughter.

"She's in the den. Why?" she asked suspiciously.

"We need to talk to her," said Stephanie, heading for the den with Jack following close behind.

They found her sitting on the couch watching cartoons. Stephanie and Jack sat on either side of her. Stephanie picked up the remote and turned the television off.

"Christina, Jack and I need to talk to you about something. Do you remember when you asked me about your daddy and I told you he died?" The little girl nodded. "I made a mistake."

"My daddy's not in heaven? Where is he? Can I see him?" Christina asked excitedly. "I have a lot of questions."

I doubt very much heaven is where your Daddy will end up. "No, sweetheart, he's not in heaven. We will try to answer your questions. Jack is your father."

"My wish came true," she said, throwing her arms around first Stephanie and then Jack. They both stared at her puzzled. Jack held his daughter in his arms and hugged her.

"You wished I could be your daddy?" he asked, smiling down at her.

She nodded enthusiastically. "I prayed every night. God does answer prayers. I wished you and Mommy would get married and you would be my daddy." He felt Stephanie stiffen beside him at their daughter's explanation. "I don't like Stanley. He's not fun like you. I don't think he likes me either."

"Honey, your dad and I aren't getting married," said Stephanie softly, "but that doesn't change the fact that he's still your dad."

She watched her daughter's face crumple and her bottom lip tremble. "We're not going to all live together?"

Jack's heart was breaking as he watched his daughter struggle to hold back her tears. She thought he and Stephanie were getting married. Christina's wish was to have a family.

You'll have it, sweetheart! You will have your mom and dad under one roof or I'm not the wolf!

"No, sweetie." The damn broke and she cried in her father's arms. When Stephanie tried to take her to comfort her, she refused to go to her mother. Instead, she clung to her father. Stephanie was stung by the rejection. She sat there watching and feeling her daughter slip away. She hadn't realized until now how much Christina wanted a father.

"I want Daddy to live with us," she cried, clinging to Jack.

"Shh, it's okay," he said, holding her and caressing her back. "I'm here, baby." His eyes met Stephanie's and he felt her anger and resentment. "Stef, can you leave us alone for a few minutes? I want to talk to Christina." She eyed him dubiously. "Please."

"Fine," she snapped, getting to her feet. "I'll be in the kitchen listening to another lecture from my mother." She closed the door behind her.

"Daddy, why can't you live here?" Christina asked tearfully.

"Honey, sometimes we can't have everything we want when we want it. Sometimes we have to be patient. You wished that I would be your father and it came true, but wishes don't always come true. Your mom and I are having some problems right now, but they will eventually work themselves out. Until that happens, you will have to be patient with us. In the meantime, sweetheart, keep praying for us to be together. One day, it just might come true."

"Really?"

"Really," said Jack, kissing her wet cheek. *You can count on it, sweetheart. I will give you that family. I will make it happen.*

* * *

"You told Christina that man is her father? How could you?" Mildred asked, shaking her head in disapproval. "I knew he was trouble. You should have listened to me."

"Would it have made a difference? If I hadn't hired Jack, he would have come up with some other way to get close to me. To answer your question, yes, Mother, we did tell Christina Jack is her father. I put it off long enough. It was time she knew the truth. She adores Jack. You know that. She's a little upset because she mistakenly thought Jack and I were getting married."

"Heaven forbid." Her mother shuddered. "Sleeping with him is bad enough, but marrying him. Please tell me you are not considering it. That man would break your heart and ruin your life. He's not for you, Stephanie. You deserve so much better."

"No, I'm not considering marrying him. I can't see it happening any more than you can. Jack and I are finished."

"Are you trying to convince me or yourself? You and Jack have only begun now that Christina knows the truth. Jack will use her at every turn to get to you. He knows how much you love your daughter and he will use it against you. Children have ways of bringing people together even when they don't want to be together."

At Christina's reluctance to say good night to her father, Stephanie invited him to join them for dinner. To everyone's surprise, Mildred stayed and Ashley came over for dinner as well.

Ashley and Christina kept the conversation going at the dinner table. Neither Stephanie nor Mildred had a lot to say.

Ashley left shortly after dinner, telling Stephanie she would call her tomorrow. She told Stephanie she was glad they told Christina the truth.

After they put Christina to bed, she and Jack went back downstairs to talk. Stephanie had nothing to say to him, but she knew she needed to hear what he had to say.

"You've heard Alexia's version of what happened with us. I think it's only fair you hear mine." He waved for her to take a seat and so did he. "We had a whirlwind courtship. My enlistment was almost over and I was trying to figure out what I wanted to do with the rest of my life. My captain came to me with a suggestion. He had an idea for a squad. We would hire ourselves out to the highest bidder mostly in South America and make quick, easy money. Alexia hit the roof when I told her what I was going to do. We had a major fight right before she took a flight to New York in her search for her father.

"Our first mission, we all made about a quarter of a million dollars each. The danger and the excitement gave me a great rush. When I got back, Alexia had moved out of our apartment. She told me she refused to live with a hired gun. I wooed her back. The next assignment was going to last about a month. Alexia was furious when I told her I would be gone that long. She told me if I left, not to bother coming back because she wouldn't be there. When I came back, she was gone. I never spoke to or saw her again."

"I don't believe you. Alexia told you she was pregnant and you left anyway. You walked away from her when she needed you most."

"Alexia called the office and left a damn message for me. She never even bothered to see if I got the message. Stephanie, I never got that message. I never knew she was pregnant."

Her disbelieving eyes locked with his. "Then what are you doing here? If you didn't get the message, how did you find out about Christina?"

"A year ago, I went with a friend to his sister's college graduation. The girl who worked in the office as the part-time receptionist was there. She asked me what we had. I was clueless and had no idea what she was talking about. When she told me about the phone call from Alexia, I was shocked and I was furious. I tried to track Alexia down and that's when I found out she died in childbirth. It took me this long to find out what happened to her and the baby. In my search, I discovered how she found Frank Luciano, her long-lost father, and how she changed her name and went to live with him. When I found out you had my daughter, I put a twenty-four-hour surveillance on you. I was waiting for the right time to make a move when I saw your advertisement for a security consultant. I needed to get close to you without arousing your suspicions. The rest you know."

Stephanie came shakily to her feet. She didn't know what to believe anymore. Jack told a convincing tale, but he was a trained professional. He was supposed to make anybody believe anything. She hugged her arms protectively around her body.

"Why didn't you tell me the truth from the beginning? Why the ruse? Jack, it didn't have to be like this."

"Would you have believed me?" he asked, moving around in front of her. "Would you? It sill doesn't have to be like this."

"I'm not sure I believe you now. You have lied to me repeatedly. When I questioned you about your daughter, you put me off and tried to avoid the subject. I gave you every opportunity to tell me the truth and you didn't. Instead, you kept lying to me. I brought you into my company and into my home knowing who and what you were. The more I got to know you, the less your past mattered to me because I knew you were not that person anymore. I was wrong, wasn't I? You are that person." She bit back her tears. She was too proud to let him see her cry again. "You are as cold and calculating as I originally thought you were."

"No, Stef, I'm not. I care about you." His hand rose to touch her and she took a step backward.

"Don't," she warned. "What do you want from me? What do you expect from me? I bared my heart and soul to you. I gave myself willingly to you and it meant nothing to you. All it meant was more information you could turn around and use against me, to manipulate me with." She wiped angrily at the tears spilling down her cheeks. "I was a fool to trust you."

"Trust me," he laughed harshly. "Is that what you call it? You never trusted me for a minute."

"I trusted you as much as I could possibly trust any man!"

"That much," he shot back. "I am so sick of your male bashing. You can't judge all men by your father! I know he hurt you but I am not him!"

His remark hit a sensitive nerve and Stephanie lost what was left of her self-control. "That's for sure! You are nothing like him! He's not a cold-blooded murderer who hires himself out to the highest bidder!" she said bitterly. "He may not have many, but at least he has some morals and values! That's more than I can say about you! Get out of my home! I want you out of my home and out of my life!"

Her words sliced through his heart. He steeled himself against the pain and his eyes became cold. "I am not going anywhere. We are not finished. We have a daughter to discuss!"

"Then have your lawyer call mine. I have nothing further to discuss with a lying pig like you! Until my lawyer tells me I have no choice, I don't want you near me or my daughter again!"

"Stephanie, don't make me take you to court or it won't stop with simple visitation rights. I will sue you for sole custody! Don't start a war with me if you're not prepared to face the consequences. I will do whatever I have to do to win. Make no mistake about that."

"Is that a threat? Go for it! What's one more body in the trail of bodies I'm sure you've already left behind?"

"What is going on in here?" Mildred asked, coming into the room. "I can hear the two of you screaming at each other upstairs. Do you want Christina to hear you?"

"Mr. Kaufman was just leaving! I don't want him anywhere near Christina or this house unless he has a court order! Hire a security guard to keep him out if you have to!"

"Stephanie!" said Mildred sharply. "Stop right there. This is not the answer. We need to discuss this."

"I'm through talking about him and to him. I mean it, Mom. Get him out of here." She limped from the room, leaving her mother and Jack staring after her.

Jack was headed to the door when Mildred stopped him. "Give her some time to calm down and she'll come around."

"I'm out of time and out of patience. Christina is my daughter. If Stephanie wants a fight, she's got one."

Mildred Mason whirled on him angrily. "Stephanie didn't start this mess," she charged. "You did. You were playing a cruel game with her. She's hurting, Jack. She's thinking with her heart and not her head. You deserve everything she has to dish out and then some. Give her some time. Let me talk to her."

Jack stared at her in question. What was she up to? "You hate my guts. Why would you do that for me?"

"Let me make something perfectly clear to you. I'm not doing anything for you. I'm doing it for my daughter and for my granddaughter. We have all seen what you are capable of. I don't want to see Stephanie or Christina caught up in an ugly custody battle. If it comes to that, there will be no winners."

"You have three days to convince Stephanie to agree to visitation rights. If you can't change her mind, then all bets are off." He watched Mildred leave the room in search of her daughter.

* * *

"Stephanie, we need to talk," said her mother, barging into the room and closing the door behind her.

Stephanie turned off the television and dropped the remote on the bed. "Mom, I'm all talked out right now."

"That's too bad," snapped her mother, grabbing her arm and jerking her to a sitting position. "I am going to talk and you are going to listen, young lady." Stephanie stared at her mother in surprise. Mildred sat down next to her on the bed. "I know you love Jack and you hate him for what he did to you. I understand, honey, believe me, I do, but you can't use Christina to punish him. Christina loves her father and he loves her. I know you are hurting and you are furious with him, but you have to think with your head, not your heart. You have to be reasonable. You more than anyone knows what Jack is capable of. Don't force his hand. Don't force him to take legal or any other action against you. If you force him to, he could very easily grab Christina and leave the country. He has the means and the know-how to disappear forever."

Her startled eyes flew to her mother's face.

"I'm not saying that's what he will do, but he has the resources if he wanted to. You can't keep him from Christina. Honey, if you are not willing to be reasonable, it could cost you everything."

"You're trying to scare me. Jack wouldn't do that. He wouldn't take Christina and run."

"Wouldn't he? Can you be sure about that? Yes, I am trying to scare you. I am trying to get you to face the severity of the situation. Jack Kaufman is not a man I would want for an enemy, and you are declaring war. He gave me three days to talk some sense into you and then he takes action. As difficult as this may be, you have got to work out some sort of custody or visitation agreement with him. You are a parent first and a woman in love second. Christina's needs have to come first. Jack Kaufman may be a lot of things, but I truly believe he loves his daughter. He has shown her more love and patience than Stanley has in the past two years. I don't know what kind of father he will be in the long run, but they both deserve the chance to find out. She needs him, Stef, and I think he needs her."

After giving the conversation a lot of thought, she knew her mother was right. Jack did love Christina and she loved him. It would be wrong to try and keep them apart.

She called Jack and set up a visitation schedule. Over the next several weeks, she made sure she was absent when he came by.

To her surprise, he asked to keep Christina overnight at his place. Stephanie had panicked at first. She thought he was going to take her and run. He must have known what she was thinking because he assured her he was not going anywhere.

This became the new pattern. Jack would come by to see her at least once a week and he would keep her every other weekend. Christina was always excited to see her father, but she cried when he dropped her off and left. Both Jack and Stephanie were more than a little affected by her distress. She was still hoping they would all live together.

Two months later, Stephanie was glad to be rid of all casts. She was 100 percent and ready to get back to work.

Stephanie froze in her tracks when she saw Jack sitting on her desk. Squaring her shoulders, she closed the door behind her and walked farther into the room.

"What are you doing in my office, Mr. Kaufman?"

Stephanie asked, throwing her briefcase in one of the empty chairs.

Jack came to his feet and moved around the desk. He stopped directly in front of her. "No need to be so formal after all we've shared," Jack said as his eyes raked over her in appreciation. The look in his smoldering eyes made her blush. Stephanie moved away from him, putting some distance between them. "Where else would I be working? You did leave me in charge. You look great, by the way. I like the new hairstyle. It suits you."

"Thank you," she said uncomfortably. "I'm back now, so you can leave. Make an appointment with my secretary and you can brief me on any changes I need to know about. Good-bye. Have a nice day," she said, dismissing him. When he didn't leave, she looked up at him. "I'm sure you have a lot of security work to catch up on."

Jack took a stack of papers from the printer and dropped them on the desk in front of her. "Call this my last act as manager. I've simplified your life. You can't do it all, Stephanie."

"There is nothing simple in my life." She picked up the organization chart and sat down. Glancing over it, she waved for Jack to take the seat on the other side of her desk. Stephanie folded her hands on her desk and waited for Jack to explain his actions.

The next thirty minutes they argued back and forth. She was furious at Jack for taking the liberty of rearranging her hotel to suit him. Her anger knew no bounds when he announced he had given all the managers a raise and put them on a bonus system, based on their job performance and hotel revenue. He also enhanced their job descriptions.

The decisions Jack made were solely to take some of the load off Stephanie. She was monitoring what the other managers should be taking responsibility for. Filling in for her the past couple of months had quickly shown him why Stephanie didn't have time for a life outside of work. She carried the weight of all the hotels on her shoulders when in truth she should have delegated the duties to the managers.

In the end, she relented. The changes made sense, she was just sorry she hadn't come up with the ideas years ago. It took the burden off her and freed up a lot of her time.

"Okay. I will approve all of it, but you should not have made these changes without discussing it with me. I have a headache now, so will you please go and close the door behind you?"

"I don't like being dismissed, but I will let it pass because this is your first day back. I'm not going anywhere. You've totally avoided me for the past three weeks. When you are there, you use Christina like a shield between us. Now that we are alone and I have your undivided attention, I was hoping we could discuss a few things."

"Been there, done that. Not doing it again." She folded her arms across her chest. "If it's not business related, I'm not discussing it with you. We have nothing left to talk about. Have a good day, Mr. Kaufman."

"I beg to differ. We have a daughter to discuss. A very distraught daughter who wants her mommy and daddy to live together."

Stephanie's blood ran cold as she turned back around to face him. "Not possible and not probable," she said quietly. "You are not moving in with us and we are not moving in with you. Just cut out the head games, Jacks. I've had enough of them to last me a lifetime. I am not going to let you use Christina to get to me. I've given you liberal visitation rights. What could you possibly want now, unless it's money?"

His eyes narrowed on her.

"How much is it going to cost me to get you out of our lives?"

Jack was stung by her question, but his expression gave nothing away of his true feelings.

"Now that you've had a taste of what it's like to be a parent, are you ready to run away with your tail tucked between your legs? Is it too much responsibility for you to handle? Are you now ready to take the money and run?"

"For that last crack, it's going to cost you everything," he said coldly. "You continue to underestimate me. I never run from a fight. I meet it head-on."

"I hate guessing games, but I'm willing to pay your price just to be rid of you. Sure, Christina will cry for a while, but then she'll forget you like the bad memory you are and life will go on. What exactly does everything mean in layman's terms? Can you be more specific? Just so we're both clear, what does everything mean to you in dollars and cents?"

"My daughter, you, and the money, in that order. Christina in my home, you in my bed, and the money in my bank account. Do you want to know what excites me the most?" His hot gaze raked over her. "You in my bed again."

Stephanie colored hotly under the intensity of his heated stare and her eyes left his momentarily. "When hell freezes over," she hissed, enunciating each word.

He dropped an envelope on the desk in front of her. "You'd better get your snow boots ready, sweetheart. There's about to be a snowstorm in hell."

"What is this?" she asked nervously. "Are you suing me for custody? I am prepared to fight you for custody of Christina. I've consulted a lawyer. She assures me no court would take a child from a loving home and turn her over to someone like you."

"Someone like me," he sneered. "What the hell does

that mean, a trained killer, a soldier? You sure as hell didn't seem to mind someone like me making love to you."

Heat suffused her face.

"You welcomed it and you enjoyed it. Who would have guessed that underneath that prim and proper facade was a wildcat in bed? I can still hear you purring and moaning in my ear and feel the scratch marks on my back."

"Stop it!" Stephanie snapped.

"Why? Does the truth hurt or does it make you all hot and bothered?"

"I really hate you."

"That's not what you said after your accident. Your last words before you lost consciousness were tell Jack I love him and I forgive him."

Stephanie paled and had to grab the desk for support. She shook her head in denial. "I never said that," she said softly, lowering her eyes. Stephanie couldn't remember saying it, but she couldn't discount what he was saying either.

"Are you sure about that? Your last thought before you lost consciousness was about me, Stef. You didn't want to die and leave me feeling guilty about it. That tells me two things. One, you do love me and two, you do believe I have a conscience."

"Or three, maybe I was trying to clear my conscience, so I was merely trying to get into heaven by saying I forgive you. Let's be clear about one thing here. I do not forgive you and I will never forget what you did to me. You made a fool out of me. You are a mercenary and there is no place for you in my life. If it were up to me and not a court of law, I wouldn't let you anywhere near Christina."

"You have no proof of what I did. There is no proof. There's no documentation of those lost two years. You can't prove a thing and neither can Miss Atkins. You think you hold all the cards. Think again, darling. I don't need custody papers, I have something even better."

She picked up the envelope and opened it. Stephanie took the paper out of the envelope and paled. She dropped down in the chair with the document still clutched in her hand. She closed her eyes and prayed she wasn't seeing what she was seeing.

"I guess this is one little detail Alexia forgot to mention to you. We were married at the time of Christina's birth and we were married at the time of Alexia's death."

She continued to stare at the marriage license in horror.

"How does it feel, Stef, to know it's all slipping away from you—Christina, the money, and the power?" Her eyes met his and he flinched at the fear in her eyes. She was afraid of him. Wasn't that what he wanted? No, that was definitely not what he wanted to see in her eyes. He remembered all too well the passion and the tenderness. "I'm sure you know what this means. My attorney assures me we can contest Alexia's will and have it overturned. You see, she forgot to mention her long-lost husband. Everything you hold dear is rightfully mine. I want everything. I will get everything. I've already set the wheels in motion. By the end of this week, I will have everything you hold near and dear."

"Alexia never told me the two of you were married. I didn't know."

"I told you that night at the Waterfords' I had been married."

"But you never told me you were married to Alexia! You can have the money and the hotels, but I will not give you my daughter. I will never give her up."

"It's not negotiable. It's all or nothing and I want it all. You don't know the meaning of the word *compromise* and neither do I. So it has to be all or nothing."

She shot angrily to her feet.

"I have a proposition for you," said Jack, moving closer

to the fuming woman. His hand brushed the hair from her face and she angrily knocked his hand away.

"I'll just bet you do," hissed Stephanie, moving backward and glaring at him. "I will not give up my child and I will not become your plaything!"

"Okay, then marry me," he suggested. He took another step closer.

Her mouth dropped open in surprise.

"Wife and mistress, they're pretty much interchangeable, aren't they? They both get paid for their favors." He caught her hand before it made contact with his face. "Nice try. So what will it be, marriage to the mercenary or a life without Christina?"

Stephanie laughed. "Marry you! You've got to be kidding! That's not a choice!"

"It's the only one I'm giving you. Marry me or lose everything."

"I would rather make love with the devil," she seethed, enunciating each word and shoving him away from her.

"You've already done that." Jack wickedly smiled, pulling her into his arms. "Several times, I might add, and you enjoyed every delicious, wicked moment of it. It's a good thing we have passion because I sure as hell hadn't planned on it being a marriage of convenience. My lawyer assures me I have a good case. Your guardianship is out the window since my deceitful dead wife didn't bother to mention me in the will. She gave away my child without my knowledge and without my written consent and I want her back. You and a multimillion-dollar empire are both huge bonuses in the deal. You have one week to decide where and when this blessed event will take place. We will be married within the month or you can walk away with nothing."

"Jack, don't do this?" she begged, pushing at his chest, but he didn't budge. "Don't make me hate you."

"If you hate as passionately as you make love, I can't wait. You are mine, Stephanie. What's mine, I keep. You gave yourself to me heart, body, and soul." His demanding mouth stopped any further protest. Stephanie angrily shoved at his chest, but he simply drew her closer. He demanded a response from her and he wasn't disappointed when she surrendered and her arms went around his neck and she returned his kiss. His hands moved over her body in a soft caress. Breathless, he ended the kiss. "I thought you'd see things my way." His head lowered again to hers as one hand slid up from her bottom to her breast. She moaned in pleasure and her nipple hardened under his massaging caress. Her hands moved over his back and then down to his strong thighs. Stephanie was coldly snatched from her fog of passion when cool air hit her hot skin. Flushed, she moved away from Jack and took a step back. Turning her back on him, she buttoned her blouse and took several deep breaths. He stepped in front of her, raising her chin to look into her troubled brown eyes. "Why fight it? It's bigger than both of us. I'll be in touch." Smiling, he left the office humming "Here Comes the Bride."

Now I'm sure I hate him. I love him and I hate him.

Chapter 9

Stephanie waited until the last possible moment before seeking out Jack with her answer. Today was the end of the week he had given her to make a decision. Her plan was to stall him or change his mind. She didn't really care which, but she needed more time to think about it.

She nervously rang the doorbell at Jack's condo. Wiping her sweaty palms on her jeans, she waited anxiously for him to open the door.

"What a pleasant surprise." Jack smiled, opening the door. He took a step back to allow her to enter. "So, to what do I owe the pleasure of this visit? Could it be you've come to your senses and decided to marry me?"

"I wouldn't exactly list marrying you as coming to my senses. More like losing the good sense God gave me," she quipped. "I've been thinking over your proposition and I have a counteroffer for you." His eyebrows rose curiously. "I'll sign over seventy-five percent of Christina's inheritance and my shares to you. I'll also give you liberal visitation rights."

"I already have liberal visitations. Seventy-five percent is a high price to pay for your freedom. Was this your idea or your attorney's? Make him a millionaire and a part-time dad and maybe he'll go away. Does the idea of being married to a mercenary make you shudder with revulsion or with pleasure? I scare you and I excite you like no man ever has before, but I'll give it some thought."

As he turned to walk away, hope flared in Stephanie's eyes. The fact that he was thinking about it at all gave her hope.

"Okay, I thought about it. The answer is still no. It's all or nothing. There is no room for compromise here. I either get everything I want or you get nothing. Maybe Christina should come live with me and I could give you liberal visitation rights." He saw her face pale and she clenched her hands together. *She wants to hit me. Prim and proper Stephanie wants to take a swing at me again. That's twice in two days.* "Take your best shot, Stef, but remember, I'm a lot quicker and stronger than you are."

"What?" Her eyes flashed with anger.

"You're dying to take a swing at me again. Go ahead. It'll make you feel better."

"You're not worth the effort it would take," she hissed. "Nothing short of you dropping off the face of the earth will make me feel better. Maybe I should have taken Stanley up on his offer."

"Is that any way to talk to your future husband?"

"It's either that or murder you myself and the idea does hold a certain appeal, so watch your back."

"I always do," laughed Jack. He walked over to the phone and picked it up. "Do I start the wheels in motion to get custody of Christina or do we take a stroll down the aisle of matrimony?"

Stephanie sighed in defeat. She had given it her best shot and lost. Jack would not compromise. She closed the distance between them, her hand trembling as she took the phone out of his hand and hung it up.

"Is that a yes?"

"You win. I'll marry you," she said softly. Her troubled gaze locked with his. Stephanie was more than a little surprised when she watched him take a black velvet box out of the drawer. He opened the box and her eyes flew to the ring. It was a beautiful two-carat diamond with baguettes on both sides. Her hand trembled as he caught it in his and slid the ring on her finger. "A perfect fit."

He kissed her hand. "Did you have any doubt? I know everything there is to know about you. I probably know you better than you know yourself. I guess this makes it official. I do have a few stipulations."

Rolling her eyes at him, she removed her hand from his. "Why doesn't that surprise me? Let's hear your stipulations."

"Number one, you play the role of loving wife with our daughter and in public. Number two, not even Ashley is to know the real reason you are marrying me. So, sweetheart, you are going to have to act your pretty little ass off to convince everyone you are madly in love with me."

Stephanie rolled her eyes at him. "You're serious. That will be a stretch," she mumbled.

He ignored her sarcasm. "Number three, your mother's free ride is over. She is more than capable of getting a job and I have one in mind for her. She will be the new interior designer for all the hotels. That should keep her busy and on the go. And on the subject of the lovely Mildred, she will be moving out before I move in."

"You expect me to kick my mother out and force her to get a job? I can't do that."

"Maybe you can't, but I can and I will. She needs a life of her own so she can stay out of ours. Stef, the woman hates my guts."

"I'm sure that line is long and distinguished. You continually antagonize her. First you lead her to believe you're a gigolo and then you shock her senseless by telling her over dinner that you're a mercenary and now you're

Christina's father. I can see how you endeared yourself to her."

"That's beside the point. She still has to go. I'm not living under the same roof with her. I don't care for the idea of sleeping with one eye open each night. Go buy her a town house or something. I don't care what you buy her as long as you get her out before I move in. Four, you will hire a regional manager to help you with the daily operations of the chain. This is also not negotiable. I want you home more with Christina. I want to come home to my wife and daughter. Her cooking an occasional dinner would be nice too."

"I have never neglected Christina," she defended.

"I didn't say you had, but you can't continue to run the chain alone and it is out of my realm. I do security, not hotel management." He caught her hand and drew her to him. "I think you are a wonderful mother. Christina is lucky to have you, but you need to spend more time with her. Last, but not least, I want a real marriage and a real family, Stephanie. I want more children, at least two, or three. A daughter who looks like you and two big strong sons who take after me."

"Little mercenaries," she mumbled, rolling her eyes at him. "I'm not sure me or the world is ready for two more like you. Would you like some fries and a shake to go with that order, sir?" He swatted her on the bottom. "Ouch!"

"Hey, I'm serious. No smart remarks allowed." His head lowered and his mouth touched hers lightly. "I've missed you."

"I've missed you too," she admitted reluctantly, slipping her arms around his waist. "I don't want to fight anymore."

"Neither do I." His mouth captured hers again, this time for a slow, thorough kiss that took her breath away. She responded wholeheartedly.

"So, when is our big day? No stalling. You have three

weeks and I'm being generous. You better run along and get busy. Shall I follow you home so we can give your mom the happy news together?"

"You mean so you can catch her when she faints."

"You mean I have to catch her?" he teased in a half-joking manner. "What are you going to tell her?"

"We are madly in love and we want to make a home for Christina. She's going to think I'm nuts for getting involved with you again. If she tries to have me committed, will you come to my rescue?"

"Always," he promised, kissing her again.

"You and I both know how badly my mother is going to take this news. Come with me to tell Christina and I will break the news as gently as I can to my mother. I don't look forward to it. I'm marrying a man she despises. I'm forcing a job on her and I am kicking her out of her home. She'll probably never speak to me again."

"And you say that like it's a bad thing, sweetheart," he replied sarcastically.

Her eyes narrowed on him, but her mother was soon forgotten as his mouth covered hers again in a steamy kiss. Pulling herself out of his arms, Stephanie moved away from him. "Let's go."

He took her in his arms. "We have time." His eyebrows rose suggestively. "Let's make the most of it. Let me show you how much I missed you." He tried to tug the ends of her shirt out of her jeans.

Stephanie caught his hands and took a step back. "Not happening today, Jack. The next time you bed me will be as my husband." She smiled coyly.

It was Jack's turn to frown. "Come on, Stef. It's been months. It will be quick. No more than an hour or two."

She laughed at his serious expression. "You have your stipulations and I have mine. Three more weeks of no sex won't kill you. It's like basic training. What doesn't kill you will make you stronger." She picked up her purse and turned back to him. "Are you coming?"

"Apparently not today," he mumbled.

Stephanie hid a smile, knowing they were talking about two totally different things.

"Lead the way." Jack was not happy as he opened the door for her and followed her outside.

When they returned to Stephanie's house, they found Christina in the kitchen with Ashley baking cookies. She ran to Jack when she saw him. Smiling, he swung her up in his arms and kissed her.

"Hi, Daddy." She rested her forehead against his.

"How's my favorite little girl?"

She giggled. "I'm your only little girl."

"True point. Your mom and I have some exciting news for you." Jack caught Stephanie's hand and drew her into the circle. "Your mom and I are getting married."

Christina let out a piercing four-year-old scream of excitement. She hugged both of them. "We will live together."

"Yes, honey, we will," answered Stephanie, turning to face her speechless sister. Ashley didn't say a word. She just stared at them in silence.

"Congratulations," said Ashley, finding her voice. She hugged both Stephanie and Jack. "I wish you both all the best. I'm just a little surprised. I don't know why, but I am."

"What on earth is going on?" asked Mildred. "I heard Christina screaming like a wild banshee. Is everything all right?"

"Mommy and Daddy . . ." Her words trailed off as Jack put his hand over her mouth. Stephanie laughed at her daughter trying to squirm free.

"We'll wait upstairs," Jack said, carrying Christina out of the room with his hand still covering her mouth. He didn't want her to let the cat out of the bag. He also didn't want Mildred to make a scene in front of Christina.

"I'll come with you," said Ashley, fleeing the room. She did not want to be around for this confrontation.

"Let's go in the den." Stephanie led the way. She needed those extra seconds to build up her courage to say what she needed to say to her mother. Stephanie waited until she heard their footsteps on the stairs. "Mom, have a seat," said Stephanie nervously. She sat down next to her mother on the sofa. "There's something I have to tell you. Please try and remain calm." She felt her mother tense beside her. Raising her hand, she showed her mother the engagement ring. "Jack and I are getting married." She waited for a reaction, but none came. Stephanie stared at her silent mother. She waved her hand in front of her face. "Mom, did you hear what I said? Jack and I are getting married in three weeks."

Without a word, Mildred got up from the sofa and left the room. Stephanie stared after her in confusion. Where was the argument she was expecting? Where was the lecture? Where was the loud outburst? She never expected quiet acceptance.

This was not like her mother. Coming to her feet, she followed her mother up the stairs to her room. She knocked softly on the bedroom door before entering. Her heart did a flip-flop when she found her mother packing her clothes. Mildred looked up at her without a word and then continued to pack her things.

"Mom, what are you doing?" Stephanie knew what she was doing, but she didn't expect it to be this easy. Her mother was packing to leave.

"What does it look like I'm doing?" She stopped folding clothes and looked at her daughter. "I knew this would happen. You are making a huge mistake marrying a man like him. He will leave you and Christina high and dry."

"I love Jack. He is Christina's father. We are going to be a family. This is what I want, Mom. Why can't you be happy for me?"

"Stephanie, you are marrying a man with a violent, questionable past. No mother would want Jack Kaufman for a son-in-law. I don't trust him and neither should you. He's going to hurt you. I can't stay here and watch this tragedy waiting to happen. Stephanie, it won't end well with a man like that. It can't and I can't live under the same roof with him."

Stephanie swallowed past the lump in her throat. "Then this is for the best," she agreed, fighting back the urge to cry. "Mom, you and Jack are like oil and water. I will not live the rest of my life playing referee between my mother and my husband. Our family as a whole couldn't survive it. Christina deserves to have a mother and a father living under the same roof."

"That's it," Mildred snapped angrily. "He wins. Jack gets to live in the fine house and you're kicking me out in the streets. You would choose that man over your own mother. I was in labor fifteen hours with you. I have loved and nurtured you for the past twenty-eight years and you choose him."

"Mom, you had a C-section. No, I'm not kicking you out in the streets. I'm not choosing sides. I'm doing what's best for my daughter and what's best for me. Find a place you like, within reason, and we will buy it for you." Stephanie folded her hands in front of her. If her mother thought this was bad, the worst was yet to come. "There's one more thing. I can no longer support you. You have to get a job."

"A what! I haven't worked in twenty years. What exactly do you expect me to do, wait tables? This is his doing, isn't it? He put you up to this! He hates me. He knows I am not fooled by him and he wants to get rid of me."

She left the room in search of Jack. She found him in Christina's room. "I have a few things I want to say to you!"

"Mom, don't." Her eyes rested on Christina.

Jack must have read her mind. "Stef, take Christina downstairs," he said, facing his furious future mother-in-law. "Now." His tone brooked no argument. Stephanie ushered Christina from the room. He waited until he was sure Stephanie and Christina were out of earshot before closing the door. "You have the floor, Mildred."

"You are not good enough to marry my daughter."

"I can bed her, but not marry her. Now I remember. You said it was okay to fool around with the hired help as long as you didn't get caught."

"You are scum and you will always be scum. You may have Stephanie fooled, but not me. One day she will see you for what you are. You are an opportunist and a fortune hunter."

"Speaking of opportunist, Mom, your gravy train just ran out. I have a job already lined up for you. You're the new interior designer for Luciano's. You get to travel all over the world spending someone else's money. I would think that's something you're quite good at. It will also keep you occupied and out of my marriage."

"You can't make me work for you."

"You're right. I can't, but what else can you do? What are you qualified to do? As far as I know, there's no salary for bitching and complaining. You have to be voted in to office for those jobs and I doubt anyone would vote you in. Luciano's will pay you a fair salary for this position. If you turn it down, you are on your own."

"You have no say in Luciano's or the finances. Stephanie is much too independent to let you tell her what to do."

"That's where you're wrong, Mildred. Legally, Luciano's and everything you see here belongs to me. Let me let you in on a little secret. Alexia was my wife at the time of her death. That means with the snap of my fingers, I could make you a pauper. Considering the way you treat me, I think I'm being quite generous in creating a position for you. I could just as easily kick you out with nothing and it wouldn't bother me a bit. Here's a news flash for you, Mildred. I love Stephanie and I love Christina. If I didn't love your daughter, I would kick you out without a backward glance. You can either accept our marriage and the job offer or you can walk out of our lives. Those are your choices."

"You would like that, wouldn't you?"

"No, I wouldn't," he said honestly. "Stephanie and Christina love you. They need you in their life just as much as you need them, but I don't need you. For their sakes, I am willing to bury the hatchet. You don't have to like me and I don't have to like you, but we do have to get along for their sakes. You can either take the job or fend for yourself. Your free ride on the Luciano gravy train is over. I'm going downstairs to celebrate my upcoming nuptials with my family. You are more than welcome to join us or not. If you do, be sure to curb your sharp tongue and pull in your fangs. I will not fight with you in front of Christina, ever."

Chapter 10

Stephanie wore a simple but elegant ivory formfitting long wedding gown. The medium-length train snapped on right above her hips. Her hair was a mass of dark curls pinned on top of her head and decorated with off-white flowers. Pearl necklace, pearl earrings, and a white rose bouquet completed her ensemble.

She had a panic attack in the bride room at the church and proceeded to hyperventilate. Ashley was there to calm her fears and talk her through it.

Stephanie had so many doubts about this wedding. Could she trust Jack? Could she trust her own judgment around Jack? She loved him, but she wasn't sure if he loved her or the money he was gaining.

All her doubts melted away when Christina walked into the room in her white satin flower girl dress. She was so excited about the wedding and the future. There was no way Stephanie could disappoint her little girl. To see the smile on Christina's face, she would put her doubts and fears aside and marry Jack.

Jack had no doubts as he and Roper waited for the wedding coordinator to come get them. He knew he was doing the right thing for everyone. It had stopped being about money a long time ago. He loved Stephanie and wanted her to be his wife. His only regret was the way he went about to achieve his goal. He had handled everything badly and it got worse instead of better over time. He pushed past mistakes aside, as he looked to the future. He couldn't redo the past, but he could do everything in his power to make sure they all had a bright future together.

Jack was more than ready for his walk down the aisle, when the wedding coordinator knocked on the door. He adjusted his tie as he stared in the mirror. He and Roper both wore black tuxedos.

Jack was all smiles as Christina walked down the isle. She looked like a little princess. She daintily dropped flower petals as she stepped. She waved at him, smiling. He waved back and blew her a kiss.

Ashley was next in a light blue tea-length silk dress. She smiled brightly and only had eyes for the best man. His eyes lit when he saw her.

The music started for the bride and the guests rose to their feet. For the first time in his life, Jack's hands started sweating.

When Stephanie came into view, the air left his lungs. The vision walking toward him took his breath away. Wow! Words could not describe how incredible she looked.

She wore no veil. The flowers in her hair sparkled in the light. As she drew near, their eyes locked. Her smile lit up the church and melted his heart. He returned her smile and held out his hand to her. Moving forward, he met her in the aisle.

Her hand trembled slightly as she caught his. The warmth of his touch calmed her nerves. They walked to the altar hand in hand.

They were married in a private ceremony with only family and a few close family friends in attendance. Stephanie's voice was loud and clear as she repeated her vows.

Jack was calm and cool during the entire ceremony. When it came time to kiss his new bride, he was more than happy to oblige by placing a passionate kiss on her lips. A kiss filled with the promise of what they would share tonight and forever.

A white stretch limousine was parked outside waiting to drive them to the hotel for the reception. Stephanie, Jack, and Christina rode in the limo.

Her mother had no say in the wedding guest list, but she made sure everyone who was anyone was invited to the lavish reception at the hotel. Jack told her for this occasion only, there was no budget. Stephanie was sure he would regret that decision after getting the bill.

When Stephanie and Jack entered the ballroom, every-one applauded the newlyweds. Jack took Stephanie in his arms and kissed her amid applauds and well-wishes. His kiss left no one in doubt of what he was thinking. Stephanie melted against him.

Stephanie smiled so much she thought her face was going to crack as they greeted their guests. Half the people, neither she nor Jack knew. They were guests of her mother.

They took all the customary pictures of the cutting of the cakes before starting the buffet line for dinner. Stephanie only got a small portion. Her stomach was in knots and she didn't know how she was going to even swallow the food in front of her.

Jack, on the other hand, loaded his plate with healthy portions of almost everything. He was going to make sure his bride ate and didn't pass out on him from exhaustion. It had been almost two months since the last time they made love, and Jack was more than a little anxious to con-summate his marriage.

As he tried new things, he put the fork to Stephanie's lips and encouraged her to try it. Soon, both their plates were empty.

* * *

"Excuse me," said Roper, speaking into the microphone. "For those of you who don't know me, and that's probably ninety-five percent of you, I'm Todd Roper, the best man. I'd like to take this time to say a few words. Most of you know Mrs. Kaufman, but you don't know Jack. Therefore, I'm here to tell you a little about Jack. I've known Jack Kaufman for about ten years now. When I first joined the navy at the young age of eighteen, he took me under his wing. He is the one true friend I have. Friends may come and go, but real friends are forever. Jack and I have literally and physically been to hell and back and it's made us stronger. He's a complex man, but he's also a good man. I would trust him with my life, and I have, and he's never let me down. I am closer to him than I am to my own brother. I am honored to be standing here today to toast him and his bride. Stephanie, I salute you for capturing his elusive heart. Cherish it and him always. Jack, may you and Stephanie have a long wonderful life together," he said, raising his glass. "To Stephanie and Jack." Everyone raised their glass in a toast to the newlyweds. "Now it's time for the first dance." Roper signaled the DJ to start the music.

Jack pulled out Stephanie's chair and led her to the dance floor as the beautiful ballad filled the air. Smiling, she went easily into his arms.

"Have I told you what a beautiful bride you are?" asked Jack, nuzzling her neck. "You look incredible."

"Yes." Stephanie smiled. "But you can tell me again." He twirled her around the dance floor. "You aren't too shabby yourself. You clean up pretty well, Mr. K. I might have to keep you." Stephanie couldn't remember ever being this happy before. She felt euphoric.

His lips brushed hers lightly. "That's the nicest thing

you've ever said to me. I'm glad I didn't show up in full combat gear. Your mom would have stroked out."

Stephanie couldn't suppress her laughter. The image was stuck in her head. "You're probably right. She loves throwing a party. Her daughter marrying a man with a shady past, not so much."

"If I didn't know better, I'd swear you were happy, Mrs. Kaufman." He spun her around before bringing her back into his arms.

"But you know better," teased Stephanie, bringing his head back down to hers for a quick kiss. "You look pretty happy yourself."

"You think?" He winked at her. Jack brought her hand to his lips and kissed it. "I will show you how much, later. I have everything I've always wanted, right here. You and Christina are my life. I will cherish and protect you both always."

The song was halfway finished when Christina ran out to the dance floor. Jack swung her up in his arms and danced with both of them.

"Well, if it isn't the blushing bride." Gloria Marshall sneered, applying lipstick to her already red lips. "Quite a man you bought with your daughter's inheritance. I can see why you dumped Stanley. Jack's some of the best human flesh money can buy. I bet he cost you a pretty penny."

Stephanie ignored her and dried her hands on a paper towel. Gloria was Stanley's latest victim. Her father was a very wealthy man. Gloria had been after Stanley for the past year. Looked like she finally snared him.

"I didn't know you were into the sinister, bad boy type. I guess little miss Goody Two-shoes is not so good after all. I hear he used to be a Navy SEAL or something. The *or something* being the key phrase here."

Stephanie stopped and turned back around to face her. "What do you want, Gloria, the inside dirt? Here's your scoop. Unlike you, I don't have to buy men or sex. Speaking of buying sex, didn't I see you sitting with Stanley? Now, there's a man after your daddy's wallet."

"Stanley loves me."

"Stanley loves money, your father's money to be exact. Without it, he wouldn't give a snotty little brat like you the time of day. Do yourself a favor and make him sign a prenuptial agreement or you will end up penniless."

"We all know he was only after your money. Why else would he want a social reject? Your daughter's money can't buy you respectability."

"Gloria, that's just one of the differences between you and me. I don't need to buy a man, or respectability. I'm not a self-centered selfish witch like you are. People only tolerate you because of who your daddy is. Without him, you're nothing. I hear Stanley's company is in trouble and he needs to marry money to save it. Does this mean I'll be hearing wedding bells soon? Has he proposed yet?"

Gloria's face fell and she tried to conceal the engagement ring on her ringer, but Stephanie saw it anyway. "You know, that looks an awful lot like the ring he gave me. If I were you, I'd get that stone appraised. It's probably not real."

"He slept with me on the night he proposed to you," she lashed out. The young woman had tears in her eyes.

Stephanie stopped and turned back to face her. "You and two hookers. My, what a busy boy he was that night. Were you before or after the hookers? In case you didn't know, Stanley has a penchant for prostitutes. I hope for your sake you used condoms when you slept with him. I was smart enough not to sleep with him. So, tell me, Gloria, did I miss anything? Was he any good or is he as boring in bed as out?" Stephanie smiled, leaving the room. *Boy, that felt good.*

Stephanie went in search of Bridget the nanny and asked

her to take Christina home. It was close to her bedtime and she was exhausted and fussy. Stephanie and Jack promised their daughter they would come by the house to see her before they left for their honeymoon.

She still had no idea where Jack was taking her. All she knew was it was out of the country because she had to put a rush on getting her passport renewed.

Stephanie watched in surprise as Jack walked over to her mother and held out his hand. *Mom, don't make a scene. Just dance with him.*

"I believe this is our dance," said Jack, taking his mother-in-law by surprise. He smiled down into her startled face and held out his hand to her. "People are watching, Mildred. Take my hand or people will talk."

"You should be used to talk, but to save my daughter the embarrassment I'll dance with you, once." She caught his hand and let him lead her to the dance floor.

"Everything is beautiful," he complimented. "You did a fantastic job. See, I knew you would be good at spending other people's money."

"And I've only just begun," she warned. "Remember, you asked for it. Oh, and by the way, if you hurt my daughter, I will make one of your secret missions look like a day at the park. You and Stephanie can spin it any way you want to, but you won't convince me that you didn't black-mail her into this marriage. I know my daughter and she was finished with you and now suddenly you two are married. If you mess up, she won't forgive you."

"I won't waste my breath denying anything you've said," he conceded. "But know this, I love your daughter and she loves me. I would move heaven and earth for both Stephanie and Christina. My family means everything to me."

"Then prove me wrong about you. Be a good father and

an even better husband. They are your responsibility now. Put them first in your life. Don't let anyone or anything come before your family."

The rest of the dance was in silence. When the song ended, they gladly went their separate ways.

Jack went back to Stephanie and enfolded her in his arms. His eyes followed hers to Roper and Ashley.

"Do I want to know what you and my mother were talking about on the dance floor?"

Jack shrugged. "Idle chitchat."

"It didn't look idle to me. It looked pretty intense. Okay. I can take a hint. I'll let it go. I don't like the way Roper and Ashley are looking at each other. They are starting to make me nervous." She watched the two of them slow-dance. The two had been inseparable since meeting a week ago.

"Why? He's a good guy. She could do a lot worse."

"She could also do a lot better. One mercenary in the family is more than enough. I'm not sure my mother's heart could take another one."

"Forget Ashley and Roper. I don't want to think about anyone else when I have you in my arms. I'm pretty sure your little sister can handle him."

"I don't want her handling him. He is not right for her."

"You're beginning to sound like your mother." He silenced her with a kiss. "Forget Roper and Ash. It's been three weeks and two days. How long are we required to stay?" asked Jack, nibbling at her ear.

"If you keep that up, not much longer," she assured him, caressing his back.

"Is that a promise? Let's say good night. I want to be alone with you. You've kept me waiting long enough. I want you so badly I ache. Put me out of my misery, Stef, and let me put you out of yours."

"Let's go." Catching hands, they walked over to the DJ.

Stopping the music, he handed Jack the microphone. He guided her to the dance floor with his arm around her waist.

"Is everyone having a good time?" Whistles and applause answered Jack's question. "That's what we wanted to hear. My beautiful bride and I want to thank all of you for coming out tonight to share this special occasion with us. Please eat, drink, and enjoy the rest of the evening, because I intend to." This was followed by hoots of laughter and whistles.

Stephanie turned red in embarrassment. She let out a surprised squeal as Jack swung her up in his arms and carried her from the room. "You can put me down now, you silly man." Stephanie smiled as Jack walked down the hallway carrying her.

"I'm not silly," he clarified. "I'm horny." They both laughed as she rested her forehead against his. "I'll put you down once we reach the honeymoon suite." Jack stopped outside the suite. "Close your eyes." Stephanie did as he requested as he unlocked the door and carried her inside. He slipped off her shoes and then set her on her feet. "Now you can open your eyes."

Stephanie marveled at the beauty around her. The entire room was covered in red rose petals. On the table sat an ice bucket and a bottle of champagne.

"It's incredible. Thank you," came her choked voice. Stephanie was touched by his thoughtfulness.

"Nothing compares to your beauty today and every day. Seeing the look on your face is thanks enough." He walked over and picked up a small package off the bed. "I'm going to shower. The package on the bed is for you." As he left the room, Stephanie walked over to the bed and sat down. Picking up the package, she smiled when she saw the name of a lingerie shop on it. She took out a silk white negligee and matching wrapper. It was exquisite. Holding it in front of her, she smiled at her reflection in the glass.

Mrs. Jack Kaufman has a nice ring to it. Stephanie Kaufman. Stephanie Mason-Kaufman. Stephanie Kaufman it is.

She unzipped her gown and hung it in the closet. Removing her panty hose, she lay back on the bed among the rose petals in her strapless bra and panties. Picking up some of the petals, she dropped them all over her body and laughed.

Minutes later, she was still covered in rose petals when Jack stepped into the room. He stood silently and watched her with a big satisfied smile on his face.

Stephanie sat up when she saw him. Her eyes trailed over his body in appreciation. He wore only a pair of paisley silk pajama bottoms. His naked torso gleamed in the soft light. She resisted the urge to reach out and touch him. She knew if she did, it would be all over. Swinging her legs off the bed, she brushed rose petals from her body.

"I must look pretty silly to you," she said, embarrassed.

"No." He shook his head. "You look delightful."

She picked up the package from the bed and held it tightly in front of her.

"I won't be long," she promised softly, slipping into the bathroom. Stephanie took a quick shower. Donning the gown and wrapper, she stared at her reflection in the mirror.

Her hand shook slightly as she turned the doorknob. Taking a deep breath, she opened it and walked through it.

Jack was lying on the bed with his back resting against the headboard. His eyes were closed, which gave Stephanie the perfect opportunity to admire her new husband's physique. He looked like a bronzed god lying on the bed among the rose petals. His chest was well defined and his arms were muscular bands of steels. His stomach was flat. Her eyes followed the trail of dark hair that disappeared into the waistband of his pajamas. She walked silently toward him and cleared her throat to get his attention.

He looked up and his breath caught in his throat when he saw her. She looked like an angel. He came slowly to his feet as she moved toward him. He poured champagne into two flutes and reached one to her.

"To new beginnings," he toasted.

"To new beginnings." She touched her glass to his. After draining her glass, she took his and set them both on the table.

Jack's eyes followed Stephanie over to the table and back. She stopped in front of him. Her hands moved to the sash in her negligee. His hands covered hers and gently pushed them aside.

This was his present to unwrap and nothing could have stayed his hands at this moment. He slowly parted the wrap and pushed it from her shoulders, letting it drop to the floor. His hands came to rest on her sides and he drew her into his embrace. Her arms went around his neck and she tiptoed to meet his hungry kiss. Stephanie's mouth parted beneath the delicious pressure of his. Jack's hands slid down her waist to her hips. He drew her near and there was no mistaking his need as he molded her body to his.

Backing her to the bed, he reached down and caught the bottom of her chemise. He raised the hem, bearing inch by inch of her skin. His eyes never left hers as he dropped it on the floor. When his eyes left hers, and moved over her body in a gentle caress, he sucked in his breath at the naked vision before him.

Stephanie untied the tie at his waist and let the pajama bottoms slide down his thighs. Her eyes darkened in passion as they glided over him in a silken caress. Her hands followed her eyes down his hairy chest. The trailed the path down his abs to that part of him that leaped with unfulfilled hunger when she touched it.

He pressed her back against the mattress and joined her on the bed. "I've dreamed about this a thousand times." His hands caressed her face. "You are perfection. You are my fantasy. My wife. My life."

Tears sprang to Stephanie's eyes at his tender words. She wanted so badly to tell him she loved him, but something held her back. She couldn't tell him with words, but she could show him with her body, until the time was right.

Taking the lead, she gently pushed him to his back. Her hands and mouth loved him in ways that left no doubt in his mind how much she did love him. She didn't have to say the words tonight. He knew how she felt and he loved her as much as she loved him.

He was overly excited and wanted the night to last. His mouth trailed a path down her neck to her shoulder blade. His tongue flicked her breast and it hardened into a pebble. He sucked the pouting nipple into the hot cavern of his mouth and his hand covered her other breast.

A soft moan escaped Stephanie's lips. Her body tingled with sensation. She wanted more. Her body craved more. His hand grazed her stomach as it ventured to her trembling thighs. Her legs parted at his featherlight touch, giving him the access he needed. His hand cupped her warmth. She gasped as one finger slipped inside her moist, hot body.

Her body was on fire as he kissed his way down her body, replacing his hand with his mouth. Every nerve in her body was pulsating at his tender assault. She squirmed under his mouth.

Stephanie was ready to explode when his body finally covered hers. She welcomed his weight and wrapped her body around his. She clung to him and her nails dug into his back as he slid smoothly into her.

They moved rhythmically together. Stephanie met and matched his every movement. They were each seeking, searching, and reaching for a little piece of heaven. Their world exploded in an array of brilliant flashes of light around them.

This was just the beginning of their night. Jack promised her a night they would both remember, and he delivered.

Chapter 11

Jack logged off his laptop and closed it. He was finished for the day. He had promised Christina he would take her to the park later. Jack also had a special dinner planned for Stephanie. Today was their three-month anniversary.

The ringing telephone interrupted his thoughts. Jack leaned over and stared at the caller ID on his cell phone. He knew that number and intuition told him he was not going to like what he was about to hear. "Hello."

"Kaufman, it's Cap," came the gruff voice on the other end. "We have a major problem. I need your expertise."

"Cap, you know I'm out of the business. I'm a family man. I have responsibilities now."

"I know, but this is a special mission. It's one you can't refuse. Todd Roper has been captured in Iran."

Jack leaped to his feet. "What? When?" He felt a knot in the pit of his stomach. "What was he thinking? Roper told me he was done with that business."

"We all say that, but the money and excitement draw us back in. He said this was his last mission. Unfortunately, that may very well be the case without your help. Roper was captured late last night. Cooper and Rodriguez are already there. They have a fix on Roper's location, but I told them not to make a move until you got there."

"I'll be on the next flight out." Jack jotted down all the pertinent information. Hanging up the phone, he turned on his laptop. He keyed in the destination and searched the airlines for the next available flight out. He booked one that left in a few hours. Quickly shutting down his computer, he went upstairs.

He entered the bedroom and headed for the closet. Jack pulled a black duffel bag from the back of the closet. Opening the bag, he took out a stack of money and checked for his passport. The bag contained about five grand, his passport, and three changes of dark clothes.

He changed into all black. To the untrained eye, there was nothing out of place with his appearance. He headed back downstairs with the bag over his shoulder.

There was one stop he had to make before he went to the hotel to see Stephanie. He called Ashley's condo to make sure she was home. He let her know he was on his way over.

Jack had to break the news to her about Roper. He hated being the bearer of bad news, but he felt she had a right to know. He also wanted her to keep an eye on Stephanie while he was gone.

He knew she would view this as his choosing Roper over his family. That was clearly not the case. Roper wasn't just his best friend; he was like a brother to him. In the past, Roper always had his back. He would never forget Roper had taken a bullet meant for him. He owed Todd Roper his life.

Jack didn't have a lot of time, so he broke the news to Ashley as gently as he could. She took it better than he thought she would. He tried to assure her he would find Roper, and bring him home. Ashley promised Jack she would check on her big sister periodically.

* * *

Stephanie stared at the home pregnancy test results. She had known even before taking the test what the results would be. Since their honeymoon night three months ago, they had taken no precautions to prevent a pregnancy.

Stephanie was happy and apprehensive. She was told after her accident, the chances of her getting pregnant were not good. Her carrying a baby to term would be a miracle. She never told any of this to her husband. Stephanie knew she had to make a doctor's appointment right way.

Jack was passionate about everything he did and making love to his wife, almost every night, was no exception. He would be thrilled about the pregnancy. She knew how he felt. He wanted more children.

She wanted this baby more than anything, but she was afraid. She was still so unsure of Jack and their future. She wanted to be happy about the baby, but something was holding her back.

She placed her hand on her stomach. *I'm going to have a baby. I should be happy. I shouldn't have any anxieties or hang-ups about it. There's a life growing inside me. One that Jack and I created. It's a part of both of us. I love my husband, but I still don't trust him the way I should. I'll tell him about the baby tonight. I'll tell him everything.*

Stephanie heard Jack's voice outside her door and dropped the pregnancy test in her wastebasket. She then pushed the basket under her desk. She needed a little more time to let the information digest before she shared it with him.

As he entered the room, she stared at his strange attire. He looked almost ready for a secret mission.

"Stef, we need to talk," he said softly, closing the door behind him. Those words sent a chill down her spine.

"No," said Stephanie, shaking her head in denial. *He was leaving!* She knew even before he said the words. "No, Jack. You promised me you were finished with that business. Don't do this." She came to her feet and rounded the desk to face him. "You gave me your word it was over."

"It is over. It's different this time, Stef. I have to go. Roper has been captured."

"You are not a superhero. Let someone else go. You can't be the only trained mercenary they have."

"I owe him."

"You owe me and Christina!"

"He saved my life, Stef. He rescued me when everyone else thought I was dead. He came back for me. I can do no less for him. I have to try and get him out of there before they kill him."

"What if something happens to you? You owe it to your daughter to be here and watch her grow up! You gave me your word you were finished with that life! I believed you! I trusted you! Now you are being sucked back in!"

"It's not like that. I owe Roper my life!"

"Your vow to me supersedes all else. I am your wife. Your place is here with Christina and me. You are not invincible no matter what you think!"

"I know it's dangerous, but I have to go. I have to try."

Fear and dread gripped her. She was losing him. "If you go, we are finished," she declared softly, wiping the tears from her face.

Her words cut him to the quick. He knew it was anger talking. She was angry and she was afraid. "You don't mean that. I know you don't."

"Yes, I do. I can't live like this. This will prove to me Christina and I don't come first in your life. We should be your number-one priority. This will prove to me I can't count on you being here for us if we need you."

"That's not fair. This is about honor. He saved my

life. He took a bullet for me. I can't walk away from that. I owe him."

"But you can walk away from us. Do you think it's fair to us what you're doing? Christina loves you. She just found you and she could lose you. If something happened to you, it would break her heart!" *And mine!*

"I know that and I will be as careful as I can be. Honey, this was not an easy decision for me, but I have no choice." He embraced her resisting body into his arms. Raising her chin, he stared down into her teary eyes. He could see the fear in her eyes. "I'll be back. I promise you I will be back as soon as humanly possible." He kissed the tears from her face. His mouth captured hers in a slow, thorough kiss. Stephanie's arms went around him and she returned his kiss. When his mouth left hers, they stood there holding each other tightly. "Please don't cry. I have to go," said Jack, pulling away from her.

"Please don't go," she begged, reaching out for him. "Please stay."

His heart constricted at her anguished cry.

"Christina needs you. I need you." The words were ripped from her heart as she cried out to him. "Please don't leave me, Jack. I need you now more than ever."

"I'm sorry, sweetheart. I promise I will be back soon. Trust me just this once. Kiss Christina for me and tell her I owe her a day at the park." He stepped back from her and walked to the door. He went back to her and swept her in his arms. His mouth covered hers again. She held on to him for dear life, returning his desperate kiss. "I love you, Stef. Don't ever doubt it or forget it." He gave her one more kiss before releasing her and disappearing out the door.

"I love you too," she whispered to the empty room. "We are going to have a baby."

Stephanie dropped down in her chair and lost what little composure she had left. She had waited a lifetime to hear those words from him. Now they meant nothing to her because he was leaving! He was going on a mission that could possibly get him killed! Did he really love her or was he only saying it to appease her?

How can you do this to me, to us? You've ruined everything. It's over! I'll never forgive you for this!

Her hand protectively covered her stomach and she cried even harder. She now had two children who could possibly lose their father. Stephanie was furious at him and at herself for not taking any precautions.

So much for him wanting a family when he wouldn't stick around long enough to be a part of one. *You wanted this baby and now you are headed to God knows where to do God knows what. I don't even know if I'll ever see you again. You may never know we have a child growing inside me. I should have been smarter. I should have used protection. I was a fool to think you could settle down, and be satisfied and happy with Christina and me. You love danger and excitement. It's part of who you are. It's what attracted me to you.*

Wiping her face and drying her tears, she came wearily to her feet. Opening the door, she noted Georgette was not there. She went back to her desk and sent her an e-mail.

Georgette
Please cancel Jack's training sessions for Maryland and Tennessee. I'm taking the rest of the day off. I'm also working from home the rest of the week. If you need me, call me at home or on my cell phone.

Stephanie needed to be with her daughter. She had to tell her Jack had taken a trip. She had to do so without falling apart or letting her sense something was wrong.

As she suspected, Christina took the news badly. She simply told her he was on a business trip and he could possibly be gone for a few weeks. She was upset he didn't say good-bye to her. Christina cried herself to sleep that night and so did Stephanie. She cursed him for a coward for not facing his daughter.

The first night was the worst for Stephanie. Sleeping alone in their big bed, she missed her husband's presence. Jack always made her feel safe and protected.

Stephanie was in the den lying on the sofa hugging a pillow to her when Ashley entered the room. When Stephanie saw her, she sat up. Ashley went to her and put her arms around her.

"Jack is gone." Stephanie sniffed. "He left me. I knew he would. I knew he couldn't escape that life."

"Stef, that's not true," chided Ashley. "He didn't leave you. He went to help out a friend in trouble. Jack will be back."

"We don't know that. He could be killed, Ashley. Todd Roper is not worth my husband's life."

"That's not fair," said Ashley softly.

"Fair! You want to talk to me about fair? I could lose my husband and Christina could lose her father because of your boyfriend's immaturity, stupidity, and greed. He has dragged my husband into this mess, when he should be home with his family. So now he's ruined my life as well as yours. Way to pick them, Ash."

"I know you are upset, so I'm not going to argue with you about this. I know you love Jack and I love Roper. You can curse Todd until you are blue in the face, but it won't change anything. He's Jack's friend and Jack will bring him back and when he does, I'll kill him myself."

The week passed slowly for Stephanie. The good news was her mother was still out of town and she didn't have to face her yet. The last thing she needed right now was to hear her mother say I told you so.

She went by her doctor's office and took a blood test, which confirmed her pregnancy. She then scheduled her first prenatal appointment.

When she got back to her office, her mother was waiting for her in her office. Stephanie was surprised to see her. "Mom, hi. When did you get back?" asked Stephanie, hugging her.

"Today. The trip was great." She smiled. "Are you okay? You look funny. Is something wrong?"

"I'm fine." Stephanie moved away from her. "I'm just a little tired. I haven't been sleeping very well." This was the truth. She had not had a good night's sleep since the day Jack left.

"Are you sure that's all? Where's that coldhearted son-in-law of mine?" Stephanie froze in apprehension. She couldn't take her mother ranting and raving about Jack right now. "I want to thank him for giving me this job. I love it. It makes me feel alive. It makes me feel appreciated."

Stephanie was floored by her words. This was her mother speaking, the woman who pitched a fit about being forced into this position. "You're kidding," said Stephanie unbelievably.

Mildred laughed at the look on her daughter's face. "No. I'm serious. I love decorating and I love to travel."

Stephanie stared blankly at her mother.

"I left a message for Jack on his cell phone a few days ago, but I haven't heard from him. I figure what the heck, I might as well bury the hatchet with him. We are family after all."

Her words brought fresh tears to Stephanie's eyes. "He's gone."

"Gone where?" Mildred asked softly, noting her daughter's distress.

"On a mission," she said, coming to her feet. "I don't even know where he went or if he will even come back. I gave him an ultimatum, this mission or his family, and he walked out. He's gone."

"Stop right there, young lady. You're telling me he left you and Christina to go pillage the countryside. This doesn't make sense. He had all the money he could possibly want. He loves you and Christina. He wouldn't just leave like that. There's something you're not saying."

"No, Mother, he's not out pillaging the countryside. He's on a rescue mission this time." Her mother sat down. "Do you remember the loud, obnoxious best man, Roper?"

Her mother nodded. "The unsavory character with the crew cut that your sister has gotten involved with. How could I forget him? What she sees in him, I'll never know. He's more uncouth than Jack."

"He was doing the pillaging in some foreign country and got caught. Jack went to rescue him. He put his life and our future on the line to save some low-life mercenary who's probably not even worth saving."

"Honey, isn't he the man who saved Jack's life?" Stephanie nodded uneasily. "Then you can't expect him to turn his back on his friend. It's in the mercenary rule book, I guess. You and Jack both owe a great deal to this man. He wouldn't be the man you love so much if he had walked away from a friend in need."

"But he would be here and he would be safe. Christina and I need him. What about our needs?"

"Stephanie, as much as it pains me to say it, we are talking about a man's life here. A man who your husband owes his life to. How could you possibly give him an ultimatum about something like this? I know you're upset he left, but you're not thinking clearly. Stop thinking about yourself and put yourself in Jack's shoes for a minute. This couldn't have been an easy decision for him. He was willing to risk his family for doing what he thinks is right."

"Why are you suddenly defending him? You hate the

ground he walks on. I thought you would break out the champagne and fine china."

"A month ago, I probably would have, but when I see the three of you together I know it's right. Stephanie, I saw the way you looked at him at your wedding. You love this man. I also saw the way he looked at you. Despite his rough exterior and atrocious manners, he adores you and Christina. I know you didn't just marry him for love. The big lug probably blackmailed you into it. Honey, if you love him as much as I think you do, don't throw away your marriage in a fit of anger. Think long and hard about this. What if you're pregnant?"

"I am pregnant," she admitted softly. "I found out right before he left and I was so angry I didn't even tell him. What if he never comes back?"

"When, not if, he comes back. You two have a lot to talk about. You and I both know Jack is not going to let you go without a fight. He'll come back, Stephanie. He'll find a way. Come here, sweetie." Mildred enfolded Stephanie in her arms and held her.

Stephanie took the mail from the mailbox and walked into the house. Dropping everything except for one large package on the coffee table, she frowned and stared at the packet in her hand. It was from Alexia's attorney. Why would he contact her after all this time?

She sat down on the sofa and tore open the package. She scanned over the letter briefly. Stephanie dumped the contents on the couch next to her. As she thumbed through the documents, her hand froze. She picked up what was a legal document. It was a certified copy of Alexia and Jack's marriage license. She turned the page and the next document made the air leave her lungs. She stared transfixed at the paper. She blinked several times to make sure she had not imagined it. Her hand trembled as she stared at the certified copy of their divorce decree. It had been dated and signed by Jack two months before Christina was born.

The paper slipped from her fingers. This document changed everything. Jack lied to her again. He and Alexia were divorced before she died.

The will was valid. Jack was bluffing about the will. He had no leverage, not even Christina, since he knew about her. If she had known about this, she would not have married him.

He had known about Christina and he had walked away before she was born. What kind of unfeeling monster would do something like that? Maybe he wasn't on a mission. Maybe he was leaving them also. This must be his way of saying good-bye.

How stupid does he think I am? Surely, he knew I would eventually find out about this. I am so stupid not to see all the signs. He wanted out and this was his way out. He ran away again. He's not coming back.

Stephanie lay back on the couch hugging her stomach. She had no idea what she was supposed to do now. She was tired of all the lies and all the games. There was no fight left in her. It was over and now she had to pick up the pieces of her life. She had to be strong for Christina and for the baby she was carrying.

As Jack sat on the plane bound for Iran, he closed his eyes and replayed his parting from Stephanie. The sight of her crying and begging him to stay tore at his heart. She said she needed him. Those were not the three words he wanted to hear from her, but he would take them because he saw the love shining in her eyes. He knew she loved him as much as he loved her. He didn't just want her love; he wanted her trust.

Don't give up on us, Stef. I will come home to you and Christina! Count on it!

When the plane landed, he followed the instructions he had received from Cooper. He was a bit taken off guard when a young Iranian girl welcomed him home and promptly kissed him. He gently set her away from him. She smiled in what Jack thought was relief. He also saw fear in her eyes. He had no idea what she was afraid of, but she was perfectly safe from him.

Catching his hand, she led him to a waiting cab. Giving the driver the directions, she appraised him. Jack studied the young girl. She was beautiful with her long dark hair and sultry eyes. She was a tiny little thing.

The cab stopped near a run-down shack and she looked at him to pay for the ride. Jack paid the fare and followed her inside the cabin.

"It's about damn time." Cooper smiled, stepping out of the shadows.

"She's all yours," said Rodriguez, indicating the girl with a nod in her direction. "Call it a late wedding present."

A smile spread across Jack's face. "As appealing as she may be, fellows, I don't play with children other than my own. Besides, I'm a happily married man. Stephanie would kill me if I looked at another woman." He shook hands and then embraced both men. "It's good to see you guys. I wish you could have made it for the wedding."

They all sat down at the dinner table. Cooper laid out a hand-drawn blueprint of where Roper was being held. "The guards rotate every three hours."

Scratching his head, Jack studied the fortress and all the guards posted around it. "What the hell was Roper thinking going in there alone?"

"He was supposed to wait for Cooper," answered Rodriguez, "but as usual he was detained by some woman."

"He should have waited for me. Roper wasn't supposed

to go in alone. We were hired to steal the guns, confiscate the drugs, and take out the top two guys in this organization. Roper got careless and they caught him snooping around. So what's the plan?" Cooper asked.

"I have a couple of different ideas, but I need to see the place first. My first thought would be to hire some locals to create a diversion. While they are doing that, you and Rodriguez sneak inside and rescue Roper. It's quick and it's painless, but it's not foolproof."

"Nothing is foolproof. We need to come up with a back-up plan just in case something goes wrong," inserted Cooper.

"Let me give it some thought. Rodriguez can show me the place when it's dark. I want to survey the area. Once I see the place, I'll decide the best way to proceed."

When night fell, Jack and Rodriguez dressed in full combat gear, with full night-vision goggles and the works. Jack got as close as he dared to the compound. He counted guards as well as calculated steps to the entrance. He sketched the compound complete with all entrances and exits.

It was after midnight when they made it back to the house. There was no shower, so Jack drew a bucket of well water and washed up for bed.

Jack was asleep when he heard the door open and the girl enter the bedroom. He quietly waited for her to make a move. When she slipped into the bed next to him, he tried to ease out of bed.

She caught his arm to stop him. "Do not trust them," she whispered in broken English.

Jack stilled and looked at her in surprise. Cooper and Rodriguez said she couldn't speak or understand English. She moved closer to him on the bed. "They lie."

Jack lay back on the bed and faced her. "What are you talking about?" he asked with raised eyebrows. "Who is lying?"

"Keep voice down," the girl whispered. "They lie about everything. They are not your friends. They are not friends to each other. Rodriguez hate Cooper."

"Lady, I don't know what the hell you are talking about, but I would trust those two with my life. Why would Rodriguez hate Cooper? They are friends."

"Cooper plot to take your life. Watch him closely. He drugged your friend Roper and took him away. He is not where they say he is. It's a trap for you."

"I was there tonight. I saw the compound where Roper is being held."

She hit him on the forehead with her hand.

"Watch that." He caught her hand. "And why would they go through all this trouble just to get me here?" he asked, playing along with her. "Why would they turn on me?"

"Money."

Jack felt the hair rise on the back of his neck.

"Cooper says you are worth millions. Your wife will pay much to get you back."

Jack lay flat on his back thinking. He had felt something was fishy from the beginning. Could what she was saying be true? Could his old comrades have set him up to extort money from Stephanie?

He vaulted off the bed, pulling the girl with him. This was ridiculous. He was letting his imagination and her get the better of him. He had known these guys for over ten years. They were like family. They wouldn't turn on him.

"You're lying," he hissed, glaring down at her. "Little girl, you have no idea who you are playing with. Cooper would kill you if he knew what you were saying about him. He may be slightly off his rocker, but he knows better than to go up against me. They both do. I take no prisoners."

"I do not lie. They will kill you and Roper. They also have my five-year old brother. They took him when they took this man Roper. They hold his life in their hands.

Why else do you think I would be here? I am trying to save your stupid life and possibly my own. They will kill me and my brother once they have no need of us."

Jack released her and paced the room. Were Rodriguez and Cooper after the Luciano fortune? Was this whole mission about him? If it was true, he had to act fast. *I have to get help to find out where they are really holding Roper and the boy. I came here to rescue my friend and I am not leaving without him.*

"Let's say I believe your story. Will you help me?" asked Jack as he faced her. "This will be very dangerous for all of us. If they catch on to us, we're dead."

"I will help you only if you agree to take me and my brother back with you to America. That is my price."

Jack's look was incredulous. What she was asking was not possible. Well, it was possible, but he had no intention of agreeing to her terms. "I can't do that. I can't be responsible for you and your brother. I have a wife and a daughter."

"So what? I can clean your house. I can cook. I can learn anything I have to, but you have to take us with you. I have a visa and passport for my brother and me, but I have no money for airline tickets. You help me and I help you. Take it or leave it, Mr. Kaufman, owner of Luciano Hotels."

"Funny how you can suddenly speak perfect English instead of the broken English you were slaughtering before."

She shrugged her shoulders.

"I guess I don't really have a choice, do I? You've already saved my life by telling me what they are planning. What's your name and how old are you?"

"I am Nina Armatage and I am . . . eighteen." She stumbled over the lie.

"You look more like fifteen," he noted, looking her up and down. "Nina, have they raped you?"

"No. I am still a virgin. I told Cooper I had a sexual disease. He said something strange about having no condoms and left me alone. What are condoms?" she asked, staring up at him innocently.

"Never mind," said Jack, actually embarrassed by her question. He was not about to have a talk with her about the birds and the bees. "Here's what I need you to do. I need you to go into town and ask around for the Scottish bar owner with fiery red hair." He sat down at the desk and wrote a short note. "I want you to give him this note and tell him I need to meet him somewhere ASAP."

"They won't let me go out at night. They don't trust me."

"Okay, then let's go to bed. We have a busy day tomorrow." He waved to the bed.

"I'm not sleeping with you," she said, primly crossing her arms over her chest. "I thought you said you were happily married."

"I am happily married, Nina. I promise I won't touch you, but we do have to share this room tonight and I'm not sleeping on the floor."

"I will sleep on the floor. I am not sharing a bed or anything else with you. I thought you were different. I thought I could trust you." Her voice rose. She let out a squeal as Jack picked her up and tossed her on the bed. His body covered hers as the door flew open.

"Ouch! You little hellcat. You bit me." He saw blood oozing from his shoulder. "Guys, can we get some privacy?" snarled Jack. "I have to teach her a lesson." Laughing, Cooper and Rodriguez both backed out of the room and closed the door. "You bit me," repeated Jack, glaring down at her. "I should put you over my knee. I guess that was convincing enough."

"Get off me," Nina hissed, shoving at him. "I did not know your intentions when you threw me on the bed. I had to defend myself."

Laughing, Jack rolled off her. "This situation is almost funny, but I don't think I'll share it with my wife. Somehow I don't think she would find me in bed with a fiery eighteen-year-old gorgeous young woman amusing. Good night, Nina, sweet dreams."

Jack felt more at ease when he read Tom's note. He had a tail on Cooper and Rodriguez. He also had someone watching his back as well as Nina's to keep her out of trouble. It also included a meeting time and place scheduled for two hours from now.

He gave Cooper the slip in town and headed for his rendezvous with Tom. He went into the restaurant and asked for the special. They led him to a room off from the kitchen. Jack and the big Scotsman embraced warmly.

"Tom, I need one more favor. I know you still have contacts in the States. I need protection for my wife and daughter." He handed him a piece of paper with their home address and the hotel. "We both know Cooper and Rodriguez didn't mastermind this. They aren't smart enough. I need a man on Cap."

"Already done. I put a tail on him when I got your note. I'll have someone on your family within the hour. My men have located Roper and the kid. They are both alive, but under heavy guard. Say the word and we go in for them."

"We go in when I know for sure my family is out of danger. While Cap is in the States, he's a threat to my wife and daughter."

"Do you want him taken out?"

"Do I have a choice? I know him. If he figures out I'm on to him, he'll use my family to get to me. Tomorrow night at eleven-thirty we make our move."

"Watch your back, Kaufman."

Chapter 12

Stephanie was lying in bed having another sleepless night. She turned off the television and tried to get some sleep. Her hand covered her stomach.

Hi, baby. I will be the best mother and father I can for you. I'm sorry your dad won't be around to see you grow up, but I will always be here for you.

The ringing telephone interrupted her thoughts. Switching on the lamp, she leaned over and picked up the telephone. "Hello."

"Mrs. Kaufman, listen carefully," said the thickly accented voice. Stephanie sat up in bed. "We have your husband. We want ten million dollars deposited into a Swiss bank account. I'll call you back on Friday with the instructions and the account information. You have three days to get the money."

Stephanie shook her head unbelievably. Jack was up to his old tricks again. He was now staging his own kidnapping to get at their daughter's inheritance.

"Then kill him," Stephanie said angrily. "I'm not paying you a dime for his return. In fact, I don't want him back. He has been nothing but trouble to me since the day he schemed his way into my life."

"Mrs. Kaufman, this is not a joke. We will kill him if we don't get the money."

"You tell that sick bastard for me there's an easier way to end a marriage. It's called a divorce. I believe he's familiar with the term, having gone through one before. And by the way, since there was no prenuptial agreement, the money is legally his to take. This whole ruse was unnecessary. Don't call here again," said Stephanie, slamming the phone down. *How could you do this? Just when I think nothing you do surprises me, something even more unbelievable comes along. How could you sink this low? How could I have been so blind and so wrong about you, Jack?*

Stephanie cried herself to sleep again that night. It had almost become a ritual with her since Jack left.

She was awakened bright and early the next morning by the ringing telephone. Staring at the caller ID, she saw it was a cellular number. She refused to answer it. The caller hung up and called back again.

"Hello," she croaked, snatching up the phone.

"Stephanie, I'm sorry to wake you. It's Tom Corbin."

She frowned as she stared at the telephone. Sitting up in bed, she looked over at the alarm clock. It registered 6:30 a.m.

"My plane landed in Dallas a few minutes ago and I'm headed to your place. I've got some news about Jack for you."

"Jack is not here. He left. I don't expect him back, ever," she said. "Sorry you made a wasted trip."

"It's not that simple. We'll talk when I get there," he said, ringing off. She stared at the phone only a few seconds before being spurred into action. She did not like Tom Corbin, or Cap as Jack referred to him. She didn't trust him as far as she could throw him. He had cold eyes and an even colder heart.

Why would he fly all the way to Dallas to see her after she

had turned down a ransom call for Jack? Something didn't add up. Could this be real? Could Jack really be in danger? What if Jack really was kidnapped? No. She didn't believe it.

Throwing back the cover, she quickly dressed and ran down the hall to wake Bridget. She wanted Bridget and Christina out of the house before Cap arrived.

"Bridget," said Stephanie, shaking Christina's nanny. "Bridget, get up."

The nanny sat up rubbing the sleep from her eyes.

"I need you to take Christina and go to my mother's town house." Stephanie placed her car keys in her palm. "This is the key to my mother's town house. The code is in my glove box."

"What's going on?" asked Bridget, pulling the cover over her head. "It's too early to get up."

Stephanie pulled the covers off her and the bed. "I don't have time to explain, but you've got to get up and move. I need you out of this house in the next fifteen minutes or less. I'll go get Christina ready. Pack a bag just in case you have to stay longer."

Stephanie packed a bag for her daughter, but didn't bother to wake her. Instead, she scooped her up with comforter and all and carried her down the stairs. She put her in the car and buckled her in. Bridget got in behind the wheel and tossed her purse and case to the passenger seat.

"I'll call you later. Bridget, if you don't hear from me, don't call or bring Christina back to the house. Stay put until Ashley or I tell you otherwise."

Stephanie stood in the driveway and watched the car drive away. As she went back inside the house, she didn't notice the car following them or the car parked almost diagonally across from her house.

When she closed the door behind her, the phone immediately started to ring. Her hand trembled as she picked it up. "Hello."

"Mrs. Kaufman, I'm a friend of a friend. I'll make this brief. Do not trust Captain Corbin. He's a dangerous man."

Stephanie gripped the phone. That much had been obvious to her from their first meeting at the rehearsal dinner.

"Do not have any contact with him. If he contacts you, let us know ASAP."

"You're a little late, friend. He's on his way here. What is going on and where is my husband?"

"Your husband is in a bit of a sticky situation. He walked right into a trap. He has the upper hand right now, because they don't know he is on to them."

Her heart constricted. Jack really was in danger.

"My job is to keep you safe. The nanny and your daughter are well protected, I had two of my men follow them."

Stephanie was having trouble taking it all in. Jack was in danger and now so was she.

"Mrs. Kaufman, I won't try and kid you, this situation is going to get worse before it gets better. He's going to try and get you to pay the ransom. I need you to stall Captain Corbin any way you can without making him suspicious. I am parked across the street at your neighbor's house. When Captain Corbin comes in, leave the front door unlocked. There is one last thing I need you to do. There are three of us out here. Unlock the back door so two of my men can come in now. They are already there; they just need you to let them in."

"How do I know you are the good guys?" she asked uneasily.

"Trust your instincts, Mrs. Kaufman. We were sent here to protect you and your daughter. If we wanted to hurt you we could have already."

Stephanie carried the cordless phone with her through to the kitchen. She unlocked the patio door and opened it. She took a step back as the two men stepped inside the kitchen. She stared at the men dressed in full combat gear down to their weapons. "They're inside."

"Okay, I'll let Norris take it from here. He's going to plant a few bugs throughout the house so I can listen in. Just follow his instructions and everything should work out."

Stephanie disconnected the call. *Should being the key phrase! Should is not very reassuring.*

"Mrs. Kaufman, I'm Norris," said the young man, extending his hand. "This is Benjamin."

She shook hands with both men.

"How much time do we have before Captain Corbin gets here?"

Stephanie looked down at her watch. "Twenty to thirty minutes at the most. It depends on which airline he used."

"Okay, give us a quick tour of the house."

After giving them a tour, Stephanie sat nervously on the couch. She called Georgette and told her she was taking the rest of the week off. Her new business manager could handle things for a few days.

God, please protect Jack and bring him back to us. Please let the kidnappers call again.

Stephanie was pacing the room when the doorbell rang. Wiping her sweating palms on her pants, she opened the door.

"Captain Corbin, hi," said Stephanie nervously, stepping back to allow him to enter. He came in carrying two black briefcases. She eyed this suspiciously.

"Come sit down. We need to talk," said Captain Corbin, walking over to the couch and sitting down.

Stephanie followed him to the sofa and sat down nervously.

"It has come to my attention that two of my trusted soldiers have gone renegade and betrayed us. They kidnapped Roper to lure Jack into a trap."

"What? Why would anyone kidnap Jack?" she asked innocently.

"I'm afraid they are holding your husband for ransom."

"Oh my God," cried Stephanie, coming to her feet and

turning away from him. Finally a chance to use those drama classes she took in college. "They phoned and I hung up on them! I told them to kill him! What if they don't call me back?" Stephanie put all her acting ability into the crocodile tears she shed. Her concern and her fear for her husband's safety were very real. She knew the man sitting next to her was a dangerous killer and she had to be civil to him. She had to pretend to trust him.

"Shh, calm down. It's okay. I'm sure they'll call back. How much did they ask for?"

"Ten million dollars." She wrung her hands nervously. "I don't have that kind of money. Why would anyone think I could possibly have that much money?"

"What about your hotels? They all seem to be doing well."

"Not that well. There is no way I can raise ten million dollars by Friday. It's impossible."

"Look, I've got two million right here to help you out. How much do you think you can raise?"

"I don't know. Maybe I could raise two or three million at most. I'd have to liquidate some assets. Sell off some stocks and maybe take out a loan." She calmed herself down. "I can't believe you would give me two million to get my husband back. You are a true friend to him."

"Jack and Roper are like family. We've been through a lot together. I would do anything for those boys."

Yet you can still have them kidnapped and killed without batting an eye. What kind of monster are you?

"I guess I'd better get busy making some phone calls in a couple of hours. Make yourself at home. I'll be in the den if you need me," said Stephanie, leaving the room. She hurried to the den. Sitting down at her desk, she let out the breath she had been holding. She spotted the note on her monitor.

You have to make it look good. Call the bank and your broker.

She was trembling as she quickly erased the note. She

pulled up her financial spreadsheet on the computer. It took her a couple of hours to figure out how to liquidate some of her assets and still keep the hotels afloat. Satisfied, she picked up the phone.

"Barbara, it's Stephanie Kaufman."

"Hi, Stephanie, I haven't heard from you in a while. What can I do for you today?"

Stephanie heard a distinct soft click as Captain Corbin picked up the phone in the living room. "Barbara, I need to liquidate all my assets. I need a total of what that comes to in today's market. I want to close out my account and Christina's."

"Stephanie, are you sure about this?"

"Yes, I'm sure. Can you total it up, call me back, and let me know how much we are talking about?"

"Sure. I can call you back in a couple of hours. For a transaction of this magnitude, I will need you to come in and sign all the paperwork before we can process the order."

She heard the soft click again and knew he had hung up the phone. "Okay. Just call me first with the total and I will let you know when I can come in. Thanks, Barbara."

Stephanie made several more calls before finally leaving the den. She frowned when she went to the living room and found Captain Corbin not there. His things were there, but he was nowhere in sight. She relaxed when he came out of the bathroom.

"I hope you like Chinese food," said Stephanie. "I was going to order some takeout. I know a great place that delivers."

"That's fine. I'll have whatever you're having."

Stephanie called in the order and they sat down and talked. She listened to Captain Corbin talk about the different missions they had been on and how successful they were each time. Stephanie said very little as she listened to the man boast about their exploits.

He pumped her for information about where Christina and the nanny were, along with how her mother and sister were doing. She calmly answered each question without giving him any concrete information. She was not about to put her family in any more danger.

She was happy when the food got there so he would just shut up. He carried the food out to the kitchen and she took it out of the bags. The minute Stephanie opened her food her stomach immediately rejected the idea of Chinese food. She rushed from the room and threw up what little breakfast she had eaten. She wasn't sure if it was her nervousness or her pregnancy that caused her to be nauseated.

Washing her face, she went back into the kitchen. She closed the lid on her Chinese food and set it aside.

"You're pregnant," he guessed, watching her pale face.

"Yes," she admitted reluctantly, going to the refrigerator. She fixed herself a sandwich and a glass of milk and sat down at the table.

"Does Jack know about this?"

"No. I found out the day he was leaving." She took a bite of her sandwich. "I was too angry at him to tell him."

"You didn't want him to go rescue his friend."

"I didn't want him to go off and get himself killed," she defended. "Jack is married and has a daughter and a baby on the way. He gave me his word he was finished with that life before I married him and now he's suddenly drawn back into it."

"Stephanie, you obviously have no concept of what a man's honor is," he stated flatly. "Roper saved Jack's life. He disregarded a direct order and went back a month later searching for him. He found him and he single-handedly rescued him from what was going to be a slow painful death. You can't ask a man to walk away from that kind of debt. He owed Roper and he had to try and rescue him."

"At what cost?" she asked furiously.

"At any cost. The bond those two have can't be broken by you and me or even death. They would die for each other. Not many people have friends like that."

Moreover, because of that bond, they will both die because of you. "This smell is making me nauseated," said Stephanie, picking up her plate and glass. "I'll finish my sandwich in the den." She had to get out of the room before she said something that would give everything away.

She read the note on her computer.

Keep a cool head, Mrs. K. We will subdue Captain Corbin when we get the okay!

The phone rang and she snatched it up. She cleared the note off her computer quickly.

"Stephanie, it's Barbara. I've got your total for you. It comes to roughly a little over a million dollars. If you come in before two and sign all the papers, we could possibly cut a check to you by Friday."

"Thanks, Barbara, but I've changed my mind." She heard the click of the phone as Captain Corbin hung up the phone. She replaced the receiver and waited for him to come into the room. She didn't have to wait long for him.

"What the hell are you doing?" he asked furiously. "Are you trying to get your husband killed?"

"I'm not paying the ransom."

"What do you mean you're not paying it?" he asked, staring at her in disbelief. "You have to pay. Otherwise, they will kill Jack."

"And he will be out of my life once and for all." She smiled coldly, coming to her feet. "You trained your boys well, Captain Corbin. Jack lied his way into my life. He blackmailed me into marrying him to keep my daughter. He lied to me over and over. I've decided I don't want him back. The price is too high. If they kill him, things go back to the way they were. I get to keep everything, my daughter, my baby, and the money. 'They' did me a favor."

She watched Captain Corbin's expression go from one of disbelief to anger in the space of a heartbeat. She had blown his little scheme sky-high by refusing to pay.

"Stephanie, if you do this, how can you live with yourself? What will you tell your daughter? What will you tell this baby you're carrying about its father?"

"He was a noble man and he died on a mission of friendship. I'm sure I'll think of something appropriate to tell them both when the time comes. I'm sorry you made a wasted trip. Just take your money and go back where you came from."

With lightning speed, he reached over the desk and grabbed her by the arm. Pulling a gun from out of his sleeve, he pointed it at her temple. Stephanie trembled as the cold metal touched her. Fear gripped her as she realized the magnitude of the danger she was in. Dragging her out to the living room, he pushed her down to the sofa.

"I don't know what you're playing at, but you will pay that ransom."

"They haven't even called back. What if 'they' never call back?" Her eyes locked with his. At that moment he knew she knew the truth.

"Jack said you were pretty sharp on the uptake. I guess I should have given you more credit. You're a lot smarter than wife number one. She was easy to manipulate. Most women are. You are all shallow, vain creatures who only think about yourself. If Alexia had half a brain, she would have tried harder to get in touch with Jack. Her first mistake was leaving him a message about her pregnancy. You see, I'm the one who intercepted her message to him about being pregnant. I destroyed the message. I couldn't let her break up the squad. She wanted him to quit. No one quits the squad. It's a lifetime commitment. Hell, I even forged his name on divorce papers. He probably doesn't even know he's divorced from her. It was only pure luck that he found out he had a kid."

Stephanie paled at the information. She had misjudged her husband again. Jack didn't lie to her about his marriage. Cap had manipulated his life for years and he never even knew. "Seems like you thought of everything," she said sarcastically.

"I always do. I don't leave anything to chance." His hand touched her face and Stephanie slapped it away from her. "If you're real nice to me, I might let you live after you get me the money."

She felt a chill go down her spine. She knew he was lying. Take no prisoners and leave no witnesses were probably his motto. "And I'm supposed to believe anything a cold-blooded killer has to say."

"Why not? You married one. Jack and I are cut from the same cloth. He would have left you eventually anyway. Jack's too wild and adventurous to settle down and be content. I just rushed his leaving you along a bit. He's a man with a certain zest for life. Like me, he likes variety. Here," he said, taking a photo out of his pocket and tossing it on the couch to her. "I have something for you."

Her hand trembled as she picked up the picture. It was a picture of Jack and a woman kissing at the airport. Tears blurred her vision as she noticed the time stamp. "It must be nice to have a woman waiting for you in every country you visit. He has great taste in women. If by some miracle the two of you survive this, I wouldn't sleep with him without him being checked out by a doctor. I hear this one carries a nasty little bug."

She made no reply as she balled up the photo and hurled it at his smiling face.

"Tears for the man who 'blackmailed' you into marrying him, the man you don't want back. Is it love or your ego that's taking a beating here?"

"I hope you rot in hell," she hissed, wiping her eyes angrily.

"I'm sure I will. I'll be sure to have my men share the news with Jack of your pregnancy and your unfortunate death, right before they kill him. Better yet, maybe I'll take you to him. We can let the last thing he sees be me raping his pregnant wife."

Stephanie shivered in fear and revulsion. "You will never beat Jack. He's too smart for you." She saw the flicker of doubt in his eyes. "He will win in the end and you will have nothing. He will take everything from you and then he will kill you."

"I'm not afraid of a dead man."

"You should be." The doorbell chimed and they both turned to look at the door. When she didn't answer it, she heard knocking.

"Shall we go see who's come to join our little party?" Grabbing her arm, he helped her to her feet.

"Stef, it's Ashley. Are you home?" She turned the knob and came in. Captain Corbin slipped the gun back up his sleeve before she entered the house. He and Stephanie both were headed toward the door. "Stef, are you okay? I rang the bell, but I guess you didn't hear me."

"I'm sorry. I was giving Captain Corbin a tour of the house. You remember Captain Corbin, don't you? He's an associate of Jack and Roper's."

"Yes, I remember. Hello," said Ashley, catching his outstretched hand.

"Hello, Ashley. Come on in and join the party." He pulled her toward him, refusing to release her hand. "I insist," said Captain Corbin, taking out the gun and aiming it at her. "And then there were two sisters. Ladies, go have a seat. Now I have leverage, Mrs. K. Call your broker back and tell her to liquidate everything. Then you will go to her office and sign whatever you need to and be back here in record timing or I have a little fun here with little sister. Then maybe just for the hell of it, I'll look up your nosy mother."

"Stephanie, what's going on?" Ashley asked, staring from Stephanie to the man holding the gun.

"I'll explain it to you while your sister makes her phone call. Have a seat." He shoved her toward the sofa. He sat down next to Ashley and put his arm around her. "Let's get better acquainted. You are a knockout. Stephanie, you'd better hurry. I'm getting horny just looking at her." Ashley tried to move away from him, but her held her tightly against him. "I like feisty women. It makes for a wild ride. You smell good too." He nuzzled her neck. "I hear you're an intern. I never had one of those. I guess it's your lucky day, little sis."

"Okay," panicked Stephanie. "Just leave her alone. I'll get you the money. You can have whatever you want, just leave my sister alone."

"I knew you would see it my way."

Stephanie picked up the phone and dialed, while keeping an eye on him.

"Barbara, it's Stephanie Kaufman again. Go ahead and liquidate. I'll be in within the hour to sign the papers."

"Are you sure about this?"

"I'm positive. Can you wire the funds to my bank by Friday?"

"Sure. I don't think that will be a problem."

"Thanks, Barbara. I'll see you in a little while." Stephanie picked up her purse and headed for the door. "I want your word of honor, such as it is, that you will not harm my sister in any way."

"Ashley and I will just sit here and chat. I can tell her about the errors of her ways for taking up with a bad boy like Roper. Oh, and take your sister's car." He took the keys from Ashley and tossed them to Stephanie. "I think you're too smart to try anything. Sign the papers and come straight back. When you get back, I want to see copies of the transactions. Don't try anything stupid or your sister will pay the price for it and so will you."

"Fine. Just don't hurt her. Ashley, I'll be back as soon as I can." Stephanie was shaking and she closed the front door behind her. She fumbled with the keys as she opened her sister's Jeep. She dropped them and kneeled down to pick them up. When she rose, she let out a squeal as a man grabbed her from behind. With his hand over her mouth, he pulled her over to his car and pushed her inside.

"It's okay, Mrs. Kaufman."

She immediately recognized the voice.

"No, it's not okay," cried Stephanie in fear and frustration. "That lunatic is in there with my sister. If I'm not back soon, God only knows what that monster will do to her."

He turned up the volume on the monitor. "I can hear everything. The first chance my men get they will take him out. He won't get the chance to hurt her."

"No!" Ashley screamed fighting him. Stephanie went cold and she heard the sound of material ripping. "I will fight you with my last breath!"

"What a little wildcat you are. I like that," said Captain Corbin. "Did you fight Roper like this? I'd heard the two of you were going pretty hot and heavy for a while. Roper's just a boy. I'll show you what a man can do. I'll make you beg for release or mercy. Who knows which one will come first? Ouch! I guess I'll have to put this down and show you who's boss."

"Roper will kill you for this. If he doesn't, Jack will."

"My dear, Roper will be dead in about thirty minutes along with your brother-in-law."

"I don't believe you," cried Ashley

"Do something!" yelled Stephanie. "He's trying to rape my sister!"

"Norris, do you have a clear shot?"

"No."

"Then get one while he's distracted. We are running out of time."

"Wait a minute, he's laying the gun down on the coffee table."

While Taggart was distracted, Stephanie grabbed his gun from the seat, threw open the car door, and ran for the front door. He caught her outside the door and moved her away from it.

"If you go bursting in there, he will kill her. Give Norris a chance. I have an idea." He led her back to her sister's car. Reaching inside, he picked up the cell phone and gave it to her. "Call her."

Her hand was trembling as she dialed her home number. The man led her back to his car so they could listen to what was going on inside.

"I have to get that," cried Ashley.

"It's probably big sister trying to make sure I haven't raped little sister. I guess if you don't answer it, she'll just keep interrupting us. Tell her you're fine and then hang up. We have some unfinished business to take care of."

"Like hell we do, you sadistic bastard."

"He's letting her up," said Norris. "He's picked up the gun again. Benjamin, he's letting her go to answer the phone. Cover the girl. He's all mine. Now!"

Stephanie jumped out of the car when she heard her sister scream and then rapid gunfire followed by silence. She was shaking as she stood by the car door. She wanted to go to her sister, but she was afraid of what she would find. "We got him."

Stephanie let out a sigh of relief and ran to the house. Tears of joy came to her eyes when she saw her sister sitting on the couch with her head in her hands.

"Ashley!" They ran to each other and embraced as they both cried tears of relief. "Are you okay? He didn't hurt you, did he?" Stephanie asked, looking her sister up and down.

"No. I'm fine," cried Ashley, returning her hug. "Who are these people and what has Jack gotten us mixed up in?"

"This isn't Jack's fault. It's Roper's," defended Stephanie through her tears. "I think you'd better call in sick today."

They both sat on the sofa as Taggart, who was the mastermind of the operation today, introduced himself. He opened the two briefcases Corbin had had with him. Sure enough, they were both filled with money. One contained his passport and a Swiss bank account number along with some cash.

He asked them not to report the incident to the police. They would get rid of the body and the car and make sure nothing could be tied back to her. Stephanie was afraid not to go along with them.

Taggart took the briefcase with the Swiss bank account and cash. He left the other one with Stephanie and Ashley. Smiling, he told her it should cover the damages to the house along with Ashley's missed day at work.

When they were gone, Stephanie packed a bag and asked Ashley to drive her to their mother's town house. She needed to see her daughter.

Ashley was speechless when Stephanie gave her the briefcase full of money minus a couple of thousands for house repairs. They made a pact not to tell their mother or anyone else anything about what had happened today.

Ashley ended up inviting them to come home with her. She warned Bridget not to be alarmed at the condition of the house. She told her the police had foiled an attempted robbery.

They were sitting on the couch at Ashley's condo watching a movie when Stephanie had her first twinge of pain. Without a word, she got up and went to the bathroom. To her horror, she found she was bleeding.

"Ashley!" yelled Stephanie, leaning against the wall. The room started spinning and she doubled over in pain. "Call an ambulance." At her sister's horrified look, blackness closed in on her and she fainted.

Chapter 13

"Cap is inside the house with your wife," said Tom. "They are waiting for our signal to move in.

"Damn!" cursed Jack, pacing the room. That was not the news he wanted to hear. "And what about my daughter?"

"She's not there. Your wife must have sensed something was wrong. She sent the nanny and your daughter to her mother's house before Cap got there. Taggart made contact with your wife. She knows Cap is dangerous and she knows he's behind your supposed kidnapping. Taggart has some men inside the house. They are just waiting for a word from us to take him out."

"Glad to hear Taggart is on the job. I trust him. It's time to make a move. If Cap hurts my wife in any way, you make damn sure he leaves my home in a body bag. I'll meet you at the cabin where Roper is being held in one hour. If anything happens and those plans change, I will send word. I need to go back and take care of Cooper and Rodriguez. Something is going on there and I need to figure out what it is. Nina doesn't think Rodriguez is a willing participant in this. I will find out the truth one way or the other. I also need to make sure Nina is safely out of harm's way before this goes down."

"You realize you have to take her with you. She can't remain here after three Americans have been living at her place for weeks. It wouldn't be safe for her."

"I know. She's coming with me. Can you get some papers for her and the boy? Have Nina's birth papers show her as fifteen and list me as her father. Aidan is five. Put me as his father also. I don't know how I can explain her to my wife, but I won't leave them behind."

"Good. I hate to see innocent victims suffer because of something totally out of their control. I'll have all the necessary papers by the time you are ready to travel. Here's the sleeping powder. Make sure she puts all of it in their food. It should keep them out for a couple of hours."

Jack slipped the packet in his pants. "Thanks, Tom, for everything. I couldn't have come this far without you." The two men clasped hands.

He was almost at the cabin when he heard Nina's blood-curdling scream. He stopped the man outside from going in with him and blowing his cover. He followed the now muffled screams to the bedroom he shared with Nina.

Throwing open the door, he became enraged when he saw Cooper on top of the fighting girl as he tried unsuccessfully to remove her underwear. Jack grabbed him off her and threw him against the wall. He untied her wrists from the rope holding them to the bedpost. She was shaking like a leaf as she tried to cover her seminaked body with the torn clothing. Wrapping the sheet around her, she scooted off the bed.

"What the hell do you think you're doing?" Jack asked, whirling on his former friend. He was tempted to beat him senseless, but he stopped himself. Too much was riding on him keeping a cool head.

"Just having a little fun," said Cooper, getting to his

feet. "I bought these on the black market today." He held up two packages of condoms. "Why should you get to have all the fun?"

"You idiot." Jack hit his hand, sending the packages flying in the air. "I could hear her screaming from outside. Are you trying to draw attention to us for a little toss in bed? Believe me, she's not worth it. Go cool off. We make our move tonight."

"I just wanted to have a little fun," Cooper sulked as he slammed out of the room. "You've had her all this time! After tonight, she's mine!" This he yelled through the closed door.

Jack turned his attention back to Nina, who was sitting on the floor rocking back and forth. She was still shaking.

He walked over and squatted down next to her. When he touched her, she flinched away from him. "Are you okay?"

She held up her face so he could see the bruise coloring her cheek. "Does it look like I'm all right? I want to cut out his heart," she hissed. Her brave facade dropped and she started to cry. Jack sat down on the floor beside her and cradled her in his arms. "I can't do this anymore. I'm scared. When will this nightmare end?" she said.

"Shh. It's almost over. Tonight it will all be over," he promised. He framed her small face with his hands. "I need you to be strong just a little while longer. You have to be strong for Aidan. Your little brother is going to need you in America." His words calmed her rattled nerves. He caught her hand and placed the sleeping powder in it. "I need you to put this in their food. Can you do that?" She nodded and wiped at her tear-streaked face. "Good girl. Come on." He got to his feet and helped her up. "You get dressed and I will go keep Cooper and Rodriguez busy. I won't let anyone hurt you."

* * *

The plan worked like a charm. Less than fifteen minutes after they devoured their food, Cooper and Rodriguez passed out at the dining table. Jack knew all their secret places and confiscated all the weapons they had hidden on their person before tying them each to a chair. He put them at opposite ends of the table.

He turned to Nina. "I want you to go to your room and stay put." He knew what the men of her country thought of her and he wanted her out of their sight while he was gone.

"I want to go with you."

"No. It's too dangerous." He caught her arm and dragged her into the bedroom. "Listen to me! I don't have time to argue with you. You have to stay here. I can't be worried about your safety when I need to rescue Roper and your brother. Promise me you will stay in this room. When I go out that door, I want to hear the lock slide into place behind me or so help me I will put you over my knee and you won't sit down for a week. Do I make myself clear?"

"I am not a child," she said defiantly. "I don't want to stay here. It's not safe for me here. You know it as well as I do."

"Then stop acting like one and do as you are told. Stay here and lock the damn door behind me. I will come back as soon as I can." As he went out the door, he heard the lock click into place. *Good girl.* He knew she was afraid to stay, but he was more afraid to take her with him.

He opened the door and waved in three of the five men watching the cabin. "Keep an eye on those two. If they try anything before I get back, shoot them. There is someone in the back room. They are packing, and they are to remain in that room until I get back."

They nodded in understanding. One of the men positioned himself in front of Nina's bedroom door. Satisfied, Jack left the cabin.

* * *

Tom and five of his men were already at the site when he got there. Their plan was to move in and strike as quickly and silently as possible. Half an hour later, they were inside with very few casualties. Jack and Tom were firm believers in immobilizing the enemy, but no lives were taken unnecessarily.

They found Roper and the boy both handcuffed to beds in separate bedrooms. Roper was bruised, bloody, and in need of a bath and shave. The little boy was just dirty and frightened. A big grin split Roper's face when he saw Jack dangling the key to the handcuffs.

"Some people will do anything for attention," Jack teased, unlocking the cuffs. They embraced warmly.

"And some people sure took their damn time about getting here." Roper smiled. "What took you so long?" He rubbed his face. "I grew a full beard waiting for you guys."

"Young pup doesn't know what gratitude is," Tom laughed, moving forward and extending his hand to Roper.

"Damn good to see you, Tom. I hope you brought food and water."

"Yeah, we can smell you from across the room. You must be Aidan," said Jack, holding his hand out to the frightened little boy. "Your sister is worried sick about you."

His face lit up like a Christmas tree. "Where is my sister?" he asked in perfect English. "Is she safe?"

"Nina's fine. She's waiting for us at the cabin." He caught the boy's hand. "I'm Jack. Come on, let's get out of here."

"Please tell me those two SOBs who are responsible for this are still alive. I want my pound of flesh."

"They are tied up and waiting at the cabin," replied Jack, reading Roper's mind. He knew that wicked glint in Roper's eyes.

"Good." Roper smiled as he took the knife from Jack's waist. "You don't mind if I borrow this, do you? I intend to show Cooper the same courtesy he bestowed on me. He's all mine."

Jack knocked three times on the door. When the guards opened it, they all went inside. Cooper and Rodriguez were slowly coming around.

Aidan yelled out for his sister and the bedroom door banged against the wall as she came flying out of the bedroom. They embraced warmly as she smothered his dirty face in kisses.

Roper did a double take when he saw Nina for the first time. "I think I'm in love. I just found the girl I'm going to marry."

"Again," replied Jack. "If I'm not mistaken, you said that before you hightailed it out of Dallas and landed in a mess in Iran. "Todd Roper, this is Nina. Nina, Roper."

Nina smiled shyly at the handsome man. She appeared to be as smitten as Roper pretended to be.

Jack took Roper aside. "I draw the line at playing chaperone. Unless your intentions are honorable, don't even think about looking her way. Nina is innocent and I intend for her to stay that way and that means keeping her away from you."

"I already told you I'm going to marry her."

"You said the same thing about Ashley. Do you remember her? About this tall," said Jack, putting his hand to his chin. "Dark brown hair, white lab coat. Very pretty young woman. My sister-in-law."

"It's different this time. I have nothing to offer Ashley. She deserves better. It's different with Nina."

"That's garbage and you know it. You sound like Mildred Mason. You have yourself to offer. You are a coward."

"She's a doctor and I don't even have a job."

"Then get one and prove to her and to yourself that you

are worth the effort. You and I both know the reason you ended up in this mess is that you were running from your feelings for Ashley. You have to face your feelings sometime. I don't want to see Nina hurt because you don't know what it is you want. Be very careful with her. Nina and Aidan are flying back with us. She is under my protection. Until there is a ring on her finger, all her clothes stay on. Get it? Got it? Good. I don't intend to have this conversation with you again."

"Who hit her?" asked Roper, looking at the bruise on her cheek.

"Cooper." Before the word was out of his mouth, Roper had walked over and punched the other man, sending him and the chair sprawling to the floor.

"That's for Nina." Roper set up the chair and hit him again, sending him and the chair backward this time. "That one was for me."

"Who the hell is Nina?" asked Cooper, spitting blood.

"I am Nina, you filthy pig," she spat, moving forward. Surprise registered on his face.

"I am your downfall. Never assume because a woman is silent, she doesn't understand what you're saying. I was only too happy to fill Jack in on what you two had planned for him."

"You bitch!" Cooper screamed. "You ruined everything!"

Roper kicked him in the chest and he grunted in pain. "Watch your mouth in the presence of a lady!" Roper jerked his chair into an upright position.

"What are you going to do with us?" asked Rodriguez, nervously eyeing the knife in Roper's hand.

"Well, Rodriguez," said Jack, leaning down to face him, "what do you think we should do with you? We could always extend the same courtesy to you that you were going to extend to us. Tell me why you are here. This is not your style. How did Cap and Cooper talk you into killing us in cold blood? You better make it good and make it the truth or I will show you no mercy."

The younger man started shaking. He knew Jack meant every word he said. "I was only following orders! This was Cap's idea! I only went along with them because they threatened to kill my parents! They needed a third person for this mission and they made me be that person! I didn't want to do it! I couldn't let them hurt my family. They have a man watching my parents' house. Cooper calls them every day. If he doesn't call them soon, they will kill my family."

Jack stared at the young man and saw the truth in his eyes. He cut the ropes holding him, but warned him not to do anything stupid.

"Damn it, Rodriguez! I told Cap you would wuss out! I'm just sorry I won't be there to help Cap put a bullet in your mother's head."

"If you don't shut up, Roper will put a bullet in your head," Jack threatened. "Roper, get Cooper's phone. Can you still do impersonations?"

"You know it. I told Cap you would wuss out!" Roper sounded just like Cooper. "How's that?"

"Make the call. Tell the man"—Jack looked at Cooper—"mission successful."

Cooper sagged against the chair.

"You are so predictable. I already know it was Cap's idea. Greed knows no bounds. Cap will pay for his treachery with his life." Jack gagged Cooper until Roper made the call to Rodriguez's parents' house. Rodriguez spoke briefly to his parents, telling them he was safe and he was coming home.

When the call ended, Jack took the cloth out of Cooper's mouth. "So will your pretty little wife," laughed Cooper. "Did I forget to mention she refused to pay the ransom for your safe return? She doesn't want you back, Jack. Not that I blame her. What would a classy lady like that want with you? She told me to kill you. Now, she's a woman after my own heart. You won't want her either when Cap finishes with her. I wonder if he's raped her yet. Too bad I wasn't there to participate. I hear she's a hot little thing."

Without blinking an eye, Jack whipped out his gun and shot him in the kneecap. He felt no remorse as he watched the younger man screaming in pain. "Get him out of my sight."

Two of the guards cut him loose and jerked him to his feet. "What do you want us to do with this one?"

"I don't care what you do with him as long as he doesn't make it back to the United States." Jack took his passport out of his back pocket. Holding it in one hand, he set fire to one end of it. "I don't think you'll be needing this, Cooper. Say hello to your new home."

"Americans don't last long in prison here," chimed in Tom. "It's a shame this one tried to rob my place and I shot him to keep him from getting away with my money. Now I guess that means he's headed for prison."

"No!" cried Cooper, trying to pull away from the men holding him up. "You can't let them do this to me! It's inhuman! They'll torture me! They'll rape me! I'll be dead within a week!"

"Less than a week if you're lucky." Roper smiled, scratching his beard. "Two at most. You know what they say about karma. It bites."

"No!" screamed Cooper. They all watched him stumble, grab the gun from one of the guards, and fire repeatedly in Jack's direction.

Jack lunged for Aidan, knocking him to the floor and covering the small body with his. Nina screamed and Roper tackled her, shielding her from the hail of bullets.

All five men opened fire on the desperate man. When the smoke cleared Cooper lay dead. One of Tom's men was injured. They all got slowly to their feet surveying the damage around them.

"Now it's over. Let's go home," said Jack to the group. "Nina, if there is anything you want to take, get it now. We need to be on the first plane out of here."

Nina and Aidan had nothing they wanted to take with them. Jack told them he would buy them whatever they needed once they got to Dallas.

They were thrilled and terrified of moving to America. Jack got Nina a seat next to his, while Roper and Aidan sat several rows behind them. Rodriguez sat somewhere toward the back. He was ashamed to face his former squad members for his role in the incident.

Chapter 14

When the plane landed, they took a cab to the house. Jack was on pins and needles as he took in the bullet holes in the wall. Tom assured him Stephanie and Christina were not hurt.

Other than the walls, everything looked exactly the same. He checked the garage. His car and motorcycle were there and so was Stephanie's car, which puzzled him because she wasn't at the house.

He told everyone to make themselves at home while he went to shower and change. He felt refreshed after the shower, but he needed to see Stephanie. Sitting down on the bed, he dialed the hotel.

"Georgette, is Stephanie there?"

"Jack?"

"Yes, it's Jack. Where's Stephanie?"

"She called in sick for the rest of the week, or rather Ashley called in for her."

"Do you have Ashley's cell number?" He jotted down the number. Walking down the stairs, he dialed Ashley's cell phone.

"Hello," whispered his sister-in-law.

"Ashley, it's Jack. Where's Stephanie and why are you whispering?"

"Jack, I'm so glad you're back. Stef is in the hospital."

His hand tightened on the phone. "What happened? They told me everything was fine. Was she hurt?"

"No, she wasn't hurt, not physically anyway, but last night she had a miscarriage. She's devastated."

He closed his eyes as the pain of her words washed over him. He collapsed on the stairs, shaken. "I'll be there as soon as I can." He disconnected the call got to his feet and continued down the staircase. He laid the phone down on the hall table. Stephanie was pregnant when he left. *That's why she was so adamant about me staying here. That's why she was afraid of losing me. She lost our baby.* "Guys, I have to go out for a while. Here's money for takeout or pizza if you get hungry." He dropped fifty dollars on the table. The front door opened and Bridget came in followed by Christina.

"Daddy!" screamed Christina excitedly, running to him. He swung her in the air and hugged her. She covered his face with kisses. "You were gone a long time. I missed you! Don't leave again. Mommy was so sad. She missed you too."

Her words cut him deeply. "I know, baby. I missed her too. I missed you." He held her close to his heart. "Hi, Bridget."

"Welcome home, Mr. K."

"Thanks. Christina, Bridget, there are some people I want you to meet. You both may remember Roper from the wedding. This is Nina and her brother, Aidan. They are going to be staying with us for a while. Nina, Aidan this is my daughter, Christina, and her nanny, Bridget." They all exchanged hellos. "Honey, I hate to skip out on you so soon after getting home, but I need to go see Mommy."

"She's in the hospital."

"I know, sweetie, but she'll be home soon. I'll be back later, okay?"

"Can I come with you? I want to see Mommy too."

"Tomorrow," said Jack, kissing her forehead. "I'll be back in time to say good night. Be a good girl for Bridget, okay?"

She nodded, hugging her father.

Jack's hand was shaking as he pushed the door open to Stephanie's room. Ashley came forward and hugged him. He returned his sister-in-law's embrace.

"Thank God you're back."

"How is she?"

"Mentally, I think she's going to be okay. Physically, she is exhausted and stressed out. Her diagnostics are way too high. I think having you home safe and sound will correct the problem. She's been worried sick about you and she hasn't been taking care of herself."

"Did she tell you about what happened yesterday?"

"She didn't have to. I was there."

He stared at his sister-in-law blankly.

"I more or less stumbled on the scene. I was taken prisoner, almost raped, and ended up a rich young woman for my trouble."

"Tell me the story later," said Jack, walking around her. Leaning over Stephanie's pale face, he brushed her lips with his in a gentle caress. He sat down in the chair Ashley had vacated. Picking up his wife's cold hand, he brought it to his lips.

"The doctor gave her something to make her sleep. Her mind and body need rest so she can recuperate. He's keeping her here one more day to try and lower her diagnostics. When she gets home, she's going to need a lot of TLC and rest."

"I'll see that she gets it."

"You'd better. Did you find Roper?" she asked worriedly.

"Yes, and he's fine. He's at the house along with two other houseguests. Nina saved Roper and me from the trap Cooper and Cap had set. Nina and her little brother, Aidan, will be staying with us indefinitely. I couldn't leave them behind when she asked me to bring them to America. They were both victims in all this as well."

"Is there anything I can do to help?"

"I'm glad you asked because there is something you can do. Nina and Aidan brought nothing with them. Could you take them shopping for me? Buy whatever they need, and send me the bill."

"Nonesense. My newfound wealth came from the spoils of Captain Corbin. It only makes sense that part of that money should go to Nina for a new start. I'll use some of it to take them shopping. The rest I will give to you to oversee for her. Please tell me they speak English."

"Perfectly. Go easy on Roper, will you? I know he left without seeing or talking to you, but he does care, Ash. He's just running scared. Believe me, I know what it's like. Get Roper whatever he needs also. I'm not sure what his plans are yet."

"Who knows with him? I can't make you any promises where he is concerned. Right now, I want to punch his lights out, but I'll try to resist the urge. I'll go pick them up. Tell Stef I'll see her tomorrow. Are you going back home tonight?"

"Yes. I told Christina I'd tuck her in."

"Good. She missed her dad."

"I missed her too. I missed both my girls." His eyes strayed to the hospital bed where Stephanie lay sleeping.

"I'll see you later," said Ashley, leaving the room. "Mom should be here soon. She flew in this afternoon."

Thanks for the warning.

Jack laid his hand on her stomach, watching Stephanie sleep. He moved his chair close to the head of her bed. He folded his arms together and laid his head on them, resting on the bed. Exhaustion overtook him and he too drifted off to sleep facing her.

The thick fog around Stephanie lifted slowly. Her eyelids fluttered open. Yesterday's events came rushing back to haunt her and fresh tears spilled down her pale cheeks.

Last night she had lost her baby, Jack's baby. Her doctor had informed her not to try again for at least another six months. Her body needed time to heal.

Turning her head to the right, she gasped. She blinked several times to make sure she was not hallucinating. Her hand rose and touched the sleeping face so close to her own. Jack roused quickly at the soft caress. Their eyes met and held for several moments, before he got up from the chair. Sitting down on the bed next to her, he opened his arms to her. Stephanie didn't even hesitate as she launched herself into his arms.

"Oh, Jack, I'm so glad you're back," she cried, clinging him. She pulled back slightly. "Are you okay? I was so worried about you."

"I'm fine," said Jack, covering her face with kisses. "I was worried about you too. Honey, I'm so sorry about the baby, about everything." He felt her freeze up in his arms and pull away. "Stephanie." He raised her tearstained face to his. "Why didn't you tell me you were pregnant?"

"Would it have made a difference?" she asked sadly. "Would you have stayed had you known?" She watched the warring emotions on his handsome face.

When his eyes closed, she had her answer. "No," he said, softly brushing the tears from her cheek with the back of his hand. She shifted away from his touch.

"Do you have any idea the hell I've been through since you've been gone?" she asked angrily. "I made myself sick worrying that Christina would grow up without her father. You could have been killed. I could have been killed. Christina was put in danger. Ashley was almost raped by that lunatic."

"I know and I'm sorry I brought him into our lives." Jack was finding it harder and harder to keep his composure. His own tears threatened to fall and he blinked then back. He tried to catch her hand, and she pulled away from him. "Honey, I love you and I'm so sorry."

"You should be. You should never have left me. We had it all and you threw it away. Or at least I thought we did, but that was a lie also. After you left, I received a packet of papers from Alexia's attorney. Among those papers were your marriage license and your divorce decree."

He frowned at her. "Alexia and I were never divorced."

"Yes, you were. Captain Corbin intercepted the package and forged your name on the papers. Two months before Christina was born he signed the divorce papers Alexia sent you. He also told me he's the reason you didn't know Alexia was pregnant. He destroyed the message she left for you. He's the reason you didn't know about your daughter."

Jack got slowly to his feet.

"He has been manipulating your life for years, Jack, and you didn't even know it. There's more," she said softly.

"This is unbelievable. I never knew any of this. I can't imagine what you must have thought when you got those papers."

Her chin rose slightly. "I believed you had lied to me again. I believed you had tricked me. I believed the worst, Jack. I thought it was all about the money. When I got the call from the kidnappers regarding you, I refused to pay. I hung up. I thought you were behind it," she confessed.

He turned back around to face her. His look was incredulous. It took several moments for him to speak. "You thought I planned this?" he asked quietly.

She could see the pain in his eyes as he waited for her answer.

"You thought I staged my own kidnapping to get money from you? You believed I walked out on you and Christina and wanted money? Stephanie, you were held at gunpoint. How could you think I had something to do with that?" He laughed without humor. "Cooper told me you refused to pay the ransom and I thought he was lying to torment me. I didn't believe him. I knew you would never choose money over me. I knew you loved me. Too bad you didn't have the same confidence in me."

"What was I supposed to think?" she defended, wiping furiously at her tears. "You have lied to me more times than you have told the truth. When I got those divorce papers, I thought it was just one more lie you had told me. You blackmailed me into marrying you. If I had known about the divorce, I wouldn't have married you."

He turned his back and moved away from the bed. He blinked away the tears that threatened to fall. He didn't know what to say or to think. The real nightmare was staring him in the face. After everything they had gone through, it came down to this.

"How could you think something like that? Have I ever asked you for one penny? Have I interfered in your handling of the finances? I haven't touched a penny of the Luciano fortune, yet you believed that's all I wanted. I don't believe this," Jack said, shaking his head sadly. "So you believed everything we shared was a lie. You believed I married you and then left you for money. I suddenly got tired of playing happy family and split. You believed I could walk away from you and from our daughter that easily. Of course you could, you believed I walked away from my pregnant wife. I am not your father! I thought you knew me better than that. I guess you really don't know me at all and I sure as hell don't know who you are. So what or who changed your mind about me?"

"One of the men you sent to watch over me told me what was going on right before Captain Corbin got to the house. They advised me to play along with him for a while and I did, but when I told him I wasn't going to pay the ransom, the game was over. He pulled a gun on me. He told me if I didn't get the money, he would kill you and then rape my mother and sister. Ashley came by and he held her at gunpoint. He would have raped her if they hadn't shot him."

"So you could trust a total stranger's word, but you couldn't trust mine," he fired back angrily.

"You have never given me any reason to trust you," she retorted. "You have been lying to me since the day you manipulated your way into my life. You blackmailed me into marrying you and then you walked out when things were going good."

"I didn't walk out. You know why I left. I told you I would be back."

"You had no way of knowing that for sure. If Captain Corbin had his way you would be dead and so would I and where would that leave our daughter?"

"And I suppose me telling you I loved you was just another of those lies? Did you think it was just a line I used on all the women I left behind before a mission?"

"You tell me. Was it a meaningless gesture?"

"I tell you I love you and you call it a meaningless gesture." He shook his head in disbelief. "Well, this just keeps getting better and better. Tell me how you really feel, Stephanie."

"Did you use it on the woman you were kissing at the airport?" she asked, angrily wiping at her tears.

He stared at her in confusion. "What woman? Since nothing you've said so far makes any sense to me, I suppose this shouldn't either. I don't have any idea what you're talking about. I'm clueless."

"The woman who greeted you at the airport upon your arrival in Iran. Captain Corbin was quite delighted to show me the photo."

Jack threw his hands in the air in defeat.

"You can't deny it, Jack. I saw the picture. You were kissing her." She leaned over and took her purse out of the drawer. Taking the crumpled photo out, she reached it to him.

Jack refused to take it as the realization of what happened hit him. Someone had taken a picture of Nina kissing him at the airport and sent it to Cap. He in turn gave it to Stephanie. She believed exactly what they wanted her to believe.

"Then take a closer look. I wasn't kissing her. She was kissing me. It was part of the plan. Nina didn't want to kiss me any more than I wanted her to. She was a victim in all this."

"You seem to leave victims wherever you go, first Alexia, then me, and now this Nina woman. How many others are there? Do you have a woman waiting in every country you visit? Did you leave her high and dry like you did the rest of us when you left her?"

"No, Stephanie, I brought her home with me."

Now it was her turn to be shocked. She stared at him in horror. "You brought your lover back with you!" she screeched. "You are unbelievable! I was here worrying myself to death about your safety and you were off having a fling. Where did you install her, the hotel?"

"No, she's at our house. You'll get to meet her tomorrow when I take you home. Doesn't that sound cozy? Ever been in a threesome?"

"You bastard!"

"Is that the best you can do? I'd think with all the

damning evidence against me you could do a little better than that for a man who staged his own kidnapping to steal money from his wife and daughter. I brought home a pretty young thing to play with so when I get tired of my wife I won't have to look far."

"How dare you?" she all but screamed at him. "You have your tramp at my home, in front of our daughter! Have you no shame, no conscience? You are the most insulting, disgusting, despicable human being I have ever had the misfortune to meet! This whole thing is your fault! You should have been here to protect me, to protect our unborn child! Maybe losing this baby was a blessing because the thought now of having your child makes me physically ill! The thought of you touching me makes me sick to my stomach. I want you out of my house and out of my life once and for all!"

Her words cut him to the core and infuriated him at the same time. "You call losing our baby a blessing! You cold-hearted witch! Now I know how you really feel about me! I am through trying to defend myself to you! Why bother? You don't believe anything I say! Talking to you is like talking to a damn brick wall!"

The door opened and her mother sailed into the room. She stared from one to the other. "What in the world is going on in here? I can hear you both all the way down the hall."

"Nothing a divorce lawyer for me and a good shrink for your daughter won't cure," hissed Jack. "Congratulations, Mildred. Your daughter has turned into you. You did a hell of a job," he said angrily, leaving the room. He leaned against the wall outside the room and took several deep, calming breaths. Closing his eyes, he knew their situation was hopeless. Their marriage was over. He refused to live his life under a microscope.

* * *

When the door closed behind him, Stephanie burst into tears. Her mother sat down on her bed and took her daughter into her arms. She held Stephanie wile she cried her heart out.

Mildred waited until the tears ceased before putting her daughter at arm's length. "Stephanie, what just happened? When did Jack get back?" Her mother spied the crinkled photo and took it out of her hand. "What is this? Who is this woman and why is she kissing Jack?"

"Her name is Nina and she's his mistress. He brought her home with him. He brought her to my home," sniffed Stephanie. "I hate him."

"No, you don't," scolded her mother. "You love him." Her mother held out the photo to her. "Take a good look at the picture. Call me naïve, but it doesn't appear as if either one of them is enjoying the kiss."

Stephanie took the picture and really looked at it. Her hand started to tremble. The woman wasn't more than a girl. It almost looked like she had tears in her eyes. Jack appeared to be setting her away from him. He seemed surprised by her kiss.

Stephanie ripped the photograph in two and dropped it in the wastebasket. She closed her eyes and lay back on the bed. It was too late for them. She had said too many horrible things to Jack to think he would stay with her. She had believed the worst about him again and again.

I pushed him away. Why can't I trust him?

"Stephanie, listen to me. Jack is not your father. Because your father walked out on me does not mean Jack will walk out on you and Christina. You can't compare all men to your father. Your father left because of me, not because of you and Ashley. It was me he didn't love, not you. It's my fault that you feel this way. You have heard me repeat over and over that men can't be trusted. Men are scum and they will eventually leave you for someone younger and prettier. I was wrong to tell you girls about the numerous affairs your father had while we were together. What I didn't tell you was my part in it. I had an affair first. Larry never forgave me and he never got over it. He didn't ruin our marriage. I did. I have wronged you and Ashley in so many ways. I've made you gun-shy about relationships and marriage. I was wrong, honey. All men are not the same. They are not all like your father. Jack loves you and he loves Christina. Stop pushing him away. Stop looking for reasons and excuses not to trust him. He's human and so are you. Human beings make mistakes all the time. We learn from them and we move on. Jack Kaufman is the one, Stef. He is your soul mate. Don't let him get away. Open your eyes to what you are doing to him. He loves you and you are using that love to hurt him, to punish him for maybe what your father did to me, to us. Do you want to be alone and bitter like I was?"

She frowned as she stared at her mother.

"That's right, honey, was. I've met someone and I am willing to open my heart again. He's a good man and he cares about me. He's made me see things in myself I never saw before. Don is a wonderful man and I'm not going to blow it this time. Don't you blow it, Stephanie. Tell Jack you love him before it's too late. You have a love and a marriage worth fighting for."

"It's already too late, Mom. You didn't hear the things I said to him. I told him that losing our baby was a blessing."

"Stephanie," gasped Mildred, "you don't mean that."

"Of course I don't mean that. I wanted our baby. I wanted to hurt him the way he hurt me. He should have been here, Mom. He should have been here and maybe this wouldn't have happened. Maybe our baby would still be alive."

"Oh, honey, this is not his fault. This isn't anyone's

fault. Things happen for a reason. It's not our place to question why."

Jack drove around for a while to calm down before he went home. Home. The word rang hollow and empty to him now. He didn't have a home. Stephanie's house was not his home.

He had a lot of thinking to do. He had no idea what to do next. His marriage was in shambles and he had just brought home two innocent people to throw into the middle of the mess he had created.

Christina was thrilled to have him home and he was not about to leave again. He had mentioned a divorce lawyer in anger, but he could not follow through with talking to one. He and Stephanie needed time to work through their problems. After everything that was said tonight he wasn't sure a reconciliation was possible. But he wasn't ready to give up just yet.

When he entered the house, Christina came running down the stairs to meet him. He picked her up and held her close.

"Can you read me a story? Please, oh, please," she begged. "You make all the stories so exciting when you read them."

Jack laughed. He placed a kiss on her forehead as he carried her up the stairs. "You bet I can. Tell Bridget good night."

"Good night, Bridget. Daddy's tucking me in and reading me a story."

"Good night, sweetie."

When he dropped her on the bed, she erupted into a fit of giggles. Kicking off his shoes, he stretched out on the bed. There wasn't much room left on the full-sized bed for her. Hopping over him, Christina went to the shelf and picked a book. She climbed back into bed and snuggled up in her father's arms.

Jack had only read a few chapters before she drifted off to sleep. Her peaceful breathing lulled him to sleep. He slept that way for a couple of hours before he woke up. Planting a kiss on her forehead, he covered her with the comforter and silently left the room.

He went downstairs in search of food. He heated a few slices of leftover pizza, grabbed a soda out of the fridge, and headed for the den. He sat down and watched the rest of the movie with Bridget.

An hour or so later, the gang returned. He and Bridget both went out to the hallway to greet them. Ashley and Nina were all smiles, but the guys looked exhausted.

"Now I remember why I don't go shopping with women," Roper complained, glaring at Ashley.

"Because you hate shopping or because you can't keep a woman?" Ashley retorted smugly.

His eyes narrowed on her and he ignored her remark. "Ashley took us in almost every damn store in the mall. Some I think were just to spite me."

"You could have tried your famous disappearing act at the mall," she snapped. "It wouldn't have surprised me this time."

Nina and Aidan watched the exchange with interest.

"That's enough, you two. I hope this is not how Aidan and Nina had to spend the day listening to the two of you bicker like children."

"Most of it," piped Nina, smiling. "Isn't love grand?"

Roper rolled his eyes at her. "Where should we put these?" he asked, ignoring her comment.

"I'll be happy to tell you where you can put them," said Ashley, walking past him. "You can shove them."

"Ashley, that's enough," interrupted Jack. "Follow me."

He led them down the hallway to the second master bedroom suite. The room was almost as big as the master and had its own private bathroom and shower/tub combination. The large walk-in closet was empty except for the hangers his mother-in-law had left when she moved out. "Nina, for now you and Aidan will have to share this room."

"It's beautiful," she said, looking around in amazement. "It's almost bigger than my whole house." She touched the soft floral-print comforter.

"Okay, you can check out the new digs later," laughed Ashley. "Everybody back out to the Jeep. We have more bags to unload. Bridget, can you run bathwater for Aidan? He looks about ready to collapse."

After unloading all the bags, Ashley helped Nina put their things away while Aidan took a bath. Roper followed Jack back downstairs to the den.

Jack walked over to the bar and fixed himself a stiff drink. He poured one for Roper and handed it to him.

"Ashley told us Stephanie had a miscarriage. Man, I'm sorry. How's Stephanie holding up?"

"Just peachy," he replied, downing his drink. He poured another rum and Coke. "I bet you never thought you would hear those words coming out of my mouth. She blames me for everything. I'm sure if the sun didn't rise or set tomorrow, she'd blame that on me too. Stephanie doesn't want me in her life. She made that perfectly clear tonight. Cooper was telling the truth when he said Stephanie refused to pay the ransom. Are you ready for this one? She thought I staged my own kidnapping to get money from her. She thought I was behind this whole thing. She has quite the imagination, my wife."

"I don't know what to say. That must have hurt like hell. I know how worried you were about her and Christina. So what are you going to do now? Where does this leave your marriage?"

"I don't know. I have made so many mistakes with her and I have lied to her so many times, she doesn't believe anything I say. It's my fault. I never really gave her a reason to trust me. Did you know I blackmailed her into marrying me?" He laughed harshly. "I told her if she didn't marry me, I'd take everything from her. She didn't care about the money or the hotels. She only wanted Christina. I used my own daughter as leverage to make her marry me." He downed his drink and poured another. "I knew the moment I walked into her office she was the one. You should have seen her face when I told her about my past. I thought she would faint." They both sat down on the sofa. "She was shocked. She was outraged and she was terrified of me. She basically threw me out of her office. I lifted her planner and made copies of it. I turned up almost everywhere she went. It was all so well planned. I lied to her repeatedly. I manipulated every situation to my benefit. Our business trip to Jamaica was the icing on the cake. I knew if I got her away from all the distractions here, I could seduce her. It worked like a charm. When I started all this, it was about the money. I had no intention of taking Christina away from her. I wanted her to think I would so she would be willing to give me whatever I wanted."

"And now?" prompted Roper.

"And now I don't give a damn about the money or the hotels. I just want Stephanie. I love her. My life is meaningless with Stef and Christina. They mean everything to me. Without them, I'm nothing. Despite my past, and despite myself, they loved me. I want my family back. I want back what I thought we had when I left, but I don't even know if that's possible."

"Anything is possible if you want it bad enough," said Ashley, wiping away her tears. They turned to see her leaning against the door watching them.

Jack wasn't sure if she was referring to him and Stephanie

or her and Roper. "How long have you been standing there?" he asked, leaning back on the sofa.

"Long enough to know how much you love my sister. Long enough to know you aren't perfect, and when you love, there are no holds barred. You play for keeps, but I knew that the moment I met you."

"And look how well that turned out. I'm my own worst enemy. I suppose you hate me too and blame me for everything."

Ashley came farther into the room. "No, Jack. I don't hate you. I'm not about to cast the first stone. True, you created the mess in your marriage, but it's not your fault you have an idiot for a friend."

"I'm not an idiot," snapped Roper. "I made a mistake, Ash. I screwed up. I'm admitting it."

"Okay, a coward for a friend," she amended. "You were running from me and ended up almost getting yourself, Jack, Stephanie, and me killed. That's not exactly something we are all going to forget overnight, Roper. Your actions caused a snowball effect. As happy as I am that you are safe, I want to kill you myself. Jack never should have been put in the position of having to choose you or his family. This is on you. Grow up." She turned back to Jack. "I don't blame you for any of this. I don't care about your reasons for coming here. I know all about your past and I couldn't care less what you did before you came here. What concerns me is the future. I love my sister and my niece, and their happiness means the world to me. You love Stephanie and she loves you. Give her some time to mourn the loss of your baby, but don't give up on her. Don't give up on your marriage. After she deals with the pain of losing the baby, I think she will understand why you did what you did. You're an honorable man, Jack Kaufman. I'm proud to have you for a brother-in-law. With that,

I will say good night. Nina and Aidan are turning in for the night."

"I'll walk you out," said Roper, coming to his feet. "I think we should talk."

Ashley kept walking as if she never heard him.

"Ashley, please."

Jack watched the two of them leave the room. He knew Roper was crazy about Ashley, but he didn't think he had anything to offer her so he had walked away from her. Ashley was furious with him and she had a stubborn streak like her sister. She would put him through the ringer before forgiving him, if she forgave him at all.

Chapter 15

The next morning Jack called the hospital to find out what time Stephanie was being released. He packed her a bag and took Christina with him to pick her up. After a tearful reunion, Stephanie went into the bathroom to get dressed. She could hear voices in the other room, but she couldn't tell who it was or what they were saying.

As she came out of the bathroom, she froze when she saw her doctor. One look at Jack's face told her everything she needed to know. Dr. Watson must have told him about her condition. Jack's face was a mask of cold fury and he wouldn't even look at her.

"Stephanie, we were just talking about you. Your husband and I were just discussing the fact that you should wait before getting pregnant again. The miscarriage did serious damage to the uterine walls. He's assured me the two of you will take precautions for at least six or seven months. Make an appointment with my office for two weeks from today. I'd like to examine you before I release you to resume marital relations."

"I'll call your office as soon as I get home," she said softly, not able to tear her gaze from her husband's.

The ride home was long and uncomfortable. Jack hadn't

spoken a single word to her. Christina chatted the whole way saying how wonderful it would be having both Mommy and Daddy home again. Stephanie and Jack made no comment.

When they got home, the place was quiet. No one was home, but the house smelled of food. Someone had prepared lunch. She figured that had been Jack's idea to make sure they were all gone when she got there.

Jack picked up the note by the phone. Bridget had take Nina and Aidan sightseeing. They would be back in time to prepare dinner.

"Why don't you go on up and lie down?" said the cold, detached voice. "I'll bring you some lunch if you're hungry."

"I'm not hungry. Where is everyone?" They both knew the everyone she was referring to was Nina.

"Can I go up with Mommy?" Christina asked, turning to her father. "I'll be quiet while she rests."

"Sure you can, honey," answered Stephanie, catching Christina's hand and leading her up the stairs.

Jack ate lunch alone in the kitchen. He changed into shorts and a T-shirt. Roper dropped by and they went outside to shoot some hoops. Nina and Aidan watched after they got back, but then lost interest and went inside.

When Jack and Roper came in, Bridget was on the phone. She found them in the den. Bridget dropped a bombshell on them. Her father had had a heart attack and she needed to leave.

Bridget had two weeks of vacation coming and Jack paid for her plane ticket to go home to Maine on the next available flight. Nina gladly piped in that she could take care of Christina while Bridget was gone.

Jack knew Stephanie would hit the roof when she found

out, but he agreed to let Nina help. He knew she wanted to feel useful and Stephanie needed bed rest.

He didn't know how he was going to break the news to Stephanie about Bridget. She hated Nina on principle and had never even met her. He knew he would have to tell her, but he wasn't going to do it her first night home.

Instead, he took Nina aside to discuss her future. Nina hinted she wanted to go to college, which pleased him immensely. Jack wanted to see her get a college degree. He told her he would take her to the college on Monday to pick up some brochures. He introduced her to the wonderful wide world of the Internet. He taught her how to look up people and search for anything with the click of a button.

He and Roper talked extensively about starting their own security consulting company. Roper was a computer genius and could hack his way into almost any company's system. They decided to go for it and meet with a lawyer to draw up the papers for a partnership. He figured Stephanie would be glad to get him out of her hotel business.

He and Roper would finish up all the work for the hotel and then freelance. For the time being, they could work out of Jack's old condo and Roper would live there.

Roper was flying home to Houston on Wednesday, so he could drive his car back to Dallas. He asked Ashley to go with him, but she declined. She wasn't ready just yet to take that step.

To Stephanie and Mildred's horror, they were madly in love. Jack and Nina were the only two who thought it was great. He thought Ashley was just what Roper needed to settle him down.

Stephanie was working a crossword puzzle while lying in bed when the door opened and Christina ran in followed by a little boy. He held back shyly as Christina hopped up on the bed.

"Come on, Aidan," she said, waving him over. "This is my Mom."

Stephanie smiled at the shy little boy. He was a handsome little guy not much taller than Christina, with the same straight black hair and soft brown complexion.

"It's okay, Aidan." Stephanie smiled, patting the bed beside Christina. He walked over and sat down. Stephanie held out her hand to him. "Hi, I'm Miss Stephanie. It's nice to finally meet you."

He hesitantly took her outstretched hand.

"Christina's told me a lot about you. So what are you two up to?"

"Just playing," he said softly. "Why do you never have dinner with us? Can you get out of bed? Are you still sick?"

"A little, but I'm getting better. In a few days I will be as good as new. I will even come down and have dinner with you."

"That's good. Mr. K was worried about you."

Stephanie felt tightness in her chest at his words. Jack. She had barely seen him since she came home from the hospital. He had come in a few nights ago to tell her Bridget had a family emergency and was gone. He also told her Nina was taking care of the kids and the house while Bridget was away. Stephanie hit the roof and adamantly vetoed the idea. Jack overruled her objection, emphatically telling her when she was able to get out of bed and take care of the house and kids, Nina would step aside.

"Mom, can we play in here for a while?" asked Christina, interrupting her thoughts. "Please. Can we stay?"

"Sure, sweetheart." Stephanie blinked back her tears. "I'll even put cartoons on for you guys."

"Yeah!" they chorused. They all leaned back against the

pillows as Stephanie turned the television to the cartoon network. A few minutes into the show, there was a soft knock on the door.

"Come in." Stephanie had not prepared herself for a face-to-face meeting with her husband's mistress so soon. She was thrown for a loop when the beautiful young girl stepped into the room. She was dressed in a pair of jeans and a T-shirt. Her hair was pulled back from her face in a ponytail and she looked all of maybe fifteen. She was a tiny little thing, about five-two, and probably didn't weigh more than a hundred pounds soaking wet.

"I'm sorry they disturbed your rest." She smiled sweetly. "Kids, back downstairs so Miss Stephanie can rest."

"It's okay," said Stephanie, forcing a smile. She didn't want the kids to sense anything was wrong. "When I get tired, I'll send them downstairs."

"I'm sorry I didn't introduce myself. I'm Nina Armatage and that handsome young man is my brother, Aidan."

"Stephanie Kaufman."

"If you need anything, Mrs. Kaufman, send one of the kids down and I'll be happy to get it for you." Turning, she left the room.

Stephanie stared after the young girl, puzzled. She certainly didn't look like a mistress. She looked more like an innocent child. Surely, she was older than she looked.

Could I have misjudged Jack again? I never gave him the chance to explain Nina's presence. I just assumed they were lovers. Jack neither denied nor confirmed my suspicions.

Jack and Roper were coming in the front door when Nina came down the stairs. They knew immediately something was wrong when she sat down at the bottom of the stairs with her head in her lap.

"What's wrong?" Roper asked, kneeling down in front of her.

"She hates me."

"Who hates you?" Jack asked, already knowing the answer to his question. The only she who it could have been was upstairs barred in her room.

"Your wife." Nina looked up at him with troubled eyes. "Why does she dislike me? She doesn't even know me."

"She thinks you're my mistress." He shrugged and started to walk away.

"But that's ridiculous. You're old enough to be my fa . . ." He turned back to Nina and his brows shot up. "Older brother," she amended. "Why would she think something like that? You did tell her she's wrong, didn't you?"

"Stephanie doesn't believe a word I have to say on any subject. Why waste my breath?"

"You are kidding, right? I'm going upstairs to tell her the truth," said Nina, headed back up the stairs.

"You are more than welcome to try, but I don't know that she will believe you any more than she will believe me. On second thought, go for it. She probably will believe you."

Stephanie was still mulling over her conversation with Nina when a few minutes later, she heard another soft rap on the door. The door opened and Nina barged in.

"Kids, go downstairs. Jack and Roper said something about pizza and ice cream for dinner," she lied to get them out of the room.

"Ice cream!" they chorused, scampering from the room.

"We need to talk about Jack," said Nina, sitting down on the bed. Stephanie stared at her, not responding. "I'm not sure what he told you about us, but you need to hear the truth."

Stephanie threw back the covers and got up from the bed. "I don't need to hear the sordid details of your affair with my husband. You are more than welcome to him, but I will ask that you refrain from continuing the affair at least while you are in my house."

"So it is true. You think I am having an affair with Jack." Nina laughed. "Why on earth would you think something like that about your husband? He loves you so much. You are all he talked about in Iran. He couldn't wait to get home to you and Christina."

Stephanie turned around to face her, shocked by her words. Their eyes locked and Stephanie looked for some sign of deceit or trickery in her bold stare, but found none.

"He talked to you about me?" she asked tightly. *Why would a man talk to his mistress about his wife?*

"Yes. He adores you. I know Jack is a man of few words, but has he bothered to tell you my role in this whole mess? Did you even ask him about me before you convicted him?" Stephanie shook her head as tears formed in her eyes. "Have a seat," said Nina, patting the mattress. "This is going to take a while."

Nina related her version of the story from beginning to end. She left out no details, including why Jack had her teeth marks on his shoulder. Stephanie listened to the girl's story and felt physically ill when she had finished.

She now knew why he brought Nina and Aidan with him and she understood. She was even more shocked when Nina told her Ashley gave her part of the money Captain Corbin left behind and had taken them shopping a few days ago. Stephanie also picked up on the way the girl blushed when she mentioned Roper. Nina had a huge crush on him.

When Nina finally left, Stephanie was convinced there was nothing going on between her husband and the young girl. Stephanie apologized to her for jumping to the wrong conclusion and Nina retorted she was not the one she owed the apology to.

They were all surprised when Stephanie came downstairs for dinner. Nina was a wonderful cook and dinner was delicious. Stephanie couldn't help but smile as she watched Nina and Roper flirt with each other. Jack watched Stephanie as she watched the entertaining duo.

After dinner, Roper helped Nina clean up the kitchen. Stephanie asked Jack to walk her back up to their bedroom.

When the door closed behind them, he watched her with a hooded expression. He knew Nina had convinced Stephanie there was nothing going on between them, but he was furious that she had to be convinced. He was hurt and angry that she couldn't bring herself to trust him. He wasn't sure she ever would.

Stephanie nervously sat down on the bed and leaned back against the headboard. She knew it was up to her to try and clear the air if it was even possible at this point.

"I should have told you everything the doctor told me."

"Yes, you should have."

"When I had the car accident there was some damage to my uterus. The doctors were not even sure I could get pregnant. They told me right before you and Mom came in. It was over between us, so there was no point in telling you."

"Yours was a high-risk pregnancy, Stephanie. I had a right to know. A baby is not worth your life. We should have taken precautions. You could have died. According to your doctor, you almost did."

"I'm sorry. What was I supposed to do, Jack? It was a no-win situation. I wasn't trying to get pregnant. I didn't even know if I could get pregnant. Once it happened, you left me. Being held at gunpoint would put stress on anyone." Stephanie took a deep breath and closed her eyes.

"I don't want to play the blame game anymore. Nina and I had a long talk this afternoon," she said quietly, meeting his eyes. "I don't know what to say. I'm sorry doesn't seem to be enough under the circumstances."

He remained silent and waited for her to finish whatever she was struggling to say.

"I wanted our baby. I didn't mean it when I said losing the baby was a blessing."

"I know you didn't, but it hurt nonetheless. You were angry and you wanted to hurt me. Well, you succeeded. It seems to be a pattern with us. Again, you can believe a complete stranger, but you couldn't take my word for anything. You refused to even listen to me, yet you calmly listened to Nina. Stef, what is wrong with this picture? I can't live like this. What do I have to do to make you trust me, to make you believe in me? Is it even possible? Was it ever possible? Is it just me or men in general you have a problem trusting?"

"I was angry and I lashed out at you. I thought you had betrayed me. I wanted you to feel the pain I was feeling."

He came forward and sat down on the edge of the bed. "I was hurting too, Stef, and feeling guilty for not being here with you. I keep telling myself if I had been here, none of this would have happened, but on the other hand, if I hadn't gone Roper, Nina, and Aidan would have all been killed. I feel like I traded our baby's life for theirs. This is what I have to live with every day for the rest of my life."

"Stop torturing yourself. This wasn't your fault," she admitted softly, and her hand covered his. "If anyone's to blame, it's me for not taking proper care of myself."

"Let's not go back down this road of who's to blame. Roper is helping me finish up the security training for all the hotels. We figure with the two of us it shouldn't take more than six weeks."

"Then what?" she asked, not sure she was going to like the answer.

"Then we start Kaufman and Roper Security Consulting. It's what I'm good at. It's what we're both good at. It's something I want to do."

"What about Luciano Hotels?"

"It's all yours. Run it however you see fit. Isn't that what you wanted, me out of your hotels and out of your hair?"

She remained silent. "I can see you've already made up your mind about this. I hope it works out for you. Do you need any financing?"

"No. We both have money set aside. If it's not enough, we'll make do. Stephanie, I know how you feel about him, but he's my friend. He is also my family. You don't have to like him, but he will also be a part of my life. To make things easier, Roper will be moving into my condo in a few days. That's where we are going to set up shop until we can find the necessary office space."

"If there's anything I can do to help?" She wanted to reach out to him, but didn't know how.

"A business referral will be enough." They both fell silent. Jack wanted to say more, but he decided against it. Instead he asked the question that had been burning in his mind. "Do you want me to move out?" As he waited for her answer, his world stood still. He didn't know how he would react if she said yes, but he knew it was a possibility.

He didn't miss the look of stark fear in her eyes. She was afraid, but he didn't know what of. He wasn't sure if she was afraid of a failed marriage like her mother or she simply didn't want to be alone. Posing the question to her had put the ball in her court.

Stephanie was taken by complete surprise at his question. She knew things were bad, but she wasn't ready to give up on her marriage. "No, that's not what I want, but I do need some time. I have some issues to work through and until I do, I can't move forward. Will you give me that time?"

"Sure, take all the time you need," Jack seethed, getting up from the bed. "You don't want me to go, but you don't really want me to stay either. You can't have it both ways, Stephanie. It's one or the other. Don't worry, when I do leave, I'll leave with exactly what I came here with, nothing. The only thing I want is access to my daughter." He slammed out of the bedroom before she could stop him.

He didn't give her a chance to explain. She needed to time to sort out some things, but she didn't need time to decide how she felt about him or their marriage. She loved him and wanted to work things out.

Stephanie hesitated only a few minutes before running after him. "Jack!" By the time she made it to the top of the stairs, she heard the screeching of tires as his motorcycle left the house.

Roper stood at the bottom of the staircase glaring up at her. As he started up the stairs, Stephanie went back to her room and slammed the door. He was the last person she wanted to talk to.

He didn't bother to knock as he stormed into the room. They stood glaring at each other.

"Roper, leave it alone," said Nina breathlessly from behind them. "Let Stephanie and Jack work this out for themselves."

"Nina, go back downstairs. Stephanie and I need to clear the air. Go!" he said sharply. Nina fled from the room.

"What could you possibly have to say to me, you pathetic excuse for a mercenary?" Her anger was now directed at the man she blamed for her problems. His greed had caused him to be captured and taken prisoner. He was the reason her husband left her.

"Some honest emotion from Ice Princess Stephanie,

that's a switch. Such open hostility. You know they say hatred eats at the soul."

"What would you know about honesty, and more importantly, what would you know about having a soul? I thought all you knew was greed. Isn't that what started this? One last job to make you set for life. Enough money so my sister wouldn't think you were the loser you are. You are not good enough for her. She deserves a hell of a lot better than you and she knows it."

"Jack's right. You do sound like your mother, but that's another story. This is not about my relationship with Ashley."

"If I have my way, you won't have a relationship with Ashley, and if she were smart she would stay as far away from you as she could get. This whole situation is one you created. You did this. You almost got us all killed and the woman you professed to love raped!"

"That's right. It was my greed and my stupidity. If you have to blame someone, then blame me. Don't blame Jack. This isn't his fault."

"He risked his life going after you. I lost my baby because of you! I blame both of you!"

"Why, because you feel he chose me over you?" He saw his remark had hit its target. "That's it, isn't it? You think he chose me over you and that's what you can't accept. There was never a contest Stephanie. You are his wife. Jack and I are friends, maybe that's something you know nothing about, but a true friend is damn hard to find. I would lay down my life for Jack and vice versa. We have been through hell together and it's made us closer. I am closer to him than my own family. I realize my life means very little to you, but it means a hell of a lot to me. Do you think Jack would have been able to live with himself if he had let me die? Do you think he would ever have looked at you the same way knowing he let me die because of you? Had he stayed, you would have lost him anyway. I'll tell you the same thing your sister told me, grow up. The world does not revolve around Stephanie Mason. Don't let your daddy issues ruin your marriage!"

"Get out of my room!" Anyone who knew her knew her father was a sore subject better left untouched. How dare this man throw it in her face? He knew nothing about her or her father.

"Not until I'm finished. Jack would do anything for his daughter. He would even put up with a self-centered head case like you to give her the family she so desperately wants. Do you think it was easy for him to leave and come after me when you were threatening to divorce him? He loves you. You and Christina are his life. I have known Jack for years and I have never seen him look the way he did when he left a few minutes ago. You are tearing him apart. You either love him or you don't. You either want him or you don't, but make up your mind soon because I don't know how much more of this he can take."

"I do love him."

"Don't tell me. Tell him." Roper yanked open the bedroom door as he left the room. It banged again the wall. Stephanie heard the front door slam and she knew he was gone also.

Your daddy issues are ruining your marriage. Don't let what happened with your father and me ruin your life. Jack is not your father.

Everyone's words were echoing in her mind. Looking in the drawer, she took out the phone number she had been fingering earlier. Picking up the phone, she called him.

Jack rode around for what seemed like hours before turning the bike for home. He opened the garage door and drove the Harley inside and let down the garage door.

He went inside the house and headed for the den. Jack found Roper reclining on the couch watching television.

"You okay?" Roper asked, coming to a sitting position.

"What do you think?" Jack dropped down to the La-Z-Boy chair and leaned back in the chair closing his eyes. "I never knew marriage was this much hard work."

"I hear the good ones always are. Having never been married, I have no personal experience to draw from. I hate to tell you this, but I think I may have made matters worse. Your wife and I had a long-overdue chat. I told her she was being unfair to you."

"And you're still alive. I'm impressed. I bet your advice went over like a ton of bricks with her. Did it kind of feel like you were beating your head against a concrete wall?"

"And then some. She ripped me a new one. I guess we now know where we stand with each other. I'm the man who ruined her life. I can live with her hostility. I'm not sure you can."

"Women. Can't live with them. Can't live without them. I'm going up to shower and get ready for bed," said Jack, getting to his feet. "I'll see you in the morning."

Stephanie was lying in the darkness of the bedroom when she heard the garage door open and close. She said a silent prayer that Jack came home safely.

There was so much she wanted and needed to say to him, but she didn't know where to begin. She could always begin by telling him how she loved him and go from there.

Stephanie was drifting off to sleep when the bedroom door opened and closed softly. She said nothing as she heard Jack enter the room and head for the bathroom. Seconds later, she heard the shower come on.

He emerged from the bathroom minutes later. She held

her breath as he slid into the bed next to her. They were both lying on their backs staring up at the ceiling.

"I love you," Stephanie said softly. Her heart was beating wildly as she waited for him to say speak.

Jack didn't respond. He didn't know what to say to her. He already knew she loved him. It was the battle she was fighting inside that frightened him. It was almost as if she were afraid to be happy. She was afraid to love and be loved in return. He knew she had abandonment issues because of her father. He didn't know how to help her fight her fear.

Stephanie turned to face him in bed. "Did you hear what I said? I love you, Jack. I don't want you to go anywhere. I want to make our marriage work."

He turned to face her in the darkness. "Prove it. Exorcise your demons, Stef. You need to come to terms with what happened with your parents. Whether you call your father or go see him, you need closure." He felt her stiffen beside him. "Don't shut me out. If you want this marriage to work, you have to let me in. You have to at least be willing to meet me halfway. I love you, sweetheart, and I'm not going anywhere."

Stephanie couldn't speak past the lump in her throat. She closed the distance between them as she moved into his outstretched arms. No more words were spoken as they fell asleep in each other's arms.

On Monday, Stephanie sat downstairs with the kids while Jack took Nina to register for a green card. They dropped by the junior college to pick up some brochures on computer classes.

After their argument on Sunday, Roper had moved his things into the condo. He told Stephanie he couldn't sit around and watch her destroy his friend.

Jack moved Aidan's things into the room Roper vacated.
From a stack of catalogs, Stephanie let Aidan choose how
he wanted his room decorated. He chose sailboats and she
ordered all the accessories for the room.

Nina tried to feign disinterest, but she was still upset
about the fight she had with Roper the night he stormed
out of the house. When he came back, he told them he was
moving out sooner than planned. Nina had run to her room
in tears.

When Stephanie went in to talk to the young girl, Nina
finally broke down and told her what was really bothering
her. It had nothing to do with her argument with Roper. It
was the secret she had been keeping from everyone.

She was really only fifteen and her sixteenth birthday
was today. Nina was terrified about what would happen to
her and Aidan now that Stephanie knew the truth.

Nina asked Stephanie to help her break the news to
Roper and Jack because she knew they would both be furious at her for lying. She told Stephanie if she hadn't told
Jack she was eighteen he might have left her and Aidan
behind.

Stephanie assured her that was not the case. She was
also delighted to know someone had pulled the wool over
Jack's and Roper's eyes. Roper most of all was in for a surprise. He was bouncing back and forth between wanting
Ashley and flirting with Nina.

Stephanie stood quietly by while Nina told Jack the
truth. Instead of becoming angry, he bubbled over with
laughter. He assured her he wasn't upset and told her he
wanted to be the one to break it to Roper.

Stephanie and Jack both assured Nina she and Aidan
were now a part of their family. They would file the necessary paperwork to become guardians to her and Aidan
to keep them in the country.

Stephanie had fallen in love with the little boy and

wanted to adopt both Aidan and Nina, but she had not broached the subject yet with Jack or Nina. It was crazy to be thinking about it when her marriage was in shambles. She would give it some time before she brought it up adopting both of them.

"Roper, come in," said Jack, handing him a double rum and Coke.

"Why are you greeting me with a drink in your hand?" he asked suspiciously. "What's wrong?"

"Let's go into the den."

Roper followed him into the den and frowned when Jack waved for him to take a seat.

"Okay, what gives? I'm sitting down. I'll even take a sip of my drink." Roper took a gulp of the fiery liquid.

"One sip isn't enough to take the edge off what I'm about to tell you." He paused for effect. "Nina's birthday is today." Jack smiled. "She turned sixteen."

Roper choked and then sputtered before he came to his feet and set the drink on the coffee table. "She's what!"

"She's sweet sixteen today. She came clean with Stephanie this morning. She thought if we knew, we would leave her behind."

"I've been lusting after a fifteen-year-old! Where is she hiding? She made a fool of me. I should put her over my knee for all the inappropriate thoughts she had running through my head."

"She's upstairs and you are not going to lay a hand on her. She was a frightened young woman. Nina did what she felt she had to do to survive. Besides, she didn't make a fool out of you. You made one out of yourself. Stef and I now have three kids we are responsible for. This makes things a little more difficult, but we can handle it. Stephanie is already in love with Aidan and she treats him like a son. I hope she can accept Nina as her daughter as easily."

"I've seen the bond between Stephanie and Nina. I don't think that will be a problem. I guess 'Uncle' Roper can still teach her how to drive."

"Oh, thank you," squealed Nina, running into the room and throwing her arms around him.

He held her at arm's length.

"Do you forgive me for lying about my age?"

"There's nothing to forgive." Roper smiled, tugging gently on her ponytail. "Happy birthday, sweetheart."

"Does that mean you're staying for cake and ice cream?" asked Stephanie, entering the room carrying a chocolate cake with sixteen candles. They all broke out in a chorus of "Happy Birthday."

Chapter 16

On Tuesday, Jack and Roper made their partnership official. Jack asked Nina to cook a special celebration dinner. Stephanie was helping in the kitchen when the doorbell rang.

"I'll get it." She looked out the peephole and froze momentarily. Taking a deep breath, she opened the door to her visitor. "Hello."

"Hello, Steffie," said Lawrence Mason, stepping inside the house. He tried to hug her, but she took a step back. "It looks like you've done well for yourself."

"Thank you for coming. If I could have come to you, I would have."

He followed her into the living room.

"Please have a seat."

He sat down, but she remained standing.

"I was pleasantly surprised when you called me and asked me to come here. You look the way I imagined you would. You're a beautiful young woman. After all the letters I wrote and phones calls I made, what made you decide to call me now?"

"Because I have a lot of unanswered questions I need answers to. I need to understand how you could walk away from us. I don't mean Mother, I mean me and Ashley. You walked away and never looked back. Why?"

"I knew one day I would have to answer these questions, but I didn't know how hard it would be. Your mother and I were so young when we got married. I was a young intern and she was a nurse. I had no desire to marry, but your mother got pregnant with you and I did the right thing. I married her. I was no more ready for a baby than I was for marriage. I tried to make it work. I really did, but I didn't love her. I was all ready to tell her I was leaving when she told me she was pregnant again."

"You think she did it on purpose both times?" Stephanie already knew the answer. She knew her mother was once a vindictive materialistic woman. That was all in the past. Her mother was a changed woman.

"Yes. I was an eligible young black doctor. She got her hooks in me and held on for dear life. I don't even think she ever really loved me. She was more in love with the idea of being a doctor's wife. She wanted the finer things in life. You know how your mother feels about money and social status. For you girls, I stuck in there as long as I could, but finally I couldn't do it anymore. I had to get away from her. It was like a dream come true when I was offered a job at a hospital in New Jersey. When I told Mildred I was leaving, she was furious. You have no idea the fight we had."

"Yes, I do because I was there."

He visible paled as he looked at her.

"I heard everything you said. You said I was a mistake that never should have happened. You told her she should have had an abortion and you wouldn't have ended up stuck with her. You said you never wanted children or her." Stephanie stopped as she wiped the tears from her face. "Why didn't you want me? Why couldn't you love me?"

"Steffie, I'm so sorry you heard that." He caught her hand. "Honey, that was anger talking. It was directed at your mother, not at you. I love you and Ashley. I stayed with Mildred for seventeen years because I loved you girls." He lovingly embraced his daughter. "Now I understand why you didn't want anything to do with me after the divorce. I thought your mother had poisoned your mind against me. I blamed her, and all along, it was me. You overheard words spoken in the heat of the moment and took them to heart." He framed her face with his hands. "I love you, Stephanie. I always will."

She cried in her father's arms. She understood words spoken in the heat of the moment. She had done the same thing to Jack about their baby.

They visited for several hours. He got a chance to meet his granddaughter, whom he fell instantly in love with. He also met Aidan and Nina. Stephanie caught him up to date on everything in her and Ashley's lives. He was thrilled to find out Ashley was an intern at one of the local hospitals. She conveniently left out the part about Jack's past and Ashley's relationship with Roper.

Jack and Roper stood outside the house. They were still both reeling from the car that had almost hit Jack.

As he stepped out of the car and started across the street to meet Roper, a dark sedan with no plates hit the gas. Jack's quick reflexes and agility were the only things that saved him from a certain death. He jumped back just in the nick of time.

"Okay. That was a bit too close for comfort," said Jack, vaulting to his feet. He brushed off his slacks.

"That wasn't an accident, Jack. He came right at you. There were no plates on the front or back," said Roper.

"This is not the first time," he confessed. "I was almost run down in the hotel parking lot a few days ago."

"Does Stephanie know about this?"

"No, and I'm not going to freak her out by telling her. I've got Taggart looking into it. Someone is out to kill me and I want to know who it is. We go inside like nothing has happened. See, there's not a scratch on me." Jack opened the door and they went inside.

Stephanie was still sitting on the sofa in her father's arms when Jack and Roper came through the front door. He did a double take when he saw them.

Stephanie and Lawrence both came to their feet. "Jack, I think you've already met my father, Lawrence Mason."

Jack stepped forward and the two men shook hands. "No, I don't think I've had the pleasure," said Lawrence, taking his son-in-law's hand. "It's nice to meet you, Jack."

"It's nice to meet you as well. I'm glad you're here." Jack knew a lot of Stephanie's abandonment issues came from her situation with her father. He couldn't meet his wife's furious eyes. He didn't need to look at her to know she was pissed off. "My friend and business partner, Todd Roper. Lawrence, please stay for dinner. We're having a celebration of sorts."

"You talked me into it. I'd love to spend more time with my daughter and her family."

"I'll see if I can get Ashley to drop by. Maybe if I took lessons in lying from my husband it wouldn't be a problem," said Stephanie, glaring at Jack.

Lawrence looked from her to Jack strangely and shook his head. "I don't get involved in domestic problems."

"I've learned my lesson too," said Roper, sliding his arm around Lawrence's shoulders and leading him from the room. "Would you like a drink?"

"I'd love one," said Lawrence, looking over his shoulder at Stephanie and Jack. He knew the look on his daughter's face meant trouble was brewing.

* * *

With arms folded across her chest, Stephanie turned to face her husband. Jack took two steps forward, which brought him directly in front of her.

"Let's hear it," he said, throwing his hands in the air. "Go ahead and get it over with. Hit me with your best shot." Jack never saw it coming as she balled up her fist and punched him in the stomach. The air left his lungs with a whoosh. "I meant that figuratively," he said, catching his breath, "but I guess I deserved that. I lied about meeting your father months ago."

Still glaring at him, Stephanie turned to leave the room. His arm looped around her waist to stop her. "Let go," she hissed between clenched teeth.

"Never," vowed Jack right before his mouth covered hers in a searing kiss. His mouth devoured hers and she returned his ardent kiss. As she moaned softly in surrender, her arms went around him and she returned his kiss. Jack pulled her closer and molded her body to his. When his mouth finally left hers, they were both breathless. Moaning in protest, Stephanie brought his head back down to hers.

"Stef, we'd better stop. How many days did the doctor say we had to wait?"

"At least two weeks."

His forehead rested against hers.

"Is there anything else I should know about? Any more secrets or surprises and I will kill you myself. No more, Jack. I can't take any more. This had better be the end of it."

"I swear. There are no more secrets. I love you and I don't want to lose you."

"You couldn't lose me if you tried," she assured him, pulling his head down for a kiss. "I'm in this for the long haul."

The doorbell rang and Jack released her with a quick

kiss. He looked down at his watch. "I invited your mother and her boyfriend for dinner. Is that going to be a problem with your father here?"

"Was World War Two a problem?" she asked sarcastically. "My parents haven't seen each other in over ten years. You get the door and I'll go warn my father."

Jack hauled her back to him for a quick kiss.

Stephanie found Roper and her father in the den. They were sitting on the couch talking.

"Guys, I hate to interrupt the male bonding, but we have unexpected guests for dinner. Mom and her date just arrived."

"Mildred is here. I need another drink," said Roper, getting to his feet.

"Make mine a double," said Lawrence, following Roper over to the bar with his empty glass.

"See, this is just one more thing you two have in common." Stephanie smiled sheepishly.

"One more thing," said Lawrence, eying her warily. "What is it you two aren't telling me?" He looked from Stephanie to Roper in question.

"Todd!" They heard Ashley coming before she got to the room. Roper met her at the door and she threw herself in his arms and kissed him. "I missed you."

Lawrence choked on his drink. All eyes turned to him as he coughed and sputtered. Stephanie smiled knowingly. Apparently, Ashley and Roper had shocked him.

"That's the other thing." Stephanie smiled, pointing in their general direction. "I feel the same way, Dad. I get all choked up too."

"Dad!" said Ashley, running to Lawrence and embracing him. "What are you doing here? Is everything okay?"

"Everything is fine," he said, clearing his throat. "Stephanie invited me. We had a long talk. We finally cleared the air. Jack invited me to dinner."

"That's great, but I just saw Jack stalling Mom and her date in the hall. She doesn't know you're here yet, obviously," laughed Ashley. "Guess who's coming to dinner?"

"That's a play on words coming from you, little sister. Wait a minute. Have you two been in contact?" asked Stephanie, taking in the easy chatter between her sister and father.

"On a regular basis. I'm not as stubborn as you are," said Ashley, hugging her father. "Dad, I'd like for you to meet Todd Roper."

"We've met. I must admit I am a little surprised." He appraised Roper's short brown military crew cut, tall yet stocky frame, and deep brown eyes. He was not at all what he had expected his baby girl to end up with.

"We could tell." Roper smiled knowingly. "I hope you don't have a problem with me being white. I love your daughter, Mr. Mason, and she loves me."

"That's what's important to me. Is this Mildred's objection?"

"Not exactly," said Stephanie, looping her arm through his, "that's only part of her objection. Let's all have a seat. This is going to take a while. Roper, you may want to get him another drink. Make it a double."

Jack walked into the room. "There's another member of the A-Team now," Stephanie said.

Jack blew Stephanie a kiss. "And you wouldn't have me any other way, babe." He sat on the arm of her chair and slipped his hand into hers. "Your mom is trying to decide if she wants to stay for dinner."

When Stephanie finished the story, her father looked from Jack to Roper without saying a word. He got up from the sofa and began pacing. Stephanie knew it was a lot to take in. She was sure both men were not exactly what any father would want for his daughters.

"For once, I'm speechless," said their father, turning to face his daughters and their mates. "I don't know what to say. I don't know what I'm supposed to say. If my daughters can accept this and live with it, so can I. I am not in a position to judge anyone's past. I didn't only regain a daughter today, but I gained a whole family."

"Thanks, Dad." Stephanie smiled at him. She saw her father freeze and knew only one woman could cause that same reaction from all three men in the room.

"Well, I couldn't have imagined this scene in my worst nightmare. Roper, Jack, and now you, Larry," said Mildred, uneasily meeting the eyes of her ex-husband.

"I feel the same way," said Lawrence as a smile easily split his lips. "You look beautiful, Mildred. The years have been kind to you."

Stephanie watched the exchange between her parents. This was not the fireworks she had expected. Maybe this was the calm before the storm.

Dinner was even more of a surprise. If she didn't know any better, she could swear her parents were into each other. They flirted and talked all during the meal. Her mother's date was forgotten as Mildred and Lawrence reconnected.

Although their family life had fallen back into place, it was still two weeks of pure hell for Stephanie and Jack. They were both on edge, as they had to live a life of celibacy until the doctor released her. Their eyes devoured each other. All either of them dared were a few light kisses.

The nights were the worst. Stephanie had all sorts of fantasies about her husband. When he was in the shower, she could envision him standing there with the water running down his chest and flat stomach. He was close enough to reach out and touch, but she was wise enough not to.

When she offered to pleasure him, his response was "when your mother starts to look good to me, I might consider it." He then repeated her statement. "If it doesn't kill me, it will make me stronger."

Stephanie was smiling as she left the doctor's office. She received a clean bill of health. She called Suzette at the hotel and booked the honeymoon suite.

She picked up the room key and took the elevator up to the tenth floor. She took a quick shower and slipped on the new outfit she had bought just for Jack.

Stephanie paced the room waiting for Jack. The purple lace teddy she wore showed more than it covered. She stopped pacing and turned down the covers on the bed. She looked down at her watch for the fifth time. He should be receiving the envelope and key right about now.

"Have you seen Stephanie? I thought she'd be back by now." Jack stared at the envelope Suzette handed him. He looked at the envelope, and then at her with raised brows.

"Actually, she asked me to give that to you. Have a nice afternoon." Suzette smiled, leaving the room.

Frowning, Jack tore open the envelope and took out the note. Unfolding it, he saw a room key.

What doesn't kill you will make you stronger? I hope you've been saving your strength. You'll need it.

Laughing, he picked up the room key and left his office. He anxiously took the elevator up to the honeymoon suit.

As he unlocked the door, the wind was knocked out of him at the sight that greeted him.

His beautiful and sexy wife stood in the middle of the room in a revealing purple teddy. He closed the door behind him, but made no move toward her.

"Wow! I guess this means you received a clean bill of health." He walked toward her slowly. "Is this a dream?"

"Come closer and find out."

He stopped directly in front of her, but still didn't touch her. Jack knew if he touched her, it would be all over. He had to think rationally right now.

"Give me two minutes to run downstairs to the vending machine in the men's restroom," he said, taking a step back.

"Why?" Stephanie asked, following him. She had a smile on her face and mischief in her eyes.

"Stef, we have to take precautions. Faithful married men don't carry condoms in their wallets."

She moved her hand from behind her back. "Which kind do you prefer, textured, ribbed, flavored, or glow-in-the-dark?" She smiled, holding the packets up for his inspection.

He quickly closed the distance between them, pulling her into his arms. His mouth covered hers in a passionate kiss, which she returned eagerly. As his mouth feasted on hers, his hands explored her body. Stephanie was busy pushing his jacket from his shoulders and unbuttoning his shirt. She stripped him in record time.

Leading him over to the bed, she slipped her arms from the teddy and pushed it down her body. She stepped out of it and into his arms. His mouth covered hers again and he pressed her backward onto the bed. Stephanie welcomed his weight. His mouth left hers to trail down to her breast. Closing her eyes in bliss, she held his head to her. Her legs parted as his hand trailed down her stomach. She sighed in pleasure when one finger slipped inside her. She arched to meet his hand.

"I can't wait," he whispered against her throat. "It's been too long since I made love to my wife."

"You don't have to wait. I want you now." She watched him lever himself off her and rip the plastic with his teeth. She took the condom from him and put it on for him. His eyes closed in pleasure beneath her caressing hand. Catching her hand, he moved over her again. Their eyes held as he slowly sheathed himself inside her. He stayed there a few seconds without moving. His mouth lowered to hers again. Her legs locked around him and she moved seductively against him. Taking her cue, Jack began a slow, steady pace that drove Stephanie closer and closer to the edge. She clung to him as his thrusts became harder and went deeper. A soft whimper escaped her lips followed by a loud gasp as her body exploded beneath his. Jack let out a guttural groan as he collapsed on top of her. He lay there for a few seconds before rolling to his side and pulling her with him. His hand stroked her back.

"I'm sorry, I couldn't wait."

Stephanie rose and leaned over and kissed him again and again. "There's nothing to be sorry about. I couldn't wait either. Besides, you have the rest of the afternoon to make it up to me," she teased, kissing him again.

He brushed the hair from her face and caressed her cheek. "I love you, Stef."

Stephanie's heart melted at those softly spoken words. She touched his face lovingly. "And I love you with all my heart."

Chapter 17

Stephanie took the roast out of the over and set the casserole dish on the stove. She removed the lid and the delicious aroma filled the air. She replaced the lid when her cell phone chimed on the counter.

She was surprised to see Stanley's number on the caller ID. "Hello."

"Stephanie, hello," came the friendly voice of her ex-fiancé. "I was just thinking about you and decided to give you a call. How are you? How's married life?"

"I'm fine. Married life is great." She and Jack were back on track and more in love than ever. "How are you? I heard you were getting married."

"Well, things didn't work out."

Couldn't get access to the trust fund, I guess. "I'm sorry to hear that," said Stephanie, rolling her eyes in disinterest.

"No one could compare to you, Stephanie. You are the love of my life. If things don't work out with that bounder you married, I will be waiting. He doesn't deserve you. He can't possibly love you as much as I do."

What you mean is no one can love money as much as you. Give it up, Stanley. "Stanley, sorry to cut this short, but I'm in the middle of preparing dinner. Did you want anything in particular?"

"I will wait for you as long as I have to. I love you. We could have had it all, Stephanie. We still can," came his desperate voice.

Stephanie hung up the phone before he could continue. She didn't know what he was going to say and didn't want to know.

"That was creepy," she whispered to the empty room. She felt a chill go down her spine for no apparent reason.

Jack finished his meeting early with Alex, the new hotel manager. He went back to his office to get his laptop. He was taking the rest of the afternoon off to surprise Stephanie.

She had had a lot of time on her hands since she turned over the day-to-day operation of the hotel to Alex. Jack had definite plans about how he wanted to spend the afternoon before it was time to pick the kids up from school and Christina from her day care.

Stephanie had enrolled Christina in day care two days a week so she would get to spend time with other kids. Next year she would start kindergarten, so they wanted her transition to be a smooth one by starting her in school now.

Jack stepped out into the sunshine and headed for his motorcycle. He started the bike and maneuvered out of the parking lot. He drove down two blocks and turned left, entering the ramp leading to the freeway. His mind was on his wife and he didn't notice the Chevy Avalanche following him. He stopped and waited for traffic to clear. He saw a meat truck coming and decided to hop on the freeway after the truck passed. His bike lurched when the truck behind him pushed his motorcycle into oncoming traffic.

Thinking fast, Jack gunned the motorcycle and dodged.
The oncoming meat truck barely missed him and several
other cars as he swerved in and out of traffic.

When he finally was out of danger, he looked behind
him to find the truck responsible and it was already exit-
ing the freeway. Jack was in the far left lane, so there was
no way he could get over and follow the truck to give the
driver a piece of his mind.

"Idiot." He dismissed the driver as he headed home.

When Jack arrived home, the house was quiet. Something smelled delicious in the kitchen. He followed his
nose, hoping to find his wife. Stephanie was nowhere in
sight. He took the stairs two at a time.

He went through the bedroom to the double doors of
the bathroom. A smile formed on his lips when he saw
Stephanie sound asleep in the Jacuzzi. He stripped off his
clothes and eased into the water.

Her eyes fluttered open when his hand covered her
breast. Stephanie smiled as his left hand disappeared in the
water. When he moved over her, her arms went around
him. Her mouth met his eagerly.

No words were spoken as they made love. None were
needed as they communicated with their mouths, bodies,
and hands.

Afterward, Jack dried her off and carried her into the
bedroom. He told her to rest, and he would pick up the kids.

Neither mentioned to the other the events of the day.
They had a nice family dinner with the children before
helping them with homework.

Jack was riding his motorcycle when he got an odd
feeling someone was following him. He changed lanes a
couple of times to be sure. Each time, the Mustang followed
his lead.

Jack sped up and then exited off the freeway. The Mustang followed him. Smiling, Jack kept going. He was meeting Taggart and the gang at a bar. Whoever was following him would be in for quite a surprise when he stopped. He pulled into the parking lot and dialed Taggart's cell phone.

"Taggart, it's me. I'm outside the bar. I have company. I picked up a tail leaving the hotel. Yellow Mustang convertible."

"We'll welcome him properly to the party. Come inside so you don't scare him away."

Jack hung up his cell phone and got off the motorcycle. As he was making his way inside, he passed Taggart going out. "Do you see him?"

"He's getting out of the car. You can look now, my men detained him."

Jack followed Taggart over to the Mustang, where Pete and Steve had the man subdued. As Jack drew closer, he recognized the man. He remembered seeing him in the hotel restaurant when he and Stephanie were eating lunch. "Who are you and why are you following me?" asked Jack, eying the short, stocky man.

"I wasn't following you," he lied smoothly. "I was stopping off to have a drink on my way home from work."

"Wrong answer. Hold him." As he struggled, Jack took his wallet out of his suit pocket. He thumbed through the contents. He held up the private eye license card. Jack was more than a little surprised. Why would a PI follow him? "I'm only going to ask you one more time. Why are you following me? Who hired you?"

"I'm not following you," answered the man nervously.

"Pete, Steve, take him out back and shoot him," bluffed Jack, turning his back to walk away. As they attempted to drag the man away, he became terrified.

"Okay, I'll talk," said the scared private eye. "I don't

know who hired me. I never met him. I'm telling the truth. I never met the man who hired me."

"What did he hire you to do?" asked Jack, studying him.

"Just to follow you and take notes. He wants to know every move you make for the next two days. He paid me in advance. He put the envelope under my door. I swear I never met the man. I'm assuming it was a man because the envelope smelled of cologne. I swear that's all I know."

"What do you think, guys?" asked Jack, looking at each man. "Do you believe him? I'm not so sure. He could be holding out on us."

"There's one way to find out," answered Taggart, eying the bar with raised eyebrows.

"Well, Nelson Freemont, today is your lucky day." Jack put his arm around the man's shoulder and led him toward the bar. "Come on, let's go have a drink."

"You're serious?" asked the disbelieving man.

"Why not? You've got nothing to hide, right? You are being paid to keep an eye on me, so you might as well have a front row seat. I'm sure you've heard the saying "keep your friends close and your enemies closer.""

Tag and the boys drank the private eye under the table. Jack rarely drank and he never had more than one when he was driving. He grilled the PI most of the night. A few hours later, he came to the conclusion the man was telling the truth.

He left the bar with a feeling of unrest. Someone had hired Freemont to follow him. He still didn't know who or for what reason.

Jack decided not to tell Stephanie about the incident. It would only worry her needlessly.

When she let it slip that Stanley had called a few days ago, Jack did not take the news well. He quizzed her about why her ex-fiancé was calling. She finally repeated the conversation to him. When he left the house abruptly,

Stephanie knew she should never have mentioned the call to him. She knew how Jack felt about Stanley. This was what she was trying to avoid.

Please don't do anything stupid, Jack. I don't want to have to bail you out of jail tonight.

Jack waited in the parking garage near Stanley's car. Stanley's footsteps faltered when he saw the silhouette of black-leather-clad Jack Kaufman leaning against his motorcycle waiting for him. Stanley's car had four flat tires and Jack was fingering a knife.

Stanley put on a brave front. "What did you do to my car? Those are new tires. I will sue you for destruction of private property."

"Your car should be the least of your worries. You're lucky I didn't set fire to it. I'll make this simple enough for even you to understand. Stay away from my family. Don't call Stephanie, don't come to my home, don't come near my wife or you will regret it. You only get one warning."

"I'm calling the police," said Stanley, fumbling with his cell phone. "I'll have you arrested for threatening my life and slicing my tires, you thug."

"Be my guest." Jack straddled the motorcycle. "Give them my regards. You can also tell them the security camera is disabled. They may want to get that fixed. You can't prove I touched your car, Stan. Heed my words or suffer the consequences."

"You are not getting away with this! I will get you for this!" yelled the angry man as Jack drove away.

Stephanie was anxiously waiting for Jack's return. She was afraid of what he could and might do to Stanley.

She breathed a sigh of relief when Jack walked into the bedroom. She studied his hands and clothing.

Good. No bruises or blood. She knew any blood would be Stanley's.

"I didn't lay a hand on him," said Jack, holding out his arms to Stephanie. She walked into them and they closed around her. She didn't need to know about the car tires. "I wanted to but I'm a peaceful family man. I did, however, issue him a warning to stay away from my family. If he doesn't heed my words, all bets are off."

A few days later, Stephanie pulled into the driveway and was surprised to find Stanley waiting for her. Puzzled, she got out of the car and walked toward him.

"Stanley, what are you doing here?" She didn't expect Jack home for a few hours, but she didn't feel comfortable with Stanley being there. Jack would rip his head off if he came home and found him there.

"I came by to see you. Can't an old friend stop by to say hello? Can I come in for a minute?"

"Sure." Frowning, Stephanie unlocked the door and he followed her inside. When the door closed, she smiled as she heard the footsteps on the stairs. Kneeling down, she waited for the dynamic duo to reach her.

"Mommy! Miss Stephanie!" Christina and Aidan came barreling down the stairs and launched themselves at Stephanie. Smiling, she hugged and kissed both of them.

"Hi, guys. Did you have a good day?" They both nodded. Christina's smile faded as her eyes slid past Stephanie to Stanley.

"What is he doing here?" she whispered loud enough for everyone to hear.

"I came to see how you and your mother were getting along," answered Stanley. "Who's your friend?"

"He's not my friend. He's my brother," she stated proudly, crossing her arms over her chest. "I have a sister too. Her name is Nina."

"What is she talking about?" asked Stanley, confused and looking around the house. "Who are these people?"

"Jack and I are in the process of adopting Nina and Aidan." Stephanie didn't miss the stricken look on Stanley's face.

"Hi, Stephanie." Nina smiled, entering the room. "Dinner is almost ready and Jack called to say he has a meeting after work and he'll be a little late."

"Thank you. My cell phone is dead. Nina, this is Stanley Jordan. He's an old friend." Stephanie knew she had to get Stanley out of the house for his own protection. She had no idea why he ignored Jack's warning.

"Hello, Mr. Jordan." Nina extended her hand to him and moved forward. "It's nice to meet you."

Stanley backed away. "You too, kid. I've got to get going," he said abruptly. "It was nice seeing you again, Stephanie. Take care."

Stephanie and Nina both stared at him puzzled. "What was that about?" asked Nina, closing the door behind him.

"I have no idea," answered Stephanie, "but I'm glad he's gone."

"I don't think he likes you either, Nina," threw in Christina, smiling.

They ate dinner and spent the rest of the evening watching a movie. Stephanie decided against telling Jack about Stanley's odd visit. There was no reason to mention it. She knew how Jack reacted when Stanley phoned. She wasn't about to tell him he came by the house.

Stephanie asked the kids not to say anything to their father about Stanley being at the house. She would just forget about it. She was already in bed and so were the kids when Jack came home.

The next few weeks, there were no more talk about Stanley and the visit was forgotten. Stephanie realized she made the right decision in keeping quiet.

"Word on the street is someone wants you dead and they are willing to pay a hundred grand for the job. Whom did you piss off this time?" asked Taggart.

"To my knowledge, no one lately. Hang on a second." Jack got up and shut the door, then sat down at his desk. "Find out who put the hit out."

"I'm already on it. I had one of my men accept the job. He's meeting the person as we speak." Taggart was already on the job.

"Thanks, Taggart."

"I've always got your back. I'll let you know who the culprit is in an hour or so," said Taggart, disconnecting the call.

Jack stared at the telephone in his hand. Slowly replacing it, he leaned back in his chair and tapped on the desk with a pen.

There's only one person I can think of who would want me dead, Stanley Jordan. He's been quiet lately. Maybe I should pay him another visit. I never liked or trusted the man. As the idea took root in his mind he picked up the phone and dialed his wife.

"Hello," said Stephanie, smiling into the phone. "I was just thinking about you. Where are you?"

"I'm at the hotel finishing up. I'm always thinking about you. How's your day going, beautiful?"

"It just got better." Stephanie walked up the stairs to the bedroom with the cordless phone in her hand.

"Then wait until tonight," he promised. "Honey, has

anything out of the ordinary happened in the past couple of days? Anything at all?"

"What do you mean out of the ordinary?" She took a deep breath. "Okay, one of the kids told you Stanley came by the house. I didn't tell you because I knew you would be livid. He didn't stay long."

"Stanley Jordan came by our house," Jack fumed, "and you didn't bother to tell me. "What did he say? What did he want?"

"I'm still not sure. He seemed upset when I told him we were adopting Nina and Aidan. He left abruptly after he met them."

"You should have told me. No secretes, Stef, that's the deal we made. Honey, I've got to take a call," he lied. "I'll see you later." Could Stanley have hired the PI to follow him, and for what reason? He drummed his fingers on the table. *Stanley was also upset to learn Stef and I were adopting the kids. Why should he care? Why should it matter to him, unless he thought with me out of the picture, Stef would turn to him? I think it's time I had another little chat with Mr. Jordan. Know your enemy. If he's planning something, I want him to know I'm ready for him.*

I think I will pay him a visit, right now. Jack left his office with a bad feeling because if it wasn't Stanley, then he was back to square one.

Stephanie was working out of the office today. She was on the phone when Jack entered her temporary office. She quickly ended the call and walked into his arms. Her mouth met his.

"I'm running out for a little while. I have some errands to run. I'll be back in a couple of hours."

"Okay. Are you still meeting me in the restaurant for lunch?" She stared up at him with questioning eyes.

"I may need a rain check. I'll see what I can do." His mouth touched hers again. "I'll see you later. I love you."

"I love you too. Jack, is everything okay? You seem distracted." Stephanie knew something was wrong. Jack was being too guarded and secretive.

"Everything is fine," he lied, brushing her lips with his. He didn't want to frighten her with the truth or his suspicions. "I'll see you later."

"I love you." Stephanie frowned as she watched him leave. She knew something was wrong, but she would wait for him tell her what it was.

Jack drove to Stanley's office in Plano. He parked his motorcycle in the parking garage. He took off his sunglasses as he walked into the building. Taking the elevator up to the fifteenth floor, he walked past the secretary.

"Sir, you can't go in there." The secretary came swiftly to her feet and ran after him.

"Watch me." He barged into the office. Stanley was nowhere in sight. "Where is that weasel hiding?"

"Mr. Jordan is out of the office for the rest of the afternoon. Give me your name and I will tell him you came by."

"No need. I'll wait. You can go now." Jack walked over to the desk and tried to open it. It was locked.

"What are you doing? I'm calling security."

He ignored her as he took the knife out of his pocket and jimmied open the locked desk. Rifling through the folders, he found what he was looking for. It was a folder with his name on it. Jack took the folder and left the drawer open.

"You can't take that! That's Mr. Jordan's private property. Give it back. I'm calling the police."

"Please do," said Jack, brushing past her. "I'm Jack

Kaufman. They can find me at the Luciano Hotel," he added, leaving the office.

His gut instinct told him Stanley was behind this. He was still after the Luciano fortune and he thought with Jack out of the way, he would stand a chance with Stephanie.

Jack drove the short distance to a nearby park. Pulling into a parking space, he opened the folder. "My, you've been a busy boy," he whistled. Staring back at him was a pretty accurate history of his life. There were also copies of his military record, credit report, and bank statement. Thumbing through the documents, he froze on the recent photos. The first one was of Nina, Aidan, and Christina in the backyard. Each child had an *x* on its face with a red marker. Today's date was written in the upper right corner of the photo.

A feeling of fear and dread filled Jack. The last picture was a wedding portrait of Stanley and Stephanie. The picture was from Jack and Stephanie's wedding, only Stanley's face replaced Jack's.

Jack picked up the phone and dialed home. He started the motorcycle and put it in gear.

"Hello. Kaufman residence. What's up, Jack?" asked Nina, smiling.

"Nina, listen carefully," he said calmly. "I need you to get Christina and Aidan and get out of the house. The keys to the SUV are on the key ring by the garage door. Get your purse and your cell phone and call me when you're away from the house."

"Jack, what's wrong?"

"Trust me, Nina. I don't have time to explain. Get the kids and head over to Roper's place. Now, Nina!" He rang off and dialed Roper. "Roper, we've got trouble. Nina and the kids are headed your way. I think Stanley Jordan has flipped out. He not only put a hit out on me, but I think he's going after the kids. He wants Stephanie and the Luciano fortune. He plans to eliminate me and the kids."

"What's the plan?" asked Roper. "What do you need me to do?"

"Take care of the kids. I'm headed back to the hotel to take care of Stephanie. Call me when the kids get there." He rang off and dialed Stephanie's office. He hung up when he got her voice mail. He dialed the front desk. "Suzette, have you seen Stephanie?"

"I think she's in the restaurant having lunch. Do you want me to give her a message?"

He let out the breath he was holding. "Let her know I won't be able to join her." He ended the call and dialed Taggart's cell phone. "Tell me you have something for me."

"The package is under wraps."

"Good. Tell me where to come." Jack jotted down the address. They were in an abandoned apartment building across town. "I'm on my way."

Chapter 18

He parked his motorcycle a block away from the old run-down building. Upon entering the building, he took the stairs up to the second floor. He knocked three times and then twice on the door; this was a code he and Taggart used often.

Taggart opened the door and waved him inside. They shook hands and then Taggart nodded toward the closed bedroom door. "We blindfolded him and tied him to a chair. He's not going anywhere." Taggart handed him a pair of plastic gloves. Jack slipped them on before opening the bedroom door.

"This won't take long," said Jack, closing the bedroom door behind him. He walked over to a bound and gagged Stanley. He removed the gag first and then the blindfold. Jack watched Stanley cringe in fear. "That's right, Stanley, be very afraid. Would you like to start with the hit you put out on me or these?" He took the photos out of his jacket pocket and dropped them on Stanley's lap. He watched the color leave the other man's face and he began to tremble. Stanley was too afraid to say anything. "The plan was to kill me, and then the children, so you could marry Stephanie. How accurate am I?"

"You can't prove anything," cried the scared voice. "None of this will stand up in court. You have no proof."

"Did I mention anything about a courtroom?" Jack asked, taking the switchblade out of his pocket. "This is your courtroom, Stanley, and I am the judge and the jury. You have been found guilty. Any last words before I cut your throat?" Jack put the knife to his throat and applied just enough pressure to scare him and make him wet his pants.

"You can't murder me in cold blood," he cried.

"Why not? That's what you were going to do to me and to my children. An eye for an eye, Stan. In my world it's kill or be killed. Welcome to my world." Jack removed the knife from his throat and slipped it back into his pocket. "I'll give you a choice of how you want to die. By my hand or yours. Those are the two choices. Either way, you are going to hell today. We're going to take a walk up to the tenth floor. When we do, I can slit your throat and push you, or you can slit your wrist and jump. It matters little to me as long as you are dead when you hit the ground."

"You can't do that! If you kill me, the kids also die. You will be signing their death certificate."

"What are you talking about?" came Jack's deadly voice as he pulled him to his feet. "The game is over, Stan. They're not in the house."

"The game is far from over if you kill me. Nina drives Stephanie's old SUV. In about five minutes, she will have a very unfortunate accident. An SUV against an eighteen-wheeler, my money's on the eighteen-wheeler."

Jack punched him. His head snapped back with the impact from the blow.

"Call it off!"

"Let me go."

"If anything happens to those children, I swear I will kill you slowly. I will peel the skin from your miserable body one inch at a time." He dialed Nina's cell phone, but got no answer. He dialed Roper's number. "Are the kids there yet?"

"No, and I'm starting to get a little worried," said Roper. "Should I go look for them?"

"Yes. Nina follows the same path you do. There's an eighteen-wheeler on her tail. Take him out."

"Done. I'm out." Roper hung up.

"You still have time to save them. All I have to do is make a phone call," Stanley bargained. "I can call it off. It's not too late to save them."

"You're a lousy liar, Stanley. You had no way of knowing the kids would be in the SUV or where they are headed. It's the house you have rigged. Where's the bomb, Stanley?"

"You mean bombs, don't you? You're so smart, Kaufman. Why would I blow up my future home or my future hotel? I had everything before you came along. Stephanie would have married me and I would be a rich man. You deserve to die. You took everything from me. It would have all been mine. The last laugh is on you. How attached are you to that black Porsche?"

All the color left Jack's face. He dialed Stephanie's office. When voice mail picked up, he called the front desk. "Suzette, I need you to find Stephanie for me."

"She just went out the front door. She said she had some errands to run."

"Stop her!" Jack yelled into the receiver. "Don't let her go near my car! Go now!" Jack was pacing and time seemed to stand still while he waited. "You stupid idiot. Stephanie is driving my car today. You'd better pray nothing happens to her or it will be a slow and very painful death."

"Jack, what's going on?" Stephanie asked breathlessly. "Suzette came running outside screaming at me."

Jack let out the breath he had been holding at the sweet sound of her voice. "Suzette gets a raise and a bonus. Honey, listen to me. There's a bomb under my car. Call the police immediately so they can defuse it. Have John keep everyone away from the parking lot. Lock down the hotel if you have to."

"A bomb! Who would put a bomb under your car?" she whispered, lowering her voice.

"You can thank your old boyfriend Stanley for that little present. It was meant for me. He's gone off the deep end."

"Stephanie, help me!"

Jack's hand covered the phone receiver.

"What was that?" asked Stephanie. "I thought I heard my name. Jack, where are you?"

"Sorry, Roper has the television up a little loud." Holding his hand over the receiver, he eased out of the room and closed the door behind him. "The kids are on their way over here. Stay at the hotel. I don't want you going to the house just yet. I'll have some of my old buddies sweep it for bombs."

"Bombs. This is insane. I can't believe this is happening. Jack, are you sure about this? Stanley is trying to kill you? Why?"

"I'm sure. His company is going under. Without you and Christina's trust fund, he's ruined. I'm in his way."

"What are you going to do?" she asked, dreading his answer.

"Get to him first." Jack didn't need to say more.

Stephanie felt a chill go down her spine at his words. She thought the danger was over when Captain Corbin was killed. This time, she had put their family in danger by dating a madman. "Be careful. I love you."

"I love you too. I've got to run. I have the situation under control. I'll be there within the hour." He disconnected the call and went back into the bedroom. "Game's over, Stanley. I win and you lose, again."

"You sent them all to your condo," he laughed. "It's too perfect. You just sent them to their deaths. It should blow in about fifteen minutes. I think we both lose. I guess I can die in peace now."

Jack grabbed him and with his head, Stanley knocked the cell phone out of his hand. It crashed to the floor. "Oops. I guess you better run out and find a phone to warn them." Jack released him and punched him again. Picking up the pieces of the phone, he rushed from the room. "If that bastard moves a muscle or even twitches, shoot him! Just don't kill him. The pleasure will be all mine. I need your phone, Taggart." Taggart tossed him the cell phone. "Keep him alive until I get back."

Stephanie called Nina's cell phone. She impatiently tapped her finger on her desk as she waited. No answer. She hung up the phone and dialed Roper. No answer. She dialed his cell phone.

"Roper, it's Stephanie. I'm looking for the kids. Have you seen or talked to them?"

"I'm looking for them also. When I find them, I'll take them to Ash's place. If Jack calls, tell him I took them to Ash's. Don't worry, I'll find them."

"Thanks. Call me when you do."

"I will."

Stephanie stared at the phone. Jack lied to her. He wasn't at Roper's place. The scream she heard wasn't the television, but Stanley. She closed her eyes. Jack had Stanley. She snatched up the phone and dialed Jack's cell phone. When it went straight to voice mail, she panicked. Stephanie knew Jack well enough to know he could and probably would kill Stanley for what he was planning. Jack would extract his own method of vengeance on Stanley. Although it was probably what he deserved, she didn't want to see her husband go to prison for murder.

Who am I kidding? If Jack kills him, no one will ever

know. They might not even find his body. Can I live with this knowledge? Can I live without my husband? is a better question.

The first call he made was to the police to have the condos next to his evacuated. Next, he called Roper. "Roper. Have you found the kids yet?"

"I see them now. There is an eighteen-wheeler on Nina's tail. I'll get between them. Hold on."

Jack was on pins and needles as he waited.

"Okay, I'm in."

"The condo is set to blow in fifteen minutes. Take them some place else. Take them to Ashley's place."

"Done. I'll take care of everything here. Call your wife."

"I'm on my way there now." He made it to the hotel in record time. Stephanie ran into his open arms. They held each other. "Are you okay?" he asked, framing her face. Stephanie nodded, holding on to him.

The knock on the door drew their attention. They looked up to see the policeman standing in the doorway.

"We disarmed the bomb under the car. We need to get a statement from both of you. Mr. Kaufman, do you have any idea who would want to see you dead?" questioned Detective Sims.

"The only enemy I have in this town is Stanley Jordan." Jack handed him the file. "I found this in his office when I went looking for him."

"Why were you looking for him?" he asked curiously.

"Word on the street has it he put a hit out on me."

"And you would know this how?" The policemen looked through the file with interest.

"He what?" yelled Stef. She took a deep breath. "Talk, Jack. You didn't tell me about this!"

"I have connections," Jack answered evasively. "Stephanie, I didn't want to upset you. I didn't have any concrete evidence until today."

"What's in the file?" Stephanie asked, filled with dread. She saw the warning look Jack shot at the detective. "Don't lie to me, Jack. What's in the file?"

"Information about my past," he said, only telling her half the truth. He didn't want her to fall apart right now. He needed her to be strong.

"What else?" She could feel there was something he was trying to hide from her. She turned to the detective. "I'd like to see it, please."

The detective looked at Jack for guidance. Jack nodded in agreement. "Stephanie, remain calm."

Those words terrified her as the detective handed her the folder. Opening the file, she paled when she saw the picture of the kids. The wedding photo of her and Stanley was chilling.

Stephanie dropped the folder as the realization of what Stanley was planning hit her. He was plotting to kill the kids and Jack so he could have her and the money.

"Where are my children?" she asked, locking eyes with Jack. "Please tell me my children are safe."

"Roper will make sure they stay safe," he assured her, taking her in his arms. "You can trust Roper." He held his wife and prayed he was right.

A few minutes later, after the detective took his statement, an APB was issued for Stanley. The detective stressed to Jack not to interfere or withhold evidence.

Stephanie and Jack waited on pins and needles for Roper to call. During that time, the police defused the bomb in Jack's condo. They also evacuated the hotel and had a bomb squad sweep it. This they knew would be a lengthy process.

When Stephanie's phone rang she jumped. Her hand

trembled as she prayed it was news about the kids. She hit the speaker button on her phone. "Hello."

"Stephanie, it's Roper. We're at Ashley's place. The kids are safe."

She closed her eyes and said a silent prayer. "Thank God. Where are they? I want to speak with them."

"They are safe. I promise. I need to speak with Jack. Is he there?"

"I'm here. I owe you one, my friend."

"No, you don't. Nina is one hell of a driver. Good thing I taught her how to drive," he laughed. "She handled herself pretty darn good."

"We're on our way," said Jack, disconnecting the call. He didn't want Roper saying anything more while on speakerphone.

When they got to Ashley's place, Nina ran to both Stephanie and Jack. They each returned her embrace. Stephanie's eyes searched for Christina and Aidan.

"They're both sleeping," Nina assured her, seeing her worried expression. Stephanie released her and went to the bedroom. She let out the breath she had been holding when she saw the sleeping duo on the bed. Leaning down, she kissed them both and sat down on the bed. Kicking off her shoes, she climbed into bed between them. She pulled them both into her arms and held them. She was afraid to let them out of her sight.

"I'm proud of you," said Jack, hugging Nina again. He led her over to the sofa and she went into his open arms. "You kept a cool head and you saved the kids' lives."

"I was so scared," Nina confessed, holding on to him. "That truck came from out of nowhere. When he tried to ram me, I switched lanes. He kept coming. I thought about you and Roper and what you would do in my situation. It gave me courage. I wanted you both to be proud of me."

He dropped a kiss on top of her head. "I am proud of you, sweetheart. You're safe now. The man responsible for trying to hurt you will pay with his life. That's a promise."

"Who would want to hurt us? I hardly know anyone in this town. Why would someone try to kill three kids? They must be heartless."

"He is heartless, but I'll take care of everything. It will never happen again," Jack promised as he held her.

A few minutes later, he peeked into the bedroom. Stephanie was lying on the bed, holding both kids in her arms. He closed the door and took Roper aside. "I have Jordan under wraps. I'll be back in an hour or so. Don't let them out of your sight."

"I'll protect them with my life. What do I tell Stephanie?" Roper tossed Jack his keys.

"Nothing. The less she knows the better," said Jack, quietly closing the door behind him.

Covering his tracks, Jack drove Roper's Jeep to the hotel and left it there. He rode his motorcycle to the abandoned building where Tag was holding Stanley.

He knocked on the door and Taggart opened it. Jack handed him the cell phone. "You can get out of here. I'll take care of this myself."

"I'll hang around and help you tidy up," said Taggart, handing him a pair of gloves. Slipping them on, Jack went into the bedroom.

"All bombs have been defused, Jordan. You lose." He took the gun out of the waistband of his pants. "Do you recognize this, Stanley? You should. It's yours. I took it from your office." He took the knife out of his pocket and cut the ropes binding the man's hands and feet. "Get up."

"No, I'm not going to let you shoot me."

"I'm not going to shoot you. You're going to shoot yourself. By the way, there's an APB out for your arrest. You are considered armed and dangerous. They are probably padlocking your office right now. You're infamous, Stanley. I can see the headlines now, once prominent psycho accountant tries to kill ex-fiancées' husband and children for money. Too bad you won't be around to write a book."

"You're bluffing. I covered my tracks too well."

"I never bluff," said Jack, aiming the gun at him. "You are an amateur, Stan. I'm a pro. When you had me investigated, you should have had them dig a little deeper. If they had, you would know I am not someone you want to mess with. I bet your report didn't tell you I was a hired killer, did it?" Stanley blanched. "Stan, you just had the bad luck to offer the hit to one of my associates. Your luck has run out. Are you ready to go to hell? My specialty is pain. I know how to inflict the most pain without killing a person or breaking the skin. I could keep you alive and in pain for days or weeks if I choose to."

Stanley began to tremble in fear.

"Have you ever heard the phrase *know your enemy*? Only one of us is going to leave this building alive. We can take a walk upstairs and you can try to make a break for it and I shoot you or I can shoot you where you sit. It matters little to me. You tried to kill my children and almost killed my wife. Those are unforgivable actions."

"Take me to the police," begged Stanley. "I'll confess to everything. I swear I will. I'll tell them how I helped your captain with the kidnapping plan. I tried to have the kids killed. I'll confess to everything, just don't kill me."

"You were working with Cap. No wonder the plan went to hell in a handbasket. You both had your own agenda.

You can't make a deal with the devil. He was going to rape and murder Stephanie. Did you know that? He's dead because he crossed me. You're next. This is Jack's justice. I'm not giving you the opportunity to slip through the judicial system or to plead temporary insanity. There is no guarantee that once you are in police custody you won't say I made you confess. Where my family is concerned, I can't leave anything to chance. I don't trust you and you are a danger to us all. You are guilty by your own admission and you are going to die for your crime. Whether you die quick or slow is up to you, but you will die. Now get on your feet. Putting a bullet in your leg or arm won't kill you and it might improve my mood a little. Move!"

Stanley was trembling as he got to his feet. He moved slowly toward the open door. He stared from Taggart to Jack before running and then diving out of the living room window.

"That was unexpected," said Jack, staring after him. "Don't let him get away."

"Stop him!" Taggart ordered to the person on the other end of the phone. They heard tires screeching and by the time they made it downstairs, Stanley was dead in the street.

"That's not exactly what I meant, but it's effective. Get out of here, Jack. We'll make sure it's logged as an accident. Give me his gun." Taggart wiped it clean and then pressed it into Stanley's hand before putting it in the waistband of Stanley's pants. "Go home and kiss that beautiful wife of yours for me. If you need me, you know how to find me."

"I'm out," said Jack, straddling his Harley. He put on his sunglasses and drove away. Jack rode to the hotel to switch his motorcycle for the Jeep.

* * *

When he walked in the door to Ashley's condo, Stephanie was pacing. She looked up when the door open. Time stood still as they stared at each other. Stephanie ran to Jack, launching herself into his arms. They held on to each other for dear life.

"Is it over?" she asked, looking him in the eye. "Tell me it's over, Jack."

He saw the desperation in her eyes. "It's over, babe." He enfolded her in his arms. Dropping a kiss on her head, he held her away from him. "Stanley Jordan is dead."

Stephanie dreaded asking, but she needed to know. "Did you?" The question died on her lips.

Jack shook his head. "No, but I wanted to. I could have. I was even there," he said honestly, "but he didn't die by my hands. It was an accident."

The doorbell chimed, interrupting their conversation. Releasing Stephanie, he opened the door.

"Mr. Kaufman, may I come in?" asked Detective Sims. Jack stepped back to allow him to enter the condo. "Mrs. Kaufman." He nodded to Stephanie and she nodded back. "I wanted to let you folks know Stanley Jordan is dead."

"Stanley's dead. I can't believe it. When did this happen? How did it happen?" Stephanie asked nervously.

"It happened about an hour ago. No need to act so surprised, Mrs. Kaufman. I assumed you already knew about the accident. A motorcycle fitting the description of yours, Mr. Kaufman, was seen leaving the scene of the accident."

"Motorcycles are a dime a dozen," Jack replied smoothly. "I actually belong to a motorcycle club. I have an alibi, Detective. I was with friends up until a few minutes ago."

"I wonder what or who scared Mr. Jordan enough to jump out of an apartment window and then run out in the middle of traffic like that."

Jack shrugged. "Maybe he had a nightmare."

"That's what I thought you'd say. Mr. Kaufman, I have

no proof you were behind what happened, but I know you were involved somehow. If I had any evidence, I would have you arrested."

"Arrested for what? Accidents happen all the time. If there was foul play, prove it. My guess is you will have your hands full trying to find the culprit."

"I doubt we would find anything. Why waste the taxpayers' money? Have a good evening, folks. Mr. Kaufman, do not take the law into your own hands again. The next policeman might not be as understanding as I am."

Stephanie immediately locked the door behind him. She let out the breath she was holding when the policeman left the condo. Jack held open his arms, and she walked into them.

"Jack, please tell me the truth. I will understand if you did. He tried to kill you. Knowing what he had planned for the kids, I would just as easily have killed him. I promise I won't judge you, but I need to know. I understand how you feel. Did you kill him?"

He saw the sincerity in her eyes. He also saw the love. He knew without a doubt she loved him despite who and what he was in his past life. She accepted him for the man he was today. Jack knew with certainty together he and Stephanie could survive anything.

"As God is my witness, Stef, I didn't kill him. I was holding him captive. I had him detained earlier today. When I stood there with a knife to his throat, the only thing that stopped me from killing him was you. It took all my willpower not to kill him. I gave him a choice, kill himself or I would kill him. He tried to escape by jumping out of the window. When he got up to run, he was hit by a car."

"And you weren't driving the car?"

Jack smiled. "No. I wasn't driving the car." He brushed the hair from her cheek. "Do you have any idea how much I love you?"

She caught his hand and brought it to her lips. "Not half as much as I love you. I knew life with you would never be dull."

"Didn't your mother say you needed some excitement in your life?" he teased, kissing her parted lips.

"I don't think she was referring to kidnappings, bullets, and bombs. You know," she said, putting her arms around his neck, "if I were a writer, this would make one heck of a movie."

"Would I be the good guy or the bad guy?" he teased.

"A bit of both, I guess, but ultimately, you are my hero. I love you, David Jack Kaufman. Let's go home."

Epilogue

Months later Stephanie and Jack were crushed when the government informed them Americans were not allowed to adopt Persian children. They could be guardians for the children, but an adoption was not possible. There sadness turned to joy as they welcomed their son a year later. Little Jack Jr. was born three hours ago, topping the scale at nine pounds and ten ounces.

Smiling, Stephanie recalled her big strong husband almost fainting at the sight of their son making his entrance into the world. Jack swore her to secrecy.

The kids were waiting outside with Ashley, Roper, and Stephanie's parents. Ashley and Roper were married six months ago and her mother and father were dating.

With the expansion of their family, Stephanie and Jack sold the hotel chain. Jack and Roper's security business was booming. Stephanie's book made the best seller list. She was now busy working on the movie script.